Sign up to my newsletter, and you will be notified when I release my next book!

Join my Patreon (patreon.com/jackbryce) to get early access to my work!

lordjackbryce@gmail.com

Cover design by: Jack Bryce

ISBN-13: 9798882922695

JACK BRYCE

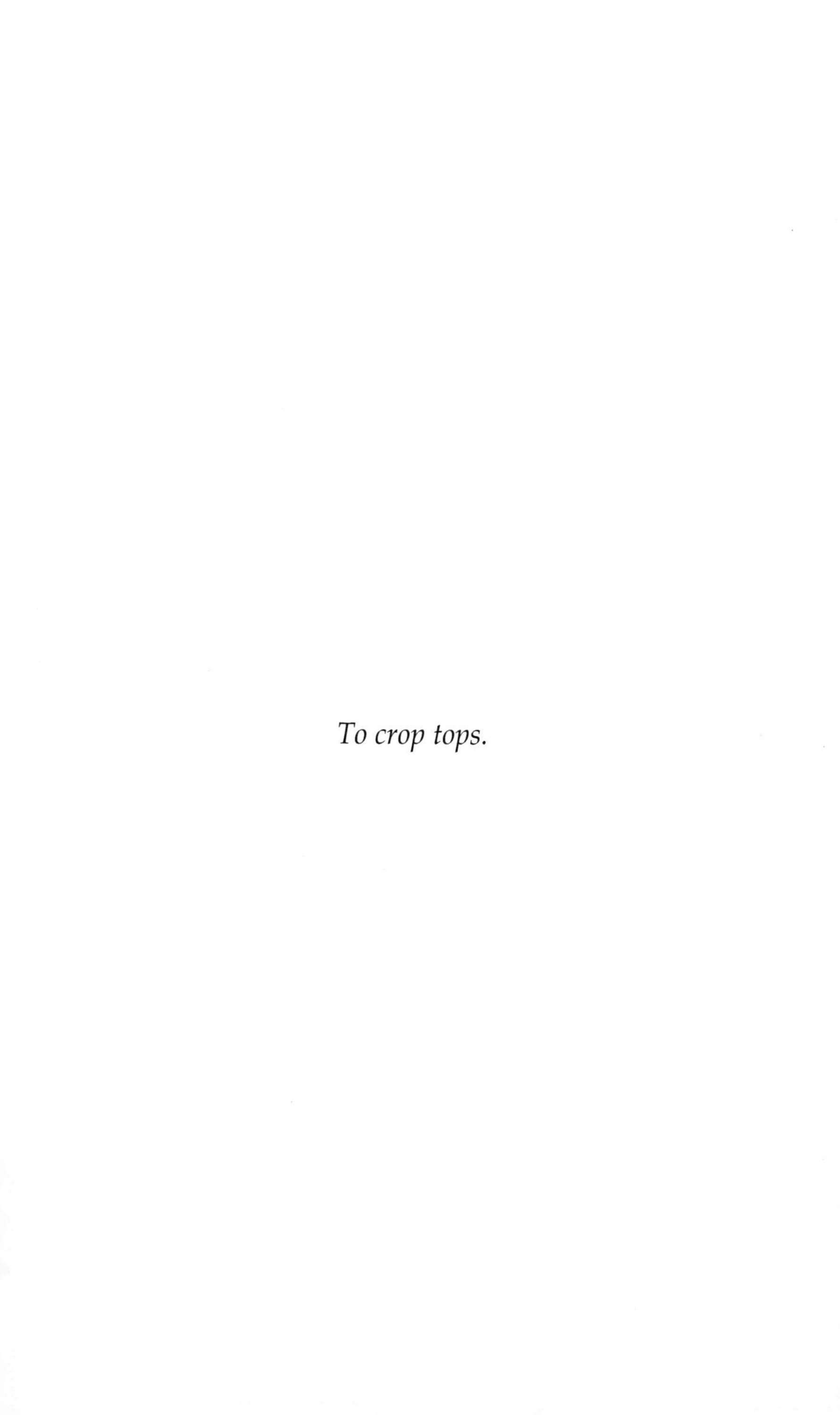

To crop tops.

Frontier Summoner 6

David's Character Sheet

Below is David's character sheet at the end of book 5.

Name: David Wilson

Class: Frontier Summoner

Level: 9

Health: 100/100

Mana: 50/50 (+10 from Hearth Treasures)

Skills:

Summon Minor Spirit — Level 21 (3 mana)

Summon Domesticant — Level 20 (5 mana)

Summon Guardian — Level 21 (7 mana)

Summon Aquana's Avatar — Level 15 (9 mana)

Summon Storm Elemental — Level 13 (10 mana)

Bind Familiar — Level 5 (15 mana)

Aura of Protection — Level 3 (4 mana)

Banish — Level 1 (6 mana)

Evolve Summon — Level 1 (4 mana)

Identify Plants — Level 16 (1 mana)

Foraging — Level 18 (1 mana)

Trapping — Level 18 (1 mana)

Alchemy — Level 22 (1 mana)

Farming — Level 9 (1 mana)

Ranching — Level 1 (1 mana)

Chapter 1

I watched with rising interest as the lithe figure of the cat girl made her way closer. I admired the way her hips swayed, but I remained cautious. Strangers on the frontier walking up to your door needed to be treated with care. Anyone could call out a name and pretend to be someone I'd heard of before.

As she approached, I narrowed my eyes at this stranger who had introduced herself as Yeska of the Wildclaws, the Bloodmage who would be able to reveal more about my Bloodline.

"Stay right there, please," I called back to her, my voice steady and firm but polite. It was imperative that I took care to ascertain that my unexpected visitor was who she claimed to be. I had little experience with catkin, and I didn't know if this could be a trickster or otherwise.

Slowly, I made my approach, each step measured and cautious. The sun was still shy, not quite ready to share its full warmth, and maybe I wasn't ready either for this sudden interference in this tranquil dawn. Yet, here she was, a catkin woman standing on my land, her eyes the color of summer leaves staring intently back at me.

The distance closed between us, and in the light of the newborn day, her features came into sharper focus. She was undoubtedly catkin, her ears twitching subtly, her tail giving a small, impulsive swish. It was unusual to feel such an immediate pull — this quickening in my pulse at her proximity. There was something raw and primal about her that spoke to my inner self.

She had not moved since revealing her identity, and now I could see the purpose etched upon her face. Yeska, this catkin woman before me, was standoffish. And yet her gaze held an intensity that beckoned me closer with an almost magnetic draw.

"Lord Vartlebeck sent me," she said, her eyes scrutinizing me. "He told me you had need of a Bloodmage."

"He told you where I lived?" I asked.

"He did," she affirmed, and now just inches away, her trait was unmistakable — that preternatural intrigue catkin held. It made them unpredictable. It was the unpredictability that stirred the air between us, her proximity sending tendrils of unforeseen possibilities through my thoughts.

"I do need a Bloodmage," I ventured, my words hanging like my breath in the cool morning air. "I need help unraveling my Bloodline."

"Yes, for your Bloodline," she repeated, licking

her lips after she had spoken, as if she enjoyed the taste of the word. Her proximity made it hard not to notice the black strands of hair that framed her face, the way they offset the green of her eyes.

"We should probably get inside," I nodded in the direction of the homestead. "Coffee?" It was an offer, but I felt it more as an escape from the open, from this sudden tension that I couldn't place.

A smile ghosted across her features at the proposal. "Coffee would be pleasant. It has been a long walk from Gladdenfield Outpost."

I smiled and nodded. "You must've gotten off to an early start?"

She grinned, flicking away an unruly lock of black hair. "Indeed," she purred.

We stood for a moment, just watching each other. The domesticants, sensing there were new dynamics in play, kept their distance. But they hovered at the edge of sight, curious and wary of this new entity now in their presence. They flitted about in silent accord, ready to provide aid if the new visitor proved hostile.

"Come," I said. "It's warm inside."

Her cloak swirled with her movement as she stepped in line with me, a whisper of a touch that was half felt, half imagined, trailed down my arm. Her interest struck as vividly as a lightning bolt, a thread of clean, sharp curiosity.

"So, what does a Bloodmage do?" I asked, seeking to make conversation while we walked.

"Oh, the things I could tell you," Yeska teased, her voice a purr of words that seemed to carry secrets and stories. It was the slight sway in her hips, the lithe grace with which she moved that drew my eyes time and again.

"I take it you enjoy your work, then?" I deflected, hoping familiarity might dull the keen edge that had colored our encounter so far.

"Enjoy isn't the word I'd pick," Yeska said. Her tone, previously light, dipped low. "It's an obsession, really — blood holds more secrets than the stars above."

We stepped onto the porch, and I shot the mysterious catkin another look. "Obsessions can be..." I paused, looking for the right way to frame it, "... consuming."

My hand found the door handle just as the sun broke fully from its slumber, spilling golden light over the homestead. Stepping back after I opened the door, I gave her the entry, an unspoken welcome.

She paused at the doorway, half turned with a silhouette etched in light. "Consuming, intriguing, compelling," she listed, stepping past the threshold but not into the house. "That's how I'd describe it."

"Then over coffee, you can tell us all about it," I said, my thoughts circling back to Leigh, Diane, and Celeste.

"Oh, there's much to discuss," Yeska agreed, moving a step closer so that the gap between us held nothing but shared air. "Sometimes, secrets are found in the most delicious places."

I chuckled and nodded, directing her to enter the home.

Chapter 2

As I entered with Yeska, the smell of coffee greeted us, blending with the homely aroma of a breakfast in progress. Warm light spilled from the kitchen, and I could hear the soft murmur of voices, the cadence of a familiar morning routine disturbed only by an unfamiliar presence.

We entered to find Diane, Leigh, and Celeste clustered around my grandparents at the kitchen table, steam from their mugs wafting up in cheerful little clouds. Waelin, a touch out of place but less rigid than before, perched on a chair with a cup in hand, his gaze casually inspecting the new arrival who trailed me.

"Good morning," I announced, a greeting that seemed to hover momentarily over the table before being absorbed into the bustle.

Diane looked up, her eyes narrowing slightly as they swept over Yeska, assessing the unannounced guest who had inserted herself into our cozy assembly.

"Everyone, this is Yeska of the Wildclaws," I began, the introduction prompting a series of nods and polite murmurings. "She's here to do some research on... Well, something to do with me."

As I spoke, Yeska moved with catlike grace to stand at my side, her green eyes flicking over the others. She took them in one by one, her beautiful features betraying nothing of what she thought.

Diane's lips tightened just a perceptible fraction,

a near-imperceptible response to the 'something' Yeska was here for — my Bloodline. Her hand found mine, a subtle reassurance, as she rose and watched the newcomer. I could sense her trepidation.

Celeste and Leigh, on the other hand, offered smiles and nods. "Welcome," Leigh beamed, always the first to speak kind words.

"Research, you say?" Grandpa asked, the tone of a man who prided himself on getting to the heart of the matter. "That sounds mighty important. Any way we can help?"

Yeska's mouth quirked into a smile. "I'm a Bloodmage," she explained almost casually. "David's lineage has... piqued my interest." There was a flicker of something in her demeanor that betrayed her own intrigues. "But it's not as simple as mere research. It's a process — a *ritual*. And a lengthy one at that."

"How lengthy?" Diane asked, her voice low.

I could tell that she wasn't looking forward to spending much time with the mysterious and — admittedly, sensual — catkin.

"Four months, at least," Yeska returned, calm as a vernal pond with hidden depths.

That won the catkin an uncomfortable shift from Diane as her eyes turned to me. I could already tell this was going to take some management…

"During this time," Yeska continued. "I'll need to be close to David — cohabitation is necessary for the duration of the ritual." This revelation hung in the air like a daring acrobat performing without a net, and I felt Diane's grip on my hand tighten.

For a second, I could almost hear the gears turning in Grandpa's head, processing this stark and unexpected piece of news.

"Cohabitation?" he echoed, looking from Yeska to me and back again as if to make sure he caught the nuance right. Then, he grinned broadly in his way. "You're gonna live with David?"

Yeska smiled with ease — or was it a challenge? — reading the mix of apprehension and curiously veiled excitement around her. "For the time being, indeed I must. It is part of the ritual," she said simply. "My presence will be... pervasive."

Grandma beamed a broad smile. "Well, isn't that

lovely! It's lucky you have a spare room, David!"

Leigh chuckled. "Well, it'll sure be nice to have another set of hands around the place. Right, Diane?" Her bright cheer cut through, dissipating the tension like the morning fog giving way to sunbeams.

Diane's smile was strained — a thin veil over the bubbling discomfort within. "Sure," she acquiesced, words wooden, her usual warmth tempered by the unexpected news. A catkin mage in our midst — and a sexy one at that.

Celeste rose with a smile and took Yeska's arm in a gesture of sisterly support. "We welcome you and your craft," she said. Her eyes met mine, and in their depths, I discerned a pool of acceptance.

"Why, thank you!" Yeska beamed.

It was already clear which relations would work right away… and which would need some work.

"Why don't we all sit down and enjoy some breakfast?" I proposed, eager to return to familiar ground. Food was the great equalizer, and the idea of sharing a meal seemed to offer a safe detour from the quagmire of emotions the morning had presented.

Yeska nodded in approval and slid gracefully into a seat. Grandpa, always ready to dispense wisdom or cornbread with equal generosity, immediately began questioning her on things that interested him — logistics, transportation, geography, and the like. Grandma listened intently, offering her two cents whenever she deemed it necessary.

One by one, everyone took our places at the table — a gathering of heartbeats and breaths in the burgeoning light of day. Diane sat across from Yeska with a measured grace, her eyes betraying her discomfort.

"I'll make us something to eat," I said, making my way toward the kitchen with my thoughts spinning.

While conversation continued at the dining table, the kitchen had a quiet about it, the kind that blanketed the room in a soft peace. I set about readying breakfast, the hissing of the frying pan gently breaking the silence.

Every now and then, I cast glances toward the dining area where conversation lulled more often than it bounced. Yeska was an enigma wrapped in a query, her presence pressing down on the usual easiness of our mornings.

I whisked eggs, my movements rhythmic and focused, trying to shake off the tension that settled in my shoulders. The eggs gave a puff and settled in the pan. I stirred them and thought of how the kitchen was the heart of our home, a place that both Leigh and Diane had filled with laughter and light.

Now, with Celeste living with us as well, it was about to become a livelier place still. However, I had just learned that — unless I would sell a hard 'no' — we'd have another newcomer for the next season. And telling Yeska 'no' meant my Bloodline would remain shrouded in mystery. That was, of course, not an option.

Luckily, Leigh, bless her heart, had a way of

cutting through awkwardness like a warm knife through butter. "Y'all always this quiet in the mornings? Or is it the fact that David's cooking that's struck you dumb?" she teased, her voice bold in the midst of restraint.

Her laughter was a balm that seemed to smooth the edges of everyone's hesitancy, and the others joined in. Especially Grandpa loved her and her sense of humor, and he guffawed happily at the joke.

Even Yeska allowed a small smile at Leigh's humor, and she regarded me more keenly, her curiosity piqued. "So, your grandfather tells me you and Celeste married just this night, is that true?" she asked, her interest a splash of color on an otherwise gray canvas.

"That's right," I replied over the sizzling pan. Flipping the eggs onto a large platter, I almost wished that the act could be as easy as flipping the switch on our moods — turning unease into comfort, questions into understanding.

Celeste nodded happily. "An elven wedding is a beautiful thing," she said. "The stars bear witness as two hearts bind beneath their light." Her eyes glowed with the remembrance of the previous night; a secret joy shared at the break of dawn.

Yeska's intriguc deepened at Celeste's description. "Elven customs are indeed fascinating," she remarked, her eyes dancing toward me. In her gaze, I saw an appetite for knowledge — or something more — that made my blood rage faster.

Diane's fork paused mid-air, her earlier grains of discomfort seeming to swell into boulders. "David and I, and Leigh, we're in an arrangement called an Elven Marriage," she explained.

It was fascinating to watch — Yeska listened with the attentiveness of someone piecing together a puzzle. "Ah, I'm familiar with the concept," she said, each word measured, "multiple women sharing one husband."

"We always knew our David was quite the charmer," Grandma joked, "but we'd never expected anything like this!"

"Ha!" Grandpa puffed. "Maybe not *you*! The boy's a Wilson!" He puffed out his chest.

Grandma gave him a skeptical look. "Well then, Mr. Albert *Wilson*... How come *you* never had an Elven Marriage?"

He turned to her with the most disarming smile ever. "My heart," he began as if he was going to make the sweetest confession, and I could see Grandma melting before he abruptly continued. "I just can't *afford* another woman!"

"Albert!" Grandma muttered, covering her mouth.

Leigh broke out laughing, and even Waelin joined in for a reserved chuckle, while Celeste gave a charming giggle. Diane, however, had a fake smile on her lips as she eyed Yeska, who in turn was watching me like she was about to pounce on me.

This was not going to be easy.

The room fell silent again as I busied myself with putting the final touches on the plates. Arranging the food neatly, I could feel the weight of their glances, the unspoken words.

I served out the scrambled eggs. The aroma of seasoning and freshly brewed coffee entwined in the air like old friends, and the food seemed to bring some calm to the table.

"Well, I hope you're all ready for some sustenance!" I declared, hoping for breakfast to help bridge whatever gaps had formed.

Diane's earlier discomfort was pushed aside as she agreed, her voice coming out firm. "Yes, let's eat."

Grandpa, ever the peacemaker, rubbed his hands in anticipation. "Nothing brings a family together like a good meal," he stated, his wisdom as solid as the oak table we gathered around.

"We still have some leftover snickerdoodles from last night!" Grandma chirped. "For those of us with a sweet tooth!"

The table filled with the clatter of cutlery against ceramic and the muffled sounds of satisfactory munching — the universal language of hunger being satisfied. Waelin joined in, the earlier stiffness around him softening in the face of my grandmother's snickerdoodles, for which he had developed a fond appreciation.

Yeska observed, each bite deliberate, her eyes

flicking from face to face as we all ate. She had an outsider's acuity, the clear view from the bank as we navigated the river.

The food seeped warmth into us. It loosened stiffness and softened edges, and even Yeska's reserve seemed to ebb away bite by bite. For a moment, the tension was diluted — there, but faint.

Grandma passed a bowl of fruit; her nurturing instincts clear as day. "Eat up, dear," she told Yeska, "No doubt you'll need your strength for this so-called ritual of yours."

"So will David!" Celeste added with a laugh. Her laughter was gentle, a balm to the remnants of the morning's earlier standoffishness. Her eyes twinkled at me from across the table, her glance a subtle reminder that we had loved under these very stars — and I still longed for more.

Diane and Leigh soon exchanged light banter with Waelin about potion mishaps and gardening woes. The awkward meeting of the morning seemed at least a little forgotten.

But still, my heart was heavy as I cleared my own plate, the delicious breakfast a reminder of this peculiar dance of the new and the familiar. I glanced at Yeska, her interest in me, the household, and especially the recent news of my marriage to Celeste, unabated.

I would have to find common ground between the girls, a way to make this work. After all, I needed Yeska and her Bloodmage abilities. I needed to find a way to make them get along.

Chapter 3

The clinking of forks and the rustle of napkin-laden laps filled the space as we dug into the breakfast I'd prepared — and, of course, the leftover snickerdoodles.

As we ate, Diane watched our guest with a hawk's intensity, her gaze barely leaving Yeska as she tucked into her own meal. I knew Diane's mind was awash with thoughts and questions; her instinct to protect our close-knit world from this new variablc was fierce.

Leigh, on the other hand, had no qualms about filling any silence with her cheerful chatter. "So, Yeska," she began, leaning forward with her usual gusto, "you're a Bloodmage, right?"

The cat girl, her mouth full at that moment, nodded with big, green eyes.

"What level, if ya don't mind my askin'?"

"Level 6," she managed around her bite of food.

"Wow!" Leigh beamed. "Level 6, huh? So, what sort of magic tricks can a level 6 Bloodmage pull out of her hat?" Her words, laced with genuine interest and a touch of her native charm, carried easily and warmly around the table.

Yeska's response came readily after she swallowed her food, as though she were used to explaining her craft. "Oh, I have some tricks," she said with a wink. "As a Bloodmage, I delve into the very essence of a person's being. Bloodlines hold histories, power, potential… and, sometimes, curses." Her lips curled into a half-smile that didn't quite reach her eyes.

Waelin set his cup down with a sound that signified the end of his participation in eating. His sharp gaze was fastened on Yeska now, as if her explanation was unlocking some private contemplation. Celeste's gentle touch on his arm drew him out of deep reverie, and he smiled warmly at his niece.

It was clear that my grandparents were out of their element. Their knitting brows and furtive glances at one another broadcasted their struggle to keep pace with this conversation. It had taken on the contours of things only understood by those who had delved deep into the workings of magic.

I peered around at the group, Yeska now the hub of our wheeling attention. As strange as it felt, there she was, seated among us as though fate had penciled her into the morning's agenda. She talked of blood magic as easily as Leigh discussed recipes for her favorite desserts.

"Bloodlines," Celeste spoke softly, almost to herself, "are like rivers that flow through time, aren't they? Connecting us to the past and the future." Her voice sang with the poetry of her elven heritage.

Leigh nodded in agreement, a quick understanding brightening her face. "Like how recipes are passed down through families," she offered, trying to connect the dots in a way that was fitting for her, and she shot my grandparents a soft smile, trying to get them to understand the topic as well. It was sweet of her.

Yeska considered Celeste and Leigh's words, her thoughtful silence insinuating a depth of knowledge and secrets bound within her practice. "Exactly," she finally said, meeting my eyes. "Like rivers — some run clear, others are shadowed and troubled by what they carry within their depths."

As breakfast drew to a close, plates cleared and cups emptied, the room hummed with the echo of our conversation. To my side, Diane's posture spoke volumes. I knew we'd need to talk, to make sense of this unexpected twist.

"Well," I broke the lingering silence, standing up from my chair with a stretch. "I think it's a fine time for a tour of the place for Yeska, don't you all agree?"

I stopped myself from adding 'since she's going to be here for a while.' After all, I wanted to talk to Diane about this first. I wasn't going to invite a new woman into our home without her assent.

Leigh bounced upright immediately, the first to take the helm of my suggestion. "I'd love to show Yeska around! C'mon, let's start with the gardens," she said, her natural exuberance finding an outlet. It earned her a thankful smile from me and an intrigued tilt of Yeska's head as she stood to follow.

Diane caught my eye, and with a subtle nod, she indicated her need to speak with me as well. It was a conversation that could not be put off, not with the day already laden with unexpected developments and travels into blood magic territory.

The clatter of dishes being stacked marked the end of the meal as Celeste began clearing up, with Waelin and my grandparents quick to rise to help her as Leigh led Yeska toward the door, her hand at the catkin's back to guide her.

"Leave it for the domesticants," I said. "They'll be here in a minute." Grandma chirped happily at that — she was most impressed by the little servants, and I knew she would love to have a domesticant herself.

Then, I took Diane's hand as the others busied themselves. "Let's head upstairs," I suggested.

Her sapphire eyes met mine, and in them, I found agreement as she nodded.

Entering the master bedroom, I closed the door behind Diane and myself, its gentle click punctuating the onset of our private conversation. The room was suffused with the soft light of the new day, the bed unmade, and the air still tinged with the lavender scent that was so distinctly Diane.

Diane walked over to the window, gazing out over the land we had come to call our own. I approached her, admiring how the light played off her black hair, catching strands here and there, turning them into glossy ribbons.

"Are you okay?" I asked, standing close to her. There was a weight to my words, my concern for her present in every syllable.

Diane turned from the window to face me, her expression thoughtful, her mouth opening then closing. "I don't know," she admitted after a moment, the words falling short like stones into still water. "Yeska... she's too familiar with you. I feel... I feel a little threatened."

I nodded, understanding her worries. Yeska's easy proximity had unsettled me as well, although perhaps in a different way. "She's just... *different*," I conceded. "New, perhaps too new."

"Not just 'new', David," Diane said, her voice taking on a firmer edge. "She knows nothing of us, of our ways here, yet she carries herself with this... assumption of intimacy. It's unsettling."

I reached out, folding my hands over Diane's, which were knotted in front of her as if she were grasping for certainty. I could feel the tension in her slim fingers, the echo of her discomfort against my skin.

"Do you want her to leave?" I asked, my eyes searching Diane's. It was important to me to honor her feelings.

Diane shook her head, a sudden firmness in her gesture that spoke volumes. "No, it's more important that we learn about your Bloodline. With Father coming," she paused, her worry clear, "we need to know what we're facing."

Her words hung there, a testament to the shared concern we all felt. Father, the powerful dragon whose shadow loomed large in our thoughts, was a danger drawing ever closer.

I squeezed Diane's hands gently in mine. I knew this was a concession for her. "Thank you, Diane," I said.

Diane managed a small smile; one I knew was hard-earned amid the turmoil. "It's not really about what *I* want. It's about keeping everyone safe." Her commitment was etching itself into the air around us. "But I cannot deny the way I feel."

"I'm going to have a word with Yeska," I promised. "And if after that, she continues to make you uncomfortable, I'll let her know that's not okay."

Diane leaned into me, her body language expressing the wariness she had yet to put into words. "I don't want to cause trouble," she confessed, her voice low.

"You're not causing trouble," I assured her, raising my hand to brush a stray strand of hair from her forehead. "You're being protective, as am I."

I watched a faint pink color bloom on the high of Diane's cheekbones, a softness seeping into her eyes. "I know she's here for a reason, but she needs to respect... *this,*" Diane said, casting a glance around the room that we had built together.

"She will," I said firmly. A determined set came to my jaw, a reflection of the resolve growing within me.

Closing the space between us, I wrapped Diane in my arms, feeling the press of her body against mine. I kissed her, the gesture filled with all the love I had for her.

"I love you," I told her as we separated, the

words a covenant between us.

Diane's lips turned upward slightly. "I love you too, David. More than anything," she hummed. Her voice was a soft echo in the large bedroom, and it surrounded us with warmth.

Sunshine bled in through the curtains, spreading patterns of light across the woody texture of the floor as we stood together by the window for a few more moments, the quiet of the room enveloping us. Outside, the world was waking up, the sounds of life from the homestead reaching our ears — a comforting symphony.

Staring out at the forest surrounding our home, I knew I was one lucky guy to have Diane at my side. We would face whatever Yeska's arrival brought together. But I would have to have the conversation with Yeska soon...

Chapter 4

After the relief and resolve from conversing with Diane, I felt a need to settle issues right away.

I stepped outside, letting the door close gently behind me. The cool morning air kissed my cheeks, providing a contrast to the warmth that lingered from our private moment upstairs. The sun had climbed higher, casting shorter shadows on the ground and painting the homestead in a clear, strong light.

Leigh and Yeska were knee-deep among the sprouts and flowers of the garden, discussing the various crops. Leigh's voice carried clearly as she explained the properties of each plant. She seemed to have taken Yeska under her wing, revealing the secrets of our magical bounty with pride. Their laughter reached me, a sound as fresh as the Magebread flowers basking under the sun nearby.

"At least those two are getting along," I mumbled to myself as I set out. Of course, that didn't surprise me one bit — Leigh could befriend a kobold berserker looking for his candle.

As I approached, Yeska's demeanor shifted slightly, her green eyes brightening even more if that were possible. The color of her irises almost shimmered with the vivacity that her interest invoked. She straightened her posture, a subtle yet unmistakable acknowledgment of my presence.

"Hello again," I greeted them both, noting Leigh's playfulness and Yeska's direct attention.

Yeska's response held a melody, an undertone of flirtatiousness. "Good morning, David. I'm learning so much about this place you have here," she said, a smile curling on her lips as her gaze lingered on me a beat longer than necessary.

I chuckled at her overt interest, feeling the corner of my mouth twitch in amusement, before I smiled at Leigh. "Thanks, Leigh," I said, "for taking the time to introduce Yeska to the workings of our homestead."

Leigh bobbed her head cheerfully, as she often did when in good spirits. "Oh, David, I was just telling Yeska here how strong and fertile the land is... just like our man at the helm," she jested, her comment holding an edge of audacity that I couldn't help but smile at.

"Leigh, you might embarrass our guest," I replied with a grin, though I suspected Yeska was not the type to be easily embarrassed.

Leigh batted the air with her hand dismissively, her laugh echoing through the rows of plants. "Clearly, ya don't know much about catkin yet, baby," she said with a wink.

I raised an eyebrow. "Oh?"

Leigh stuck out her tongue and wagged her finger. "Very different from elves," she just said, and Yeska chuckled at that before turning to me.

"I don't mind one bit," she said. "We catkin, we admire strength and... vitality," she said, her words heavy with subtle implication. Her tail flicked playfully, betraying, perhaps, her true thoughts.

I caught Leigh's gaze and gave her a small nod, communicating without words my need to speak with Yeska alone. Quick on the uptake, Leigh clapped her hands together. "Right, I'll leave you two to chat. I've got some herb blends to assemble," she said, turning her attention back to the garden with practiced ease.

Leigh wandered off, but I watched her for a moment longer, grateful for her understanding. She was absolutely the best.

Then, I turned to Yeska. "Yeska, about earlier," I started, catching her attention as she turned to face me fully. "I'm truly glad you've come. Your expertise will be invaluable, especially with... what we might face soon," I said, alluding to the dragon Father whose potential for destruction lurked ever in the back of my mind.

Yeska tilted her head slightly, considering my words, her posture open and attentive.

"But there is something I need to address," I continued, hoping my straightforward approach would resonate with her. "Diane seemed a bit uncomfortable with your… *familiarity*." I chose my words carefully. "If you're going to stay with us for a while — which I hope you do — I think it's important to maintain a sense of respect and boundaries."

A shadow flickered across Yeska's features; a sign that suggested she was taking my words to heart. "You're right, David," she agreed, her voice softer now. "I don't mean to cause disruption or discomfort. I will be more mindful. It is… it is something we catkin do." She bit her lip for a heart-stopping moment, flashing a cute canine. "We… *express* interest."

I nodded, fighting for composure myself as well. There was a magnetism between us that I found hard to ignore. "I appreciate that," I said, and I hoped she didn't notice my voice was a little more hoarse than before.

She let out a sigh, and in that exhalation, I detected a mingling of resignation and something else — a deeper longing, perhaps. "To be honest, I envy Diane. You have an effect on me that no man has had before," she confided, dropping her gaze for a moment.

That confession caught me off guard, causing a moment of hesitation. Yeska's honesty was raw. Perhaps another thing of the catkin, and I simply didn't know how to respond.

She looked up at me, then her eyes smiled — her mouth soon following — when she realized there was a cultural gap between us.

"You know," she began, a teasing purr to her voice, "when you receive a compliment and do not know how to respond or do not want to delve into the meaning of that compliment, there is a customary thing to say… At least, among us catkin."

I cleared my throat. "Oh? And what is that?"

Her eyes blazed on me a moment longer. "*Sal-Chalur kalssi*," she said. "It means something like..." At this point, she touched her plump bottom lip with a slender finger, eyes narrowing as she thought. "Well... Something like 'you flatter me,' I guess..."

"*Sal-chalur kalssi*," I said with a grin.

She licked her lips and giggled, as if I said it in a funny way. We stood like that for a moment longer, her green eyes searching me, the air between us charged.

Yes, I could already sense that Yeska and I were going to like each other. Now, all that remained was to make sure the others would accept her as well.

After a moment of staring at me, Yeska's expression turned a little more serious. "But tell me, David," she prompted, "what is your Class? You wield such command over this land and its creatures. It is quite… captivating."

The question prompted a grin from me, a natural reaction to her interest, which felt strangely affirming. "I'm a Frontier Summoner," I revealed, watching her carefully for her response.

"A Frontier Summoner, you say?" she purred. "How extraordinary. I've read the treatises, scoured the lore — I never actually met one before," she remarked, her voice reflective. Her curiosity about my class seemed to stem from a genuine place of surprise and interest.

"I know it's rare," I replied, watching as she delicately brushed a strand of her raven hair behind her ear. The sunlight played off the slight point of her cat ears, marking the exotic beauty of this alluring woman. She didn't just look the part of a Bloodmage; there was something about her demeanor that radiated a subtle but deep knowledge.

"Tell me more, David," she hummed. "Where did you come from?"

"Well, I spent most of my life in New Springfield," I continued, "and for a long time, I didn't have a class. But Caldwell of the Frontier Division — the very same one you might be familiar with — he helped awaken my class through an elven ritual." The memory of Caldwell and the ceremony brought a hint of nostalgia; the way my life had changed afterward still felt surreal at times.

She purred, a sound that didn't seem quite human. "Caldwell the Magebreaker, hmm? He's credited with scouting numerous talents. Remarkable, really." Her interest seemed piqued by the mention of Caldwell, as if my connection to him added another layer to her unfolding understanding of me.

I shifted my weight from one foot to the other, recalling more of my past as she listened attentively. "Both my parents had Classes. They were adventurers," I explained, my voice trailing off as the memories became hazier. "But they disappeared after the Upheaval. Life took quite an unexpected turn after that, and I lived with my grandparents for some time — the ones you just met."

Yeska's green eyes seemed to shimmer as she processed the information. Her intense gaze now had a glint of enthusiasm, a flicker of an almost childlike interest in the unknown. "Disappeared, you say? How tragic, yet such events often leave the most intriguing imprints."

"I suppose they do," I acknowledged. The notion of imprints — literal and figurative — had a haunting resonance. For all the power and stability I had amassed here on the frontier, my past still seemed wrapped in an enigma.

"Lord Vartlebeck told me your Bloodline was one that allowed rapid advancements," she prompted me. "And you fought a dragon at Hrothgar's Hope?"

"We did," I affirmed. "It was a juvenile one, and it called me 'Goldblood.' It had something to do with my Bloodline, I am sure, and Celeste told me there is mention of 'Goldbloods' in elven myth… powerful warriors, although she knew little more."

"*Goldblood*?" she hummed. "How fascinating." The way she leaned in when saying 'Goldblood,' as if the word held secrets only she could unlock, made the shadows around us feel heavier somehow.

I nodded at her reaction. "Yes, that's what it said. I've been trying to understand what it means — what that dragon knew about me."

Her response was an audible hum; the purring sound present again. "Discovering the meaning behind 'Goldblood' will be a most captivating journey — and one I'm all too eager to undertake." Her conviction had an almost predatory sharpness to it, a focused intent that her feline nature mirrored so well.

I smiled and nodded. "Have any ideas?"

"I have *some* theories," Yeska confessed as she traced an abstract pattern on the palm of her hand. It was a habit that hinted at restlessness, a mind forever churning with thoughts and deductions.

A knowing look passed between us as if to seal an unspoken partnership. "I look forward to hearing them," I said, "and to your research into my Bloodline."

A smile quirked at the edge of her mouth, pulling her lips into a mischievous curl. "Oh, *thorough* research is the cornerstone of my practice."

My own smile mirrored hers, the ease with which we were slipping into a rapport surprising me. The promise of unraveling mysteries about myself, the understanding of 'Goldblood,' and its implications was indeed alluring.

"So, what kind of research are we talking about?" I pressed on, the notion prickling at my curiosity.

Yeska's tail swayed behind her in a slow, hypnotic tempo, emphasizing her words as she spoke them. "Everything in-depth, David," she reaffirmed, her eyes holding mine, "from your Bloodline properties to the very fiber of your abilities as a Frontier Summoner."

It dawned on me that having Yeska so close, a stranger yet not, in the months to come, would challenge the tranquility of our lives here in more than one way. But the mutual understanding that whatever loyalty lay behind her inscrutable eyes could be the key to safeguarding our future against the shadow of Father, the dragon.

"Then we'll explore 'Goldblood' together, try to figure out what it truly signifies," I suggested, reaching a decision that felt important.

Yeska nodded once, sharply as if slicing through the uncertainty. "Together," she agreed, her poise unfaltering. "I'm excited to begin, David. This is a unique opportunity — for both of us."

As if she sensed that we had reached an end to our conversation, Leigh strolled over with a smile on her plump lips to rejoin us. Yeska and I exchanged one more look of understanding before turning to the bubbly blonde.

Chapter 5

Standing outside with Leigh and Yeska, I caught sight of the domesticants zipping about. I decided it was time to make introductions to the more ethereal members of our homestead, and I mentally commanded them and Mr. Drizzles over.

The late morning air was decidedly crisp as we

waited there, a comfortable silence enveloping us for a moment. It was an ordinary, tranquil day interrupted only by the presence of the new face among us.

Yeska's eyes were bright, a clear sign of her curiosity piqued by the surroundings, and she gave a pleased purr as the domesticants approached.

"These little guys here are Ghostie and Sir Boozles," I explained when the two domesticants came over, my voice warm with affection for the floating specters.

They darted around happily, their gleeful chirping almost like a cheerful greeting to our guest.

Yeska's eyes followed their movements, a smile tugging at the corner of her lips. "They're quite… lively," she commented, her observation underlined with a reserved amusement that hinted at a levity I hadn't seen in her before.

"They help around the homestead," I said. "I bound them to me as familiars." Then, I gestured as Mr. Drizzles emerged from the path and closed in.

Mr. Drizzles made its presence known by allowing a stray arc of lightning to snap into the air. Yeska stepped back, her eyes widening not in fear but fascination.

"And this is Mr. Drizzles," I went on, "our resident storm elemental. Another of my familiars. He helps keep the property safe."

Yeska tilted her head, an almost inaudible hum resonating from her throat as she studied the crackling cloud of energy that was Mr. Drizzles. "A storm elemental — remarkable," she said, her tone suggesting she understood the significance of such a creature and what its presence said about my skill as a summoner.

Then, she laughed. "That name, though!"

I replied by rolling my eyes. "I know," I muttered.

"Hey!" Leigh chided her good-naturedly. "Mr. Drizzles is a good name!"

Yeska giggled, and Leigh joined in before she clapped her hands together, her face breaking into her customary grin. "You haven't seen the best part yet. C'mon, let's show her the larroling," she urged, eager as ever to share everything our life out here had to offer.

As Yeska and I followed, the domesticants continued their boisterous zipping around. It felt homely, that simple dance of everyday living entwining with the morning routine.

The larroling loomed into view, its bulk majestic against the backdrop of the forest. Leigh approached it without hesitation, scratching under its chin where I knew it loved to be scratched. "Meet the biggest guy around — ain't he something?"

Yeska furrowed her brow, but a smile still managed to find its way onto her face as she watched the larroling respond to Leigh's affection. "He's quite a force," she said, her voice reflecting surprise and recognition of the animal's strength and stature.

Leigh beamed, puffing up with pride. "Yep, ya won't find another creature like him for miles around!"

The larroling snuffled in agreement. Or at least, I liked to think it was agreement, its deep snuffling sounds resonating in the clear morning air.

Our little tour of the grounds continued with occasional stops; each new sight seemingly more attractive to Yeska than the last. We didn't speak much; it wasn't necessary. The land around us offered enough conversation in its quiet and serene way.

Before long we reached the bank of the Silverthread River. Its soothing waters were a sight I had always cherished, a constant reminder of the natural beauty we were surrounded by. "We do a lot of fishing here," I told her, nodding toward the river's placid surface.

Yeska's eyes lit up with childlike excitement. "I do enjoy a good fish meal," she said, her smile spreading at the prospect of what the river had to offer. "I'm thinking the coming months won't be dull, will they?"

From the corner of my eye, I caught Leigh's amused expression. Her questioning look made me almost laugh outright. Of course, we'd make sure Yeska was well-provided for — there was no shortage here, and Leigh's skills in the kitchen ensured it. And there was plenty to do.

"They won't be dull at all," I said.

We enjoyed the sight of the Silverthread for a while, each of us reflecting in our own way. It was Leigh who spoke up first.

"Why does it have to take so long, though?" she asked, her head cocked to the side. When she saw Yeska blink confused, she added, "I mean, this ritual of yours."

Yeska paused, carefully picking her words. "A Bloodline ritual calls for observation in multiple scenarios — emotions, stress levels, the presence of magic," she explained, a hint of her usual intensity coloring her voice. "It's intricate work, you see."

"Oh, alright," Leigh said. "Not that I object to havin' you around, mind you… Just being curious."

Yeska smiled. "No offense taken," she said. "The ritual can be quicker if you're willing to shed substantial amounts of blood," Yeska added, her gaze momentarily darting to me, an edge of wildness creeping into her tone.

I laughed at that; it couldn't be helped. "Let's

stick with the slow path if that's alright," I said, chuckling more at our expressions than the idea of letting the cat girl loose on my veins.

Yeska shook her head in amusement. "Very well, the slow and steady path it is," she conceded, joining in the laughter that bubbled up from within me.

Leigh clapped her hands in evident agreement. "Yes, let's not get too hasty," she said, her eyes twinkling with merriment. "We need David functionin' around here!"

The morning had warmed considerably as we had done the grand tour of the homestead grounds. I glanced at the sky, noting the sun's climb higher still — an unspoken marker of the day's progression.

"I suppose we should grab some lunch soon," I mentioned, eyeing Leigh and Yeska, who both nodded in agreement.

As we walked back, close enough to see the house now, I couldn't help reflecting on the morning's events. The conversation we had, the peculiar tension of conflicting customs and lifestyles — Yeska's new slate in our book.

The very thought caused a smirk to curve my lips. As Yeska had suggested, the coming months wouldn't be boring, to say the least.

Chapter 6

The midday sun had climbed high enough to pour a generous glow through the kitchen windows, warming the wooden floors and casting a homely glow on the faces gathering within.

Leigh, Yeska, and I returned indoors to find Waelin and my grandparents settled into an easy banter around the dining table. Their laughter and the fluid exchange of stories were pleasant to witness — another affirmation that we had bridged some serious cultural gaps yesterday by bringing them closer together.

Diane entered through the swinging kitchen door; her arms filled with an assortment of greens freshly picked from our garden. Her movements were efficient, yet a shadow of earlier apprehensions lingered in her swift strides. The presence of Yeska had introduced a wrinkle into the fabric of her comfort — one that, despite her best efforts, still pressed visibly upon her.

With the fish that was to be our lunch in mind, Leigh and Diane set about their preparations. I watched them work in tandem, their practiced motions a familiar dance that I found both comforting and grounding. Diane hummed a tune, soft and low, while Leigh focused intently on filleting with precision that spoke volumes of her mastery in the kitchen.

I pulled out a chair from the dining table, signaling Yeska and Celeste to join. Across from me, Waelin and my grandparents were deep in discussion about the many plants — and the few stray magical creatures — that had found their way into our vicinity since the Upheaval blended our worlds together.

Surrounded by the conviviality of family and the new guest, I allowed myself to relax in the chair. Celeste settled next to me, her hand finding mine, a silent exchange of support and shared contentment between us. Yeska sat opposite, observing the dynamic of our home with an unobtrusive gaze.

The conversation looped around various topics, from the laughter-inducing incident of the domesticants playfully chasing a butterfly to more serious matters concerning the well-being of the homestead. In between, Waelin and my grandparents peppered me with questions about our lives here.

As the talk meandered back to family matters, Grandma turned to me with a smile that seemed to strip away the layers of concern. "David," she began, her voice softened by affection and curiosity, "have you and Celeste thought about when you'd like to have your marriage celebration?"

The question piqued the attention of everyone at the table, turning expectant eyes toward me. Celeste gave my hand a gentle squeeze under the table, her silent way of saying this was a decision we had pondered together already.

"We were thinking next spring," I said. "It's a beautiful time, with the world coming back to life all around us. We don't want to do it now or in winter."

My grandfather nodded approvingly, his eyes twinkling — a testament to his shared joy in our plans. "Spring is indeed a fine season for weddings, with flowers in bloom and the land full of hope."

Waelin regarded us with a look that somehow melded formality with a touch of personal regard. "Springtime suits both human and elven customs well," he conceded. "It symbolizes renewal, the perfect backdrop for you and Celeste to affirm your bond for friends and family."

Of course, she and I were already formally

married in accordance with elven custom. But it was also custom to celebrate with friends and family, and I would use the occasion to marry Diane and Leigh as well, since they had both accepted my rings of shimmerstone. By then, Diane's belly would be properly swollen…

The warmth that had been building at the table seemed to blossom at the mention of spring, a collective envisioning of a day filled with laughter, love, and the promise of fresh beginnings. Yeska remained silent but attentive throughout, her eyes betraying no specific emotion regarding our plans.

Soon enough, the kitchen filled with the rich aroma of fish cooking to perfection, indicating that lunch was progressing well under Diane and Leigh's skilled hands. Their efficiency was a melody that played alongside the table's harmony, reaffirming the ties that bound us.

Faint sizzling sounds punctuated the lull in our conversation as I reflected on the coming ceremony in spring. There were measures to be taken, friends to be invited, and a covenant with Celeste to be celebrated. It felt both exhilarating and daunting, the sheer enormity of it.

Waelin's voice called us back from our individual reflections. "Preparing for a wedding is a considerable undertaking, but I assure you, I will lend whatever assistance I can," he offered, a show of solidarity that was gratefully received.

My grandmother echoed his sentiments, her face alight with the gentle vigor that family and festivity always stoked in her. "We'll all pull together, won't we? Such a special day for our David — and for his lovely brides, of course."

Celeste leaned closer to me, whispering words like a secret meant only for my ears. "Spring will be magical," she murmured, and I could feel her excitement mirroring my own — a shared anticipation blossoming within us both.

Diane glanced towards us, her lips quirking in a semblance of a smile. Despite her earlier reticence, it was clear her thoughts had already turned to making the day memorable.

Lunch was nearing readiness, Diane's previously sunken spirits lifted by the task at hand. One could see her easing back into the comfort of routine, the act of creating and serving food as much a part of our family's traditions as any wood elven rite.

Waelin and my grandparents continued to converse, their topic now circling around the shared experiences of their respective lives. The dialogue unfolded and branched, treading down memory lanes and across fields of mutual merriment.

As the morning inched towards afternoon, I reflected on how my grandparents and Waelin had quickly become a part of the fabric of our homestead. Despite the rocky start, they had woven themselves into the pattern of our days.

I felt a tug at my heart at the thought that their rides home would arrive later in the afternoon — stretching the fabric, perhaps, but not tearing it. I would miss them, that was certain, but hopefully, it wouldn't be long before we'd welcome them back again.

As the midday sun climbed to its zenith, Diane and Leigh set the table with the lunch they had prepared. The sizzling fish, garnished with the freshest greens from our garden, made a delightful display that seemed almost to brighten the room.

Yeska surveyed the spread with an air of appreciation, a soft purring sound arising from her throat at the sight. "This looks marvelous," she said, her eyes fixed on the fish. "What a feast!"

I released a breath I hadn't realized I was holding, hoping the compliment would help pave the way to smoother interactions between Diane and our guest.

Diane managed a smile at Yeska's praise, nodding her thanks while busy distributing the plates. Her earlier caution appeared, for the moment, replaced by the satisfaction of a job well done.

The domesticants, in their typical fashion, zipped around the room energetically, picking up fallen crumbs and tidying as we settled down to eat. Their chirps and whirs lent a lighthearted backdrop to the lunchtime gathering.

We dug into the meal with genuine relish, the simple act of eating together smoothing over the morning's wrinkles. Waelin and my grandparents chatted merrily, expressing their joy at having visited and at having seen the home and happiness we had created. The affection in their words was palpable, casting a familial warmth over the gathering.

"It's been a true delight, this visit," Grandpa said, glancing around at each of us with that look he gets when he's particularly pleased. "You've made a fine life for yourselves out here."

Grandma echoed his sentiment, her face a picture of contentment. "We're so proud of you, David, and your dear ladies," she added. "It's been an absolute pleasure to be here."

Celeste replied first, her voice carrying the little melody it always seemed to have, "You've both been wonderful guests — part of the family now." Her grace and hospitality visibly touched Grandma, who reached out to pat Celeste's hand in an affectionate gesture.

I joined in, feeling a swell of gratitude for their

presence and their easy acceptance of us all. "You know, you're welcome any time. This home is as much yours as it is ours," I told them, and Diane and Leigh nodded heartily in agreement, their expressions open and inviting.

As lunch wound down, plates cleared and appetites sated, we lingered at the table, indulging in easy conversation that spun from one subject to the next. It showed how well the day had turned around, from uncertain beginnings to closing on a note of companionship and understanding. Still, there was work to do in bringing Diane and Yeska closer to one another, but we had changed a poor start, and that was often the hardest part.

I noticed the time, the afternoon pushing on, and realized that the vehicles to pick up Waelin and my grandparents would be due soon. It saddened me more than I was willing to admit.

"I think your rides are going to be here soon," I told them. "Perhaps we should get ready."

Grandpa chuckled, shaking his head. "Oh, we already packed everything, but thanks, son. It's high time we let you kids get on with your lives without us old folks lingering too long."

"You ain't been nothin' but a pleasure," Leigh said, beaming at my grandparents.

"Leigh is right," Diane agreed. "You have been a joy to host."

"Indeed!" Celeste said. "Making your acquaintance has been most enjoyable!"

Grandpa chuckled and Grandma patted Diane on the hand with a thankful smile.

I nodded at Waelin. "And the same goes for you, Waelin," I said sincerely. "I know we had our differences, but I truly enjoyed your presence."

A little more formal with Waelin than with my grandparents, my women nodded their agreement and spoke soft words, with Celeste patting her uncle on the forearm with a grateful smile gracing her lips.

"Thank you, David," Waelin said, "and likewise. It has been an unexpected joy."

Leigh, ever the one with the ideas, rose with a grin. "How about one last stroll around the property before your ride gets here?" she suggested, beaming at the idea like it was a grand adventure.

Everyone agreed, and we rose from the table. I scanned everyone's faces — Celeste's serenity, Waelin's reserved calm, my grandparents' genial smiles. We headed out into the gentle thrum of afternoon life at the homestead.

Outside, the world had warmed under the sun's gentle auspices. We walked together, pointing out small things we enjoyed on the property, making small talk about the beautiful weather, enjoying our time together like a family.

Waelin lingered beside me, quietly observing the plants and the layout of the land. Leigh took it upon herself to narrate every little detail to my grandparents, who listened with nodding heads and occasional laughter.

Diane walked beside them, and Yeska hung back a little, not wanting to intrude. However, she regularly joined the discourse between me and Waelin when it came to the land's arcane properties.

The warmth of the day echoed the warmth in my chest, a comforting glow that came from seeing my grandparents so at ease in the world we had built. It felt right, and a part of me wished they could stay longer.

As we rounded the back of the house, my grandmother leaned into my side. "You've done good," she whispered, a hint of mischief in her eyes before she moved to join Grandpa.

The casual stroll slowly led us back to the front of the house. As reluctant as I was to see the visit end, I knew my grandparents and Waelin had their own lives waiting for them, just as we had ours here.

A comfortable silence settled among us as we reached the front porch. I stepped up, savoring the feel of the familiar wood beneath my shoes, and absorbed the scene before me — one I knew would start evolving again as soon as our visitors left, for there was much work to do.

The sound of approaching vehicles broke through the quiet, the crunch of gravel loud in the still scene. Yeska, Celeste, Leigh, Diane, and I turned towards it, while Waelin and my grandparents took it as their cue to bring out their things.

Chapter 7

The crunch of wheels on gravel signaled the awaiting vehicles outside the homestead. I watched Grandpa and Grandma gather their light jackets and hats, the former patting down his pockets in search of something probably forgotten. Their easy manner, a comfortable fit in our lives here, would be sorely missed.

And I had to admit, part of me was hoping to bring them around here for good. It would be nice to have them closer.

Grandma found her way to me first, her hands reaching up to cup my face. "Oh, David," she said, her voice thick with emotion. "Everything about this place — it's so full of love." Her eyes glistened, brimming with unshed tears, the weight of her pride and happiness heavy in her gaze as she looked at me.

Grandpa stood a step behind Grandma, a steady presence as always. His eyes met mine, and there was a silent exchange, an understanding of the changes and challenges that we navigated to build a life here. "You keep those lovely girls of yours happy, you hear?" he stated, his voice a rumble filled with warmth and a fatherly insistence.

Diane came over then, her smile for my grandparents a mirror of their own affection. She thanked them for the visit, her words sincere and filled with the promise of regular communication, of photos and letters and shared stories to keep the fabric of family strong. Grandma happily touched her stomach, teary-eyed, and wished her good luck in the coming months.

Leigh followed suit, her own goodbye laced with laughter and an offhand promise to whip up more of her special dessert the next time they came. It was a casual assurance that there would be a next time, a future gathering where we would all come together again.

Celeste approached last, her farewell a gentler one, a soft-spoken thank you that carried the weight of her gratitude for their acceptance and shared joy. Grandma pulled her into a tight embrace, whispering something that made Celeste nod and smile through tears of her own.

Meanwhile, Waelin hung back a touch, his distance bridged as he stepped forward to extend his hand to me. His grip was firm, his usually stoic face softened with what I thought was approval. "Celeste has found true happiness with you," he said, his voice low and gruff with emotion. "I see it in her eyes."

His handshake lingered for a moment longer

than expected, his eyes holding mine. It was a goodbye but also an acknowledgment of the shared understanding, the respect that had developed between us during the visit.

As we all moved toward the front porch, I found Yeska standing close, her eyes hooded yet observant, her hand lifted in a wave to my grandparents and Waelin, who bade her goodbye in turn. Kind words were exchanged.

"I'm thinkin' we'll see more of you," Grandpa said with a grin, followed by a wink for me, hinting he had noticed the little spark between me and the cat girl.

I smiled, then raised a hand. "Oh, wait!"

My grandparents halted, and all eyes were on me as I swiftly cast my Summon Domesticant spell, then bound it using my Bind Familiar spell. It was a cute little thing, and I mentally instructed it to obey every order from my grandparents.

"There," I said, smiling at my grandparents. "This little guy will be joining you to help around. How's that sound?"

Grandma clapped her hands in front of her

mouth. "Oh, David!" she said. "You didn't have to do that!"

"Aw, we don't need that, son," Grandpa said.

"Sure you do," I laughed. "I'm a mage, Grandma. I can help make your lives a little easier like this, so please let me! It's my pleasure, and I insist!"

"Well," Grandpa said, shrugging with a grin. "Ain't gonna deny a little extra help is good. Little feller can get me a beer and my slippers."

"Oh, Albert!" Grandma laughed, and my women and Waelin joined her with heartfelt laughter.

"Go on," I said, chuckling as I gave them both one more hug then shooed them aboard the vehicle. "We'll be in touch!"

Agreeing and waving, they entered. The little domesticant hopped into the car with them at Grandma's first — albeit hesitant — command.

The passengers were settled now, my grandparents in one vehicle, Waelin ducking into the other. We stood on the porch, a line of figures waving as the engines revved gently, and the cars began to roll down the driveway.

Grandpa leaned out the window, shouting something about not being strangers now and to expect a box of his favorite fishing lures in the mail. His laughter carried back to us, mingling with the crunch of tires on gravel.

Grandma blew kisses, her eyes bright and cheery despite the tears that stood in the corners. She called out reassurances, reminding us that we were always in her thoughts, always in her heart.

Waelin gave us a solemn nod as his vehicle pulled away, a final salute of sorts before he disappeared around the bend in the drive. It was an ending and a beginning, the conclusion of a visit that had woven new threads into the pattern of our lives.

Standing beside me, Diane took a deep breath, exhaling slowly as she watched the vehicles turn onto the main road and vanish from view. "Sad to see them go," she said.

I put an arm around Diane's shoulder, my own eyes following the retreating cars. "They'll be back before we know it," I said.

Celeste's hand found mine again, squeezing

gently. "It's been a beautiful time with them," she murmured, her voice a balm to the subdued mood that lingered as the silence of the departing cars settled over us.

I nodded, feeling the full weight of Celeste's sentiment. It had been beautiful, indeed. The presence of family, the conversations, the shared meals — it had filled the homestead with an energy that would not soon be forgotten.

We lingered, the breeze carrying the scent of the fields, birds chirping their midday songs. Life around us continued, unperturbed, carried forward by the rhythm of nature.

With the wedding over, it was time for things at the homestead to get back to normal. Although, I wondered how 'normal' would look now that Yeska was here.

Chapter 8

Once our guests were gone, a quiet hush fell back over the homestead. We headed inside to find a space as neat as a new pin, the domesticants having whisked away any signs of the earlier meal. A sense of bareness hung in the rooms, which just moments ago had been filled with the familiar faces and voices of family.

The five of us sat down at the now gleaming kitchen table, the wood still warm from where plates and cups had rested. I took in the clean tabletop, the smooth surfaces speaking of domesticants' diligent labor. The air still carried the warmth of baked bread and cinnamon from this morning's breakfast.

"So, you've seen the place and a bit of the work that gets done," I began, addressing Yeska directly. Her green eyes settled on me, sharp and attentive. The domesticants hovered nearby, their occasional chirps and whirs a comforting backdrop to our conversation.

"If you're going to be staying with us for a while, you should know we can easily provide for you," I said to Yeska, folding my hands together on the table. "But I was wondering if you'll be helping out around here. Can you focus on more than just the ritual, or will it take all of your time? And will you charge anything for your services as a Bloodmage?"

Yeska's posture shifted as she absorbed the

question. She leaned back in her chair, considering her response. "I can help," she offered after a thoughtful pause. "I know nothing about farming or growing crops, but I can hunt. I can fish a little. And while the rituals will take an hour or two most days, outside of that, I can assist. I'm rather adept with a bow. As for costs…" She smiled a little wickedly and shrugged. "I may require a little bit of blood every now and then for some of my spells, but nothing you will miss."

"Blood?" I asked, eyebrow raised.

"Hm-hm," she purred, once again letting her bedroom eyes drift over me without mercy. "Blood fuels the most potent of my abilities. And the more potent the blood, the better. If you have a powerful Bloodline, as Lord Vartlebeck hinted you had, then some of your blood could aid my powers. That would be all I ask."

"How much blood is 'some blood'?" Diane asked, scrutinizing the cat girl with a fire in her eyes.

Yeska smiled. "Just a few vials. He won't miss it."

Diane was about to object, but I raised my hand. "It's fine, Diane," I said. "I'll work this out with Yeska." I turned my eyes back to the cat girl. "And you'll help around the homestead?"

The corner of her mouth twitched into an almost-smile, a hint of mirth amidst the seriousness. "Certainly. And I can learn," she added. "I'm curious about your way of life here." Her fingers tapped lightly on the table, her gaze sweeping the room as though imagining herself in this new, unfamiliar world.

Diane's eyes met mine across the table, a silent question lingering in their depths. Celeste's hand rested lightly on my arm, her touch a steadying presence.

Leigh, seated closest to Yeska, gave a thumbs-up, her expression a mix of encouragement and mischief. I was pretty sure she liked Yeska — their playful sides matched up perfectly.

"But to complete the ritual to learn the truth of your Bloodline, there's more to be observed," Yeska said, her attention shifting to encompass Celeste, Leigh, and Diane. "More... situations besides farm work." A subtle emphasis colored the word "situations" with innuendo.

The room's temperature seemed to rise a few degrees at her insinuation. Celeste's cheeks flushed a delicate pink, while Diane's gaze darted away, briefly finding interest in the grain of the wood table. Leigh responded with a playful wink, not one to be easily embarrassed or outdone.

The exchange felt weightier than mere words. There was suggestion there, one that might tug at the lines that bound us together, testing their strength. Diane was unsettled, Celeste intrigued, and Leigh, as ever, ready to take the bait and run with it.

"You'll get to see how we work together," I said, trying to steer the conversation back to safer waters. But Yeska's presence changed the balance like a new instrument introduced in a familiar song.

"I'm going to need to accompany you on a Dungeon expedition as well," Yeska continued. Her eyes were alight with an eagerness that was hard to miss. "Only through a range of experiences can I observe you fully."

I could almost feel the room hold its breath at her pronouncement. Venturing into a Dungeon was no small matter, always fraught with danger and unknowns. The prospect, while necessary, hung over us with a certain heaviness.

"Alright," I said, never one to shy away from a challenge. "We'll need to find a suitable challenge for all of us. I'm level 9, while you, Leigh, and Diane are level 6. Celeste is level 4. The average is around level 6-7, so we should look for a challenge in that range."

"Very well," Yeska purred. "Looking forward to it."

Leigh stretched out her legs under the table, her casual demeanor a mask for the seriousness of Yeska's request. "Guess we'll be breakin' out the weapons and satchels again soon," she said.

Celeste nodded in agreement, though her hand gripped my arm a bit tighter. "Whatever is needed," she said, her voice betraying none of the anxiousness that tinged her touch.

I let out a slow breath. "We'll plan for it," I

assured the group. "As we always do. We need to be prepared."

Yeska's demeanor was unflappable as she sat there, the newest member of our compact. She had yet to find her place at the table in ways beyond the physical sense, but she had taken a bold stance that I liked, even if Diane still had to get used to it.

"I'm looking forward to understanding more about the powers of a Frontier Summoner as well," Yeska said, her voice a low purr that seemed to vibrate through the room. "Understanding you."

Her words hung in the air, their meaning rippling through me. I felt the binding between us tighten — a mixture of anticipation and a hint of dread. The future seemed closer at that moment, pregnant with the possibility of revelation or upheaval.

Leigh leaned against the countertop, watching us with bright eyes. "I think the next four months are going to be quite interesting around here," she quipped, her tone teasing.

We all felt it, a shift caused by Yeska's presence and her intentions. The air of the homestead was filled with unspoken promises and uncertainties, the hidden dynamics of our relationships unfolding anew.

Standing there with all of them, I felt something else — a vague premonition that aligned with what Leigh had said.

Perhaps autumn and winter would not be as homey and calm as I had expected they would be…

As we all sat digesting the morning's revelations, Celeste leaned forward with a spark of curiosity in her eyes. "Yeska," she began, her voice steady with genuine wonder, "what exactly can Bloodmages do? The stories are so varied and so... atmospheric." She had a way of phrasing things that made them sound more like discoveries than inquiries.

Yeska placed her cup down on the table with gentle precision. "Bloodmages," she said, her tone clinical as she delved into explanation, "have the ability to manipulate the vital essence of living beings. It's not merely the physical blood, but the life force it represents."

"Primarily, we can provide 'passive buffs,' enhancing a person's natural capabilities at the cost of draining some of their vitality, their Health." As she talked, Yeska's fingers traced the rim of her teacup lightly, a visual accompaniment to the lesson. "We can also cast 'curses,' for lack of a better term, causing gradual harm over time. And in fact, the 'blood' part of my Class's name is actually a misnomer. The magic focuses on essence, Health, regardless of whether there is actual blood involved."

Her explanation felt antiseptic, detached, and yet a tingle of intrigue made its way around the table.

"So, it works on the undead?" I asked.

"Exactly," she said as gaze flicked from face to face as she added, "My abilities are generally proportional to the strength of the target's Bloodline and the augments of blood, or Health, that we use."

"So, someone with a strong Bloodline would be more... affected by your magic, both positively and negatively?" Diane asked, and I could hear the effort she put into keeping her voice neutral.

"Exactly," Yeska replied. She seemed to appreciate the grasp Diane was taking on the complexities of her art. "That's what makes Bloodmages particularly suited for combating powerful entities — bosses — within Dungeons, for example."

The room was still, each of us contemplating the implications. I looked at Yeska, wondering about the untapped potential of such powers, especially considering the enemies we might face.

"Could you then, theoretically, be more effective against a creature like Father, if he possesses a powerful Bloodline?" I asked, the thought of the dragon causing an involuntary tightening of my shoulders.

Her eyes stayed fixed on me, unblinking. "If Father has a Bloodline — and I can't imagine such a being wouldn't — it stands to reason that my spells would indeed work more potently against him," Yeska confirmed, her voice betraying nothing of the fire her words kindled in my chest.

The possibility lingered in the air, inviting analysis and strategy. We all considered this, the idea of turning Yeska's unique talents against such a formidable adversary opened up new pathways in our planning. If Father was the challenge I expected him to be, then we might need Yeska to join our adventuring party.

"I sense there's a great deal for us to weigh," I said at last. "It's a promising thought." The sentiment was echoed in soft murmurs of assent from around the table.

As the conversation trailed off, I felt a tugging need to get things in order, to prepare for the challenges we would surely face. "I'll go and sort out a room for you," I told Yeska, standing from my chair with a glance toward the unallocated space on the first floor.

She nodded graciously. "Thank you, David. I appreciate your hospitality."

"We can do that!" Celeste put in.

I smiled and shook my head. "You get

acquainted, and I'll be right back."

Chapter 9

My mind was churning as I made my way upstairs to the room we had set aside for Yeska, the spare bedroom that Waelin had occupied during his brief stay. The quiet of the house followed me, a comforting companion as I entered the space that would be hers for the coming months.

Sunlight streamed through the open window, bathing the room in a placid glow. I paused at the threshold, taking in this canvas soon to be splashed with the presence of a Bloodmage — a thought that intrigued me.

The bed stood in the corner, its frame sturdy and expectant. I fetched fresh linens from the linen closet — crisp and neat, with the subtle scent of lavender from the sachets Diane liked to tuck between the sheets.

As I stripped the bed of its old dressings, my thoughts meandered through the day's events — the quiet breakfast, the not-so-quiet farewells, and Yeska with her green-eyed gaze that seemed to cut straight to the marrow, announcing a presence that would change things up a little around here.

I tossed the used sheets into a corner, intending to deal with them later. A new ally like Yeska could be vital — her knowledge of rituals and her ability to dive into the life force of beings; these were tools that could tip the scales in our favor.

I unfurled the fitted sheet, tugging it tight around the mattress corners. This act, something done so frequently, now felt imbued with greater meaning – preparing a haven for someone who might be our wild card against Father.

The top sheet followed, billowing like a soft sail, then settling gently in place. As I worked, I turned the presence of Yeska over in my head. Having her here would certainly prove exciting, an infusion of unknown energy into the rhythm of our daily life. Her assertiveness, her dominant nature, it wasn't something we were used to here.

I fluffed the pillows, tucking them in clean cases as my mind continued wandering while I performed the simple task. Was I ready to trust her, to allow her into the inner workings of this place we held so dear? Trust is earned in actions and time, not just in the necessity of the moment.

As I draped the quilt over the bed, smoothing out any wrinkles, I considered the delicate balance of our home. Yeska's strong energy – would it mesh with the harmonies we had so carefully composed?

The thought lingered as I stood back to survey my work. The bed was made up neatly, almost professionally — a small corner of orderliness in the anticipation of chaos.

Diane, with her perceptive eye and protective heart, might clash with Yeska's forwardness. And Celeste, well, she seemed intrigued, but I knew we all felt the friction. It would take care to navigate these new waters. I was less worried about Leigh, who herself had confidence and playfulness in spades and was never worried by the appearance of a newcomer.

I smiled at the thought of each of them being so different and unique. The caring and loving nature of Diane, albeit slightly protective; the playful and bouncy energy of Leigh, full of lust for life; and the gentle and creative forces that fueled Celeste's soaring spirit.

And now there was the fiery, challenging, and perhaps slightly maniacal presence of Yeska. I grinned and shook my head, sincerely looking forward to what time would soon tell.

As I left the bed to gather the discarded linens, my movement echoed slightly against the walls. It was vital to maintain open communication with my women — Celeste, Diane, and Leigh. Everyone needed to be on the same page, especially with Yeska in the picture.

I would also need to talk to Yeska more, to understand her beyond the fog of mystery that seemed to encompass Bloodmages. Communication — that was key.

As much as Yeska drew the eye, a figure of both allure and power, the others held my core. Diane, Celeste, and Leigh — they were my grounding, my north star in this expanding universe. I would stay true to them and make sure that they accepted Yeska before I would ask her to join our party.

I carried the used linens out of the room, my mind still wandering. These were more than just fabrics to be washed and reused; they were the tangible remnants of the day's transitions.

Pausing at the door, I took one last look at the room. Sunlight and shadows played across the bedspread, a silent piano of light and dark. It felt ready to welcome our guest, to welcome the turn our lives would take with her in it.

I closed the door behind me, a soft click in the

solitude that filled the hallway. My mind was cleared in the simple task, and I headed back downstairs — to where the others waited, ready to embrace whatever came next.

Chapter 10

Over the next two days, I took it upon myself to help Yeska adjust to the intricacies of frontier life. It was somewhat out of her depth, clearly more accustomed to the alchemical studies and patient observances a Bloodmage's work entailed, but here she was, gamely shouldering traps and wandering around the outskirts with me.

"Trapping," I explained, as we checked another contraption I had set up, "isn't just about catching prey. It's a bit like... predicting the future, really. Anticipating where and how these animals will move."

Yeska watched intently, her eyes taking in the mechanism, the bait, the signs of recent activity. "Not much different than working a ritual, I would imagine," she murmured, nodding. "And I am a good huntress," she added with a pointed look.

I chuckled. "Trapping and hunting are very different," I said. "You might be able to bag some game with bow and arrow, but we rarely do that around the homestead. Trapping is different, but you'll see."

Despite her insight, Yeska was all thumbs when it came to resetting the traps, her movements awkward as she tried to balance the delicate tension necessary to keep them set. I stepped in to guide her hands through the motions, telling her, "You'll get the hang of it."

When it came to tending the crops, however,

Yeska's inexperience was even more pronounced. She stooped beside me amid Magebread flowers, her attempts to pull weeds ending in uprooting a bit of the precious crop itself. "Oh," she gasped softly, a frown creasing her brow.

"Don't worry about it," I reassured her, though I was mentally counting the loss. "This one... is a bit beyond repair, but it happens to the best of us."

As we moved on, me showing her the rows of tomatoes and beans, her hand tentatively reached for a ripe tomato. But as she tugged, the vine gave an unexpected jerk, and a small cluster of unripe fruit plopped onto the ground. She looked up at me, mortified.

"Yeska, really, it's alright," I insisted, though my tone held a bit less conviction this time. I was quickly learning where her aptitudes lay — and the garden wasn't one.

The chopping block for firewood didn't fare any better. Yeska hefted the axe with determination, but each swing seemed to bounce off the wood as if repelled by an invisible shield. After several attempts and zero results, she let out a frustrated sigh.

"Here, let me show you," I said, taking the axe and demonstrating how to align and deliver a solid, splitting blow. "It's all about where you focus your strength."

Her next attempt managed to wedge the axe into the log, but it stopped short of cleaving it in two. She tugged at the handle; cheeks flushed with exertion. "How do you make this look so easy?" she puffed out the question between breaths.

"Practice — and maybe a bit of stubbornness," I joked, trying to lighten her mood. "We might stick with trapping for now. You've got a good eye for it."

She nodded, watching me retrieve the axe and neatly split the log in two. "Trapping it is," she said, and I thought I saw a flicker of relief in her eyes.

By evening of the second day, as Yeska and I ambled back toward the house with a weighty haul of wood scraps she managed to gather, we were both quiet, reflective. This crash course had been more informative for me than for her, I felt. She had been almost boastful about her skills as a huntress and her ability to learn, but she hadn't made much progress.

Leigh and Diane had kept busy as well during those two days. Returning to find the aftermath of their toil was a comfort — the land cared for, the results of their work tangible in the freshly moved earth and the bucket of gleaming fish ready for the smokehouse.

Celeste, too, found her rhythm, managing the household with a grace that belied the hard work involved. The house had the aroma of a well-timed meal, and the cleanliness of the rooms spoke of attentive hands. Of course, the domesticants helped her, and they did much, but Celeste had some easing into the rhythm of her own to do — after all, she had lain comatose for a long time and had lived a pampered life before that.

The dinner conversation was light, the fatigue of the day leaving most of us more inclined to listen than to speak. Diane and Leigh shared their accomplishments, the beans that were harvested, the fish that didn't get away.

Celeste added her own quieter achievements — the laundry washed and dried, the floors swept, the meals she'd conjured from the staples in our store. I felt a surge of pride for what they managed to achieve day in, day out.

Yeska contributed her experiences in learning the lay of the land from me, expressing a clear, respectful admiration for the others' know-how. The women exchanged a few good-natured barbs about Yeska's initiation into frontier life. Luckily, she could take a joke, and things were starting to get easier around the table already.

I had one more plan for Yeska — one more activity we could test her on, and it was one I hoped would match up perfectly with her catkin nature.

When the meal ended, I spoke up. "Tomorrow," I began, rubbing my hands together in anticipation. "I thought we could all take our visitor here on a proper fishing trip."

Diane raised her eyebrows, a smile tugging at the corner of her mouth. "Fishing, huh? That should be interesting. Yeska, have you ever done any fishing?"

Yeska inclined her head with a playful glint in her eyes. "I may not be a farmhand or a lumberjack, but give me a rod or a spear, and I'll show you how the catkin fish."

Celeste nodded, always supportive. "It'll be nice to get out together." Her voice held a note of quiet excitement.

Leigh clapped her hands together, beaming. "Oh, a fishin' trip! This is gonna be so much fun! I can't wait!"

As the idea settled among us, a mixture of laughter and chatter bubbling up. I couldn't help but wonder how this trip might turn out with Yeska in tow. The thought of the four of us out there gave me a sense of shared curiosity and a flicker of unease.

It could either strengthen our bond or highlight the rifts. Only time would tell.

"So, you've done a lot of fishing before?" Diane asked Yeska, referring to the boast the cat girl had just made.

"Plenty," Yeska said with an air of confidence. "I'm good enough at it."

I exchanged a look with Diane. Teaching Yeska anything other than trapping would be too much work since she had no talent for the more rustic skills. However, if we could get her on fishing duty, she would certainly contribute in a meaningful way. After all, fish sold well in Gladdenfield, and we often dined on them.

Leigh's enthusiasm was a spark ready to ignite a flame, her bright disposition infectious. "Oh, it's settled then! We're going fishing, and it'll be grand. You'll see, Yeska. There ain't nothin' like the Silverthread River in the mornin' light."

I nodded. "And we'll hit Gladdenfield on the way back. Yeska needs to observe me in a Dungeon, so maybe there's word of a quest we could pick up."

Diane took a more measured approach, her eyes flicking to mine for a shared understanding. "It sounds nice," she murmured, "A day by the river could be good for us all. And I guess a visit to Gladdenfield wouldn't hurt either." Her reluctant smile was a small victory in itself.

Celeste, ever the thoughtful companion, added softly, "Yes, a day outside, away from the routine, might bring a new perspective."

I nodded, feeling a sense of purpose crystallize among us. "Great, then it's settled." The idea of venturing into a challenge, with our new Bloodmage along, injected an undercurrent of anticipation throughout the room.

After a brief, companionable silence, I voiced another thought. "Maybe Darny or Mayor Wilhelm can lead us to a suitable Dungeon for our combined strength."

Yeska leaned forward, her interest clear. "A Dungeon adventure sounds thrilling," she said, a hint of fervor coloring her tone. "To witness your skills in a more... challenging setting would be enlightening."

Leigh's head was bobbing enthusiastically, her shoulder brushing against Yeska's, spreading her vivacious mood. "That's the spirit! We'll have a real adventure, just you wait."

Celeste's response was a serene nod, the promise of navigating the unknown with the company she trusted offering her a sense of tranquil audacity. It was reassuring to see her come around, bolstered by our shared decision.

I felt the excitement begin to thrum beneath my tranquil exterior at the thought of our upcoming outing. Some good, old-fashioned fishing followed by a trip to Gladdenfield — it sounded like the perfect way to understand our new companion better.

I voiced a final thought that had been nagging at me since Yeska's arrival, seeing how easily the cat girl had slipped through our defenses. "And since we'll be leaving the homestead for the day, I've been thinking about summoning and binding an extra Storm Elemental just to be on the safe side."

"An extra Storm Elemental?" Leigh whistled softly. "Look at you, living the high mage life, David. But sure, nothin' wrong with an additional layer of protection."

I agreed with a small nod. The homestead was rugged and well-guarded but leaving it unattended while we were all away felt like tempting fate. It was best to be cautious.

"Alright, ladies," I said. "Let's pack up and get ready!"

In the following hour, we pulled together the essentials — fishing tackle, baskets, and a small cooler for whatever we might catch. Celeste gathered blankets and picnic supplies, while Diane made sure we had enough water.

Yeska observed us plan and pack, her gaze traveling over the items we laid out. "Seems I'll need to pack as well," she mused, motioning to her belt where a sheathed dagger hung — her only weapon.

"You don't fight with traditional weapons?" I asked, my curiosity piqued.

"No," she shook her head. "Bloodmages rarely do. Our strength lies in our spells. But I do carry a dagger, just in case." Her hand brushed the dagger's hilt, a silent show of readiness.

With all our items laid out to pack, I glanced

around at my companions brimming with quiet determination. We were each other's strength, ready to support one another in whatever awaited beyond the boundaries of the homestead.

I methodically checked each item; Celeste's carefully prepared food packs, Diane's sturdy crossbow, and Leigh's trusted revolver and dagger. My semi-automatic rifle and handgun felt familiar and reassuring in my hands as I prepared them.

Yeska stood beside me, her gaze lingering on my weapons. "Impressive arsenal," she commented with a nod of approval. "Preparation is key, after all."

Evening settled over the homestead with a hushed promise, the transition from day to dusk filled with the rustle of leaves and the soft clinking of our gear as we packed it away.

I looked over at Celeste, her expression calm yet filled with that gentle excitement of hers that bubbled under the surface. I could not help but smile, her enthusiasm contagious.

The finality of our plans brought a new energy to the group, and we all seemed ready for the promise of tomorrow's dawn. With our fishing trip and excursion to Gladdenfield on the horizon, there was an undercurrent of anticipation as we cleaned up for the night.

Already, Celeste and Diane fared better with the reality of Yeska staying with us for a while, her dedication to aiding our cause easing the shift. Leigh, always the life of any gathering, seemed undaunted by the challenges ahead, her face lit by the soft glow of lamplight as she finished stowing her gear.

Yeska, too, presented an enigmatic figure, her catkin grace hinting that she had to have *some* talents. Of course, as I watched her, I could guess one activity someone with her body would excel at... But that was not an activity that would really help the homestead much.

Come morning, we would see if there was any truth to her boasts.

Chapter 11

The next day, I was awake before the others. I pushed back the coverlet carefully, reluctant to disturb the tranquil sight of my sleeping companions.

I stood up and stretched, feeling the satisfying crack of my spine. Stepping lightly across the smooth oak floorboards, I glanced back at the bed: Diane's dark hair splayed across her pillow, Leigh's arm flung wide in carefree abandon, Celeste's face serene as though she was lost in a pleasant dream. Slowly, they were murmuring their sleepy sounds and waking up.

The sight of them all peaceful and groggy from sleep brought a quiet smile to my lips, and I headed towards Yeska's room, my hand pausing on the doorknob before rapping gently — a courteous summons for the day we had planned.

"Good morning, Yeska," I called softly through the door. "We have a big day ahead." There was only a moment's wait before a muffled acknowledgment came.

The kitchen awaited me, still and expectant in the early light; it was the heart of the household where each new day was inaugurated with the aroma of coffee and the promise of sustenance.

I set about preparing breakfast for the five of us, moving almost by muscle memory through the routine of firing the stove and setting out our sturdiest skillets. The scent of coffee soon filled the space, robust and welcoming as an old friend.

Diane, Leigh, and Celeste made their way downstairs, each in varying degrees of wakefulness but united by a common thread of eagerness that hung palpable in the air.

They greeted me with soft murmurs and sleepy smiles while I cracked eggs into the pan, watching them whiten and solidify.

"I can almost taste those trout we're going to catch," Leigh said, her voice picking up in volume as her excitement spilled over.

"Let's not count them just yet," Diane reminded her, although her tone was more playful than admonishing.

Celeste nudged Diane with a shoulder, "Who knows? We might surprise ourselves out there today."

Yeska joined us soon after, her night's rest chasing away any vestige of unfamiliarity in the kitchen as she easily blended into the fabric of our morning.

Her excitement mirrored that of the others, a shared anticipation for the day that lay ahead of us, the collective hope for a haul of fish swimming just beneath her calm exterior.

We sat and shared the humble breakfast, the food serving as both fuel for the body and kindling for the spirit of camaraderie that bound us together.

With the ritual of the meal completed, we distributed the tasks of preparing for our venture. Leigh checked the fishing gear while Diane assembled a small first aid kit.

Celeste wrapped up the remaining snacks, her fingers swift and sure as she packed away what we might need for a meal on the riverbank.

Yeska offered to carry the heaviest tackle box, her earlier endeavors at the chopping block a forgotten comedy next to the earnestness with which she undertook this new challenge.

We gathered our things and stepped outside, the freshness of the day wrapping around us like a soft shawl. I took the lead, energized by the prospect of what the day might hold.

"I have a good feeling about this," I said, my voice carrying a trace of the optimism that saturated the very air. I sensed that we were all looking forward to this little expedition.

The others agreed, the murmur of their assent a gentle undertow to the crunch of our boots against the earth as we walked.

"Could be the last time this season we have a day as pleasant as this for an outing," I observed, the words edged with a touch of wistful knowledge.

They all nodded, understanding the days of beautiful and sunny weather would soon be over – the unspoken acknowledgment that soon the bite of winter would put an end to such activities.

Outside, the Silverthread River awaited us, its clear waters an open promise. The time for fishing and something more just around the riverbend, for I had a good spot in mind.

The morning air held a freshness that invigorated the spirit, a tangible sense of the day's potential as we walked along the Silverthread River. The gentle murmur of water accompanied our steps, a soothing soundtrack to our journey through the Springfield Forest.

"There's a spot I know, Pakauley Lake, a few hours from here," I said, pointing ahead and downstream of the river. "The water gathers into a small lake, teeming with fish. It's a perfect place for a day like today."

Diane walked beside Yeska, a hint of her earlier reservations still clinging to her like morning dew but gradually dissipating with each stride and shared conversation about the joys of fishing.

"It's all about patience and knowing the waters," Diane explained, her words reflecting a quiet confidence born of experience. Yeska listened, her interest genuine as she nodded and asked thoughtful questions.

The forest around us was alive with the whispers of leaves and the occasional call of a distant bird. We tread past ferns and moss-covered stones, ensconced in the verdant embrace of nature.

As our discussion wove through topics of lure and line, Yeska described her own ventures into fishing, her tales shaped by far different waters and a different kind of prey than what Diane knew.

Celeste, ever observant, picked up small details of the forest's character, noting the subtle variations in the flora that indicated the health of this woodland expanse. Her appreciation for such nuances was clear in the smile that graced her lips with each discovery.

"You see that poplar over there?" I pointed to a tall tree with bright, fluttering leaves. "Always a good indicator of water nearby."

Leigh, in her element, chimed in with a joke. "David has a sixth sense for wetness," she hummed, shooting me a naughty look.

That made Yeska laugh, a sound that was light and honest, hinting at a bond that was slowly forming between these souls. I chuckled along with the joke, although I wasn't sure if Diane enjoyed this kind of innuendo as she was more careful with Yeska.

Walking as a group, united by this patchwork of experiences and skills, each of us bore our own connection to the waters we sought. Our conversation meandered like the river path, natural and unforced.

When talk lapsed into silence, it felt like breathing space — an interlude for us to simply absorb the world. The quiet was its own form of dialogue, filled with meaning for those who listened.

And then, as if inspired by the serenity around us, Celeste's voice lifted in song, a gentle, lilting melody that seemed to belong to the woods themselves.

Diane joined in, their voices harmonizing in an impromptu celebration of the moment, their song a spontaneous outpouring of being alive in this wilderness.

I listened, letting the beauty of their shared voices wash over me as I walked, the tune a simple one that spoke of rippling waters and dancing light.

"By the river's gentle sway,
We will find our catch today.
Sunlight breaks on dappled waves,
treasure hidden in watery caves."

"Hooks and lines, we cast them long,
waiting patient, hopeful, strong.
Nature's bounty soon to hold,
the river's tale in silver, gold."

As the final note faded, a hush settled in the air, a collective pause that held us in its grasp as if the world approved of their reverence for its beauty.

It was Leigh who broke the reverie with sweet praise of the little song that the two had come up with. Yeska, too, spoke her approval, and we laughed as the girls made absurd variation of the song. Their laughter was a sound that seemed right and fitting as we continued our journey towards the fishing haven I had promised.

The sun ascended, casting its benevolence over our trek, warming my back through the layers of my shirt as I led the way, my steps measured and sure.

Around me, the forest seemed to breathe, a living entity aware of our transit, indifferent and eternal in its stoic grandeur.

We passed a small clearing where shafts of sunlight filtered through the leafy canopy, spotlighting a family of deer that glanced our way with idle curiosity before bounding off into the underbrush.

Yeska gestured to the scene with a smile, a shared appreciation for the encounter brightening her features, and I nodded in agreement.

The trees began to thin, a hint of openness ahead that signaled the approaching end of our woodsy corridor, the babbling crescendo of the river pulling us forward.

Through the screen of greenery, I could see the sheen of a vast expanse of water through gaps in the trees, the anticipation in my chest blooming into excitement.

Holding up my hand for a pause, I smiled at my companions, my voice low and full of promise, "We've arrived at our spot, and it is looking to be a beautiful day."

Chapter 12

The forest gave way to the clear expanse of Pakauley Lake, the sun high in the sky, painting the surface of the water with strokes of light. We arrived, our feet shuffling the pebbles on the beach, a sound as satisfying as the view that opened up in front of us.

Leigh was the first to drop her gear, a playful spark in her eyes as she scanned the area. "This'll do perfectly," she declared, hands on her hips as she considered the optimal spot for our makeshift camp.

Celeste joined in, her nimble fingers already pulling items from her backpack — blankets, a collapsible shade, and the components of a portable picnic table. Her movements were precise, the habitual motions of someone who had turned setting up camp into a personal art form.

I watched for a moment, our bonds a comfortable blanket in the cool morning air. But Leigh caught my eye, her lips curving in a knowing smile.

"Go on, David," she said with a gentle push. "Take Yeska and Diane to the water. We got this covered."

I hesitated, a part of me reluctant to leave them to the labor. But there was a wisdom to Leigh's nudge, an unspoken encouragement to foster the budding dynamics within our group.

"Alright," I agreed, turning to Yeska and Diane. They looked back at me, an unreadable mixture of anticipation in their shared glances. "Shall we see what the lake holds for us?"

Yeska nodded, her lithe fingers reaching for the tackle box. Her earlier clumsiness forgotten, there was a newfound eagerness in her posture. Diane, for her part, had gathered the rods, her pretty face thoughtful as she considered the day's potential.

We made our way to the beach, the cool water lapping at the shore in gentle invitation. Folding chairs were set up in a line, a silent row of sentinels waiting for occupants.

Diane, with methodical care, began assembling her fishing pole, the components clicking together with the satisfaction of well-maintained equipment. She glanced at Yeska, who was obviously unfamiliar with our relatively advanced gear, and she offered a small tutorial. "The reel goes on like this, see?"

Yeska watched and mimicked Diane's actions, her features focused. A small furrow appeared between her brows as she worked, showing her concentration. Diane corrected her hold, guiding Yeska's hand with a patience that was touching.

I set up my own chair between them, the comfortable familiarity of the lake calming my spirits. It was good to be here, away from home, in a place as soothing as any I knew.

Yeska made a commendable effort, and after a few adjustments, her rod was ready. She grinned at Diane, a look of triumph in her eyes. "Like this?" she asked.

Diane nodded. "Exactly like that." Her approval was plain, and for a moment, I saw a softening in her expression, an opening perhaps for the bond I hoped they would forge.

We settled into our chairs, the coolness of the metal a contrast to the warm pebbles underfoot. The lake stretched out, an open canvas for our day's pursuits.

The sound of Leigh and Celeste's laughter carried over, a reassuring note that underpinned the tranquility. I could hear the snap of the shade being set, the rustle of the wind through its fabric.

Diane caught a tiny fish on her first attempt, her skill as undeniable as the pride that swelled in her chest. She held it up for Yeska to see, the silver flash of it a brief spectacle before she released it back into the water.

"Too small, but humble beginnings are best," she purred.

I chuckled and watched Yeska as she stood. There was a balance to her stance, a readiness in her posture as she cast the line. She caught nothing yet, but her determination didn't waver. Still, she seemed a little impatient.

"I'm better with spear in the shallows," she said. "I... With this rod I can't really see them."

"It's about patience," Diane reminded her. "Waiting for that perfect moment. You'll get it."

I sat back, watching the two of them interact. Yeska's earlier intensity had tempered into a steady resolve, the morning's awkwardness was replaced by the shared goal of a successful catch.

As the minutes stretched, the water's surface undisturbed by a bite, Yeska's earlier confidence — and what little patience she had — waned. But Diane was there, her encouragement a quiet force. "It's just about time," she said, and something in her tone hinted she knew the lake's secrets well.

Then, with a sudden jerk, Yeska's line . She stood swiftly, reeling in with a focus that transformed her. As she drew the fish closer, a look of astounded satisfaction crossed her features — a mirror image of Diane's earlier excitement.

With a triumphant flourish, Yeska pulled the fish from the water, her first catch glowing in the bright sunlight. Diane clapped, a genuine cheer that bloomed like a flower in the air.

They looked at each other, Yeska's catch creating a kinship that hadn't been there before. A bond had been formed, fragile but real in the joy of the moment.

I watched them, hopeful. They had shared in an activity, found a common ground that might become the foundation for something more. Yeska and Diane, laughing by the water's edge, offered a glimpse of what might be possible.

"Great work, girls," I said. "Now let's see if we can't fill a bucket!"

The gentle sway of the reeds by Pakauley Lake accompanied our moments of expectation, each of us poised with a rod in hand, watching the dance of the fishing lines on the water's surface. The lake's serenity seemed a world apart, its stillness only occasionally broken by the hopeful bob of a float.

Yeska watched her line with an intensity that bordered on focus and frustration. Beside her, Diane's gaze held a more measured patience, a silent acknowledgment that nature often made its own schedule, unaffected by our desires.

I recalled the particular satisfaction of fishing here, the simple joy of a successful catch, and the silent companionship that spoke louder than any conversation. But the fish beneath the shimmering surface were elusive today, uninterested in our offerings.

"They're not biting," Yeska observed, her voice a

mix of disappointment and challenge. "But it's a beautiful day, regardless."

"I could use my Fishing skill," Diane mentioned, her tone matter-of-fact, though it held a hint of pride. Her revelation seemed to shake Yeska from her drowsiness, who turned to look at her with renewed interest.

"A skill?" Yeska repeated. "As part of your Scout Class, you mean?"

Diane nodded and explained, "It's an ability that helps me to better understand the habits and preferences of the fish. It usually makes catching them a bit more... predictable."

I leaned back in my chair, amused at Yeska's furrowed brow. "And I could summon a minor water spirit," I added. "They can herd the fish to make catching them easier, but I think we should try to catch fish on our own first. Like with any skill, we should be competent at the basics before we try tricks."

Yeska laughed lightly. "Fair enough, David. I prefer doing things more directly anyway."

Diane stood, examining the water's edge before

turning to us with determination. "There's a better spot around that bend where the water runs a bit deeper. They might be more active there."

We gathered our chairs and gear, making our way to the location Diane suggested. As a Scout, her understanding of the land and its creatures often led to spots ripe with potential, hidden from untrained eyes.

Once at the new spot, we set up again, the background rhythm of the forest providing a calming soundtrack. This time, when we cast our lines, the ripples seemed to sing with promise.

Yeska's line tensed suddenly, and with a swift reaction, she reeled in a struggling fish. The surprise and pride in her eyes were mirrored in Diane's pleased smile as she watched her catch.

Not to be outdone, Diane's rod dipped moments later, a sign of her own success. With expert movements, she brought in her catch, holding it up for Yeska to see before depositing it in the bucket.

"Not bad," Yeska said, her usual confidence bolstered by the day's victories.

As Diane helped Yeska with her reel, I watched,

a quiet contentment filling me. Whether or not the fish continued to bite, the day had already delivered some small treasures.

It was then that something peculiar happened – a fish leaped from the water, high enough to glint in the sunlight, and with impeccable comedic timing, it splashed back down, sending a spray of water right onto Yeska's face.

Startled, Yeska let out a yelp, wiping her face with the back of her hand in a most cat-like manner while Diane burst into laughter. My own chuckles joined them, buoyed by the infectious nature of the moment.

"I didn't know fishing included a free shower," Yeska quipped, a wry smile tugging at her lips despite the surprise dousing.

"Only for the most dedicated fishermen," I said, winking back at her.

The laughter seemed to bond them together, a shared joke that found fertile ground in the common experience of being soaked unexpectedly.

As our chuckles receded into soft sighs of amusement, Leigh's voice carried across from where she was preparing for lunch. "Lunchtime, everyone! Hope you worked up an appetite!"

I stood and extended a hand to Yeska, "Time to see what culinary surprises Leigh has in store for us."

We made our way back to where Leigh had set up an inviting array of lunch by the edge of the lake. The food smelled delightful, a perfect accompaniment to our morning efforts.

Chapter 13

We settled into our makeshift picnic area by the lakeside, where Leigh and Celeste had laid out a spread of food. They had woven together the comforting smells of our homestead kitchen with the invigorating scent of the open air, creating an ambiance that couldn't have been more perfect.

The sandwiches were thick and generous, stuffed with freshly sliced tomatoes and lettuce that still had traces of dew on them. Yeska took a bite, and her eyes closed as if she wanted to savor every taste, every sensation that the simple yet delicious meal offered.

"This is fantastic," she mumbled between bites. The corners of her lips turned up in a heartfelt smile. "Really hits the spot after a morning out here."

Diane chuckled, nudging Yeska with her elbow. "Wait until you try Leigh's coleslaw," she said, passing a bowl of the creamy, tangy concoction towards our guest.

Yeska took a spoonful, her initial hesitation giving way to an appreciative nod as she chewed. "You could've warned me," she joked, "I might not want to leave after getting a taste of this."

I watched the exchange, a gentle feeling of contentment growing inside me. Leigh's coleslaw was a bit of a legend — I knew once Yeska had a taste, she'd be hooked.

Leigh sat back with a self-assured grin that was

all warmth. "We could trade secrets," she proposed, "your Bloodmage skills for my kitchen prowess."

The table erupted into laughter, and it was easy, it was natural. For a moment, nothing else mattered — not the worries, not the what-ifs — just the here and now, the friendships forming over a shared table.

Diane speared a pickle with her fork, her movements nonchalant as she shared the little accident from this morning with Yeska. "She almost had a whole school of fish on her line, but instead, she got a shower."

Yeska rolled her eyes in good humor, joining in on the fun. "I *did* catch one afterwards," she reminded us, her pride evident even as she played along with Diane's teasing.

"With a little assistance," Diane added slyly, and again, we laughed. There were no undercurrents, no barbs — just the simple joy of shared experiences and new memories.

Celeste reached for a bunch of grapes, her motions as smooth and delicate as if she were painting a picture with her movements. "Poor Yeska!" she exclaimed, smiling.

"You should've seen it," I said. "A true fisherman's baptism. The poor girl looked pretty surprised… Like a wet kitten."

Yeska chuckled and stuck out her tongue at me, and the blaze in her pretty eyes told me she liked the gentle ribbing. I grinned at her, happy that she was finding her place.

Lunch slowly wound down, Leigh and Celeste collecting the empty containers and shaking out the picnic blankets. Their chatter, low and easy, blended with the sounds of the lake and the breeze rustling through the trees.

"We'll take care of the clean-up," Celeste said, her tone leaving no room for protest. "You three enjoy the afternoon. Catch some more fish!"

Diane stood, dusting off her hands on her pants before giving a brief, grateful squeeze to Celeste's shoulder. "Thanks," she said.

Yeska and I rose as well, following Diane's lead. "We'll leave you to it then," I said, not unkindly.

The thought of returning to our little fishing

haven felt just as comforting as the meals we'd just consumed. And I knew the girls were doing it to allow Diane and Yeska to bond a little more. It was really sweet of them; they wanted us all to get along.

Yeska hoisted the tackle box with a fluid motion, adjusting it in her hands as she walked. "Fishing seems more my speed than farming," she said over her shoulder, and the lightness in her voice was refreshing.

The path back to the fishing spot was known now, familiar under our feet. It prompted a sense of routine, and I found myself looking forward to the calm rhythm of casting lines and waiting for bites.

Diane cast a glance back at Leigh and Celeste, who were still tidying up the picnic spot. "It's nice, isn't it?" she said, a small smile quirking her lips. "Days like these?"

"It is," I agreed, matching her stride. "Nothing to do but enjoy the afternoon."

Yeska seemed to slip into contemplation, her eyes on the lake's gentle waves. There was a quiet assurance about her, a sense of being exactly where she wanted to be.

We spread out along the pebbly beach once more, each finding a comfortable spot to settle into the patience fishing required. The sun caressed our backs as we cast lines out into the lake's silvery expanse.

I looked at Yeska and Diane to my left and right, their profiles etched against the tranquil scenery, the lines dancing on the water, and felt a surge of gratitude for this moment. I hoped that the afternoon would help our bonds improve even more.

With our rods in hand, we returned to our strategic positions along the pebbled shores of Pakauley Lake. Diane took her spot to my right, casting her line with a smooth, practiced flick of her wrist.

Yeska positioned herself to my left, watching Diane's technique closely before attempting to mimic it. The peace of the gentle waves against the shore was our metronome, guiding the rhythm of our casts.

The air was cool, carrying with it the fresh scent of the surrounding forest, just enough to invigorate the senses without chilling the bones. I watched the way the water undulated, carrying our bobbers in a soft dance. Diane's line was the first to suggest a nibble, a subtle bob and weave of the float indicating a curious fish, teasing the bait before darting away.

Yeska was patient, her eyes never leaving the water's surface, her body tense in anticipation. She adjusted the grip on her rod, fingers tightening as if to command the fish to her will. The quiet focus was a sharp contrast to her earlier inexperience, revealing an adaptability that spoke of intelligence and perseverance.

She may have been somewhat unfamiliar with our more modern tools, but she definitely had the makings of a fisherwoman.

My own line remained unmoving, a test of patience that I accepted as part of the experience. It wasn't simply the act of catching that brought me pleasure, but the act of waiting, the expectation, the quiet communion with both nature and companions.

As time passed with the three of us waiting in silent accord, I couldn't help but smile at the thought of the robust laughter and warm chatter during lunch. Those moments of ease and simplicity would carry me through days less tranquil than this.

Occasionally, my gaze wandered back to our base campsite, where Celeste and Leigh had stayed behind to tidy up from our lunch. They moved with seamless coordination, a muted ballet of efficiency amidst the natural splendor that surrounded us.

They seemed to be having a good time, even while tidying up and doing chores. Leigh's laughter carried across the lake, a silvery thread that managed to weave its way into our quiet fishing alcove. Celeste was humming a soft tune, adding a soundtrack to our silent wait.

As I glanced back yet again to the campsite, I

noticed Celeste and Leigh disappearing into the tent, still caught up in their private amusement. Their tranquility was infectious, emanating across the distance and settling upon our little fishing trio with a reassuring touch.

"Now what are those two up to?" I mumbled to myself.

Yeska adjusted her position — a slight shuffle on the pebbles that caught my attention. She glanced sideways at me, catching one of my frequent looks to the campsite. "Leigh seems to enjoy herself no matter what she's doing," she said. "And Celeste seems the same."

"They're a good-natured duo, alright," I admitted, watching as another fish made an attempt at my bait, a half-hearted nibble before retreating to the depths of the lake, denying me the satisfaction of a catch.

Moments later, Celeste and Leigh emerged from the tent. And how!

My mouth went dry, and my hands slackened on the fishing rod as I saw they had changed into thong bikinis, the fabric hugging their curves in a way that drew the eye irresistibly.

Leigh's freckles stood out, charming against her sun-kissed skin. The blonde hair fell around her bare shoulders like lines of spun gold. Celeste was a vision, her amber hair tumbling over her shoulders as she followed Leigh out, looking as serene as the lake beside us.

And those pretty behinds in those skimpy thong bikinis…

Swimwear like that wasn't something that most women would wear to a public beach, but by the naughty blaze in Leigh's baby-blue eyes, I could tell this was her little plan for the day, and she had involved Celeste! They looked absolutely delicious, and I felt my attention move away from fishing — however fun — to wanting to run my hands over those curves.

Giggling, the two women spread towels some distance from us, easing down onto them to catch the sun while we waited for the fish to bite. Leigh turned back to wave at us, a joyous grin splitting her face.

Celeste lay back, letting the sun caress her pale

skin. They stretched out languidly, the grace of their movements seizing my attention, holding it captive. The sight affected me in ways both innocent and not so innocent, stirring warmth within me that transcended the sunlight.

I struggled to refocus on the lake, on the fish that had to be down there, somewhere beneath the calm surface. But my gaze was pulled again and again to the perfect picture they made against the backdrop of green and blue.

Yeska cleared her throat gently, and when I turned to her, I found her expression held a knowing amusement. "You are a lucky man, aren't you?" She nodded in the direction of Celeste and Leigh, her voice underscored with a tease. "To have such beauty gracing your life."

"I am," I agreed, feeling the rush surge through me. It was embedded in every look, every smile they shared, the pleasure they took in the simple act of lying in the sun.

It was no small task to pull my attention back to my line, back to the gentle sway of reed and water, the occasional plop of a curious fish breaking the surface. Yet the peaceful activity felt starkly inadequate compared to the allure of sun-kissed skin, oiled-up bodies, and playful laughter.

Diane caught a bass, her efficient movements drawing it from the lake, smiling at her victory. She tossed it in the bucket, which was filled mainly with the girls' catches. Yeska watched, learning from every successful catch, honing her own technique.

And all the while, despite our serene surroundings, the soft laughter from the two sunbathing beauties played like a siren's song, pulling at me with an irresistible force.

Diane caught my distracted glances, and though she said nothing, I could read the understanding in her eyes. It was as clear as the water we fished in, as undeniable as the catch of the day.

Quiet prevailed among us, a silent agreement to savor the tranquility of the moment, the perfect pause before returning to the urgency and challenges of daily life.

But that pause was interrupted by a call from Leigh, her voice lifting across the distance, laced with mirth. "David! Mind coming over here for a sec?"

I set my rod down, and Yeska and Diane both smiled at me. "Don't worry!" Diane said. "We'll fill that bucket."

"Alright," I said. "I'll be right back."

I walked back towards the campsite, towards Leigh and Celeste on their towels, who watched me approach, a hint of mischief playing on their lips.

My heart quickened, and my breath caught as the sight of Leigh and Celeste in their bikinis filled my vision. And judging by the naughty light in their eyes, they had a little plan all cooked up and ready to go.

Chapter 14

I made my way over to Leigh and Celeste as they beckoned, their laughter soft and inviting against the backdrop of the sun-drenched lake. The gravel crunched beneath my feet, each step an echo of the heart beating more intensely within my chest.

The afternoon air, carrying the scent of water and

warmth, seemed to press against my skin as I approached.

They lay side by side, their bodies glistening faintly with the sheen of the sun's affection, and their faces tilted up to bask in its glow. Leigh propped herself up on her elbows, revealing the smooth expanse of her back as she handed me the bottle of lotion with a playful glint in her eye.

"Would you mind?" she asked, her tone as melodious as the ripple of the water nearby. "Can't get burned."

Celeste's giggle floated in the air, a hint of shared secrets and unspoken delights. I smiled at her, surveying the prize of these two beauties in their thong bikinis.

I accepted the bottle, feeling the cool plastic against my palm. I poured some of the lotion onto my hand, the creamy texture contrasting with the warmth of my skin, ready to attend to the task at hand.

I lowered myself to straddle Leigh, resting just under the curvature of her perfect bottom, hugged tight by her thong bikini. The delicious scent of her sun-touched skin met my nostrils.

I reached out, my hand gliding over the soft freckles that dusted Leigh's sun-kissed shoulders. The lotion spread under my touch, and I worked it into her skin with a care that belied the casual nature of the act. My fingers moved in small circles, the lotion warming as her skin absorbed it.

Leigh let out a soft hum of approval, her body relaxing under my ministrations. "That feels really nice," she murmured, her voice a low purr that resonated with contentment.

Celeste watched us with an indulgent smile, her green eyes reflecting sunlight and shadows. During our moments of quiet concentration, she said, "It's good to see them smiling together," referring to Yeska and Diane, who sat a short distance away by the water's edge.

I glanced over to Diane and Yeska, witnessing a laughter shared between them as they enjoyed the simplicity of fishing. Their earlier unease had ebbed to a point where you could catch glimpses of understanding, maybe even the start of a friendship.

"It looks like things are going better between them now," I replied, glimpsing the progress that had taken root. Yeska held a fishing rod with growing confidence, and Diane seemed to take pleasure in Yeska's company — laughter and activities with a slight competitive edge had a way of bridging divides.

Leigh's eyes twinkled mischievously over her shoulder. "But who knows how long that will last?" she teased, bringing my attention back to her. "They might need you to mediate again."

Celeste chuckled, her feet kicking up softly, as though entertained by Leigh's jest. "They'll be fine," she said with a wisdom that was part of her charm. "They're finding their way."

With a last smooth stroke across Leigh's lower back, I capped the bottle of lotion. As I sat back, taking in the sight of Leigh's bronzed skin now protected against the sun, she stretched out, languorous and satisfied.

"All done?" she asked, the question more of an opening to further possibilities than an inquiry.

"All done," I confirmed, wiping excess lotion on

a towel. My own imagination began to wander, led astray by the twinkle of suggestion in Leigh's gaze, the playful shadows of what might unfold.

Celeste sat up then, brushing her hair back with elegantly long fingers. Her look was thoughtful, and her voice held a whimsical note when she said, "The afternoon is still young."

Leigh's look transformed into a full-blown beckoning as she bit her lip gently. "David, why don't you stay here with us for a while?" she suggested. "Give those two a little time alone. They seem to be having fun. Best let 'em ride that wave, baby."

I laughed at the proposition, amused and touched by her inclusive spirit. "And what will I do with you two, now that my task of reconciliating Diane and Yeska is done for the moment?" I asked, intrigued by the invitation implicit in her words.

Leigh's answered with a smirk that promised mischief. "Oh, we have an idea or two," she said, a spark of adventure lighting up her words.

Celeste's giggle was the perfect accompaniment

to Leigh's impish proposal. It was light and teasing, a sound that made the prospect of the afternoon even more enticing.

"That so?" I said, my desire rising as my eyes roamed over Leigh's perfect backside once more.

The breeze carried distant laughter from where Diane and Yeska stood, remnants of their easy conversation drifting towards us. It was a soothing melody, one that spoke of burgeoning friendships amid the day's simplicity.

"Hm-hm," Leigh hummed. "Celeste and I can keep you occupied, baby. Can't we, Celeste?"

Celeste nodded, biting her plump bottom lip. The elven beauty in her skimpy thong bikini quickened my heart even more, and even though the last few nights had been full of nighttime activities, my lust already rose.

"Well then," I said, "no harm in hanging around here for a bit, then..."

Chapter 15

Taking a deep breath filled with the lake's intoxicating blend of sun, water, and the faint linger of sun lotion, I found myself lost in the glow of Leigh's bronzed skin. I glided my fingers along her shoulder blades as she lay with her back to me, tracing the landscape of her sun-kissed back. My fingertips danced along her spine, caressing each perfect curve, before resting on the swell of her full behind, the slick thong disappearing between her cheeks.

"Oh, David," she moaned. "That feels so good."

As I continued to knead the firm flesh beneath my hands, Celeste moved closer on my other side. My heart thundered in my chest as I felt a soft touch on the front of my pants, feather-light, tantalizing.

Shivering with anticipation, I glanced down to see her slender, artistic hands at my waist. I grinned at the sight of the coy glint in her eyes, pleased she was growing bolder in the bedroom, so to speak.

"Now, Celeste," I said, shaking my head with mock disapproval. "Is this any way to act out in the open? With Diane and Yeska just a stone's throw away?" Of course, my tone of voice was teasing.

The soft murmur of her giggle was electric, sending shivers rushing down my spine. "I shall be silent," she said, her eyes big in feigned innocence. "That is, if *you* are too."

Meanwhile, Leigh squirmed beneath my touch as she gave a playful giggle, the reaction eliciting an inaudible gasp from my lips. Her oiled-up skin and the scent of her in the sun like this drove me wild.

"Both of you are just full of tricks today, aren't you?" I murmured, my hands exploring more intimately down the curve of Leigh's waist and over the flare of her hips.

Leigh's bikini was little more than a teasing suggestion, leaving her voluptuous beauty at the mercy of my touch. The way her thong ran between her luscious butt cheeks made my cock harden. My palms roved, gliding over the slippery lotion-covered flesh, the scent of the sun adding to the intoxication.

Meanwhile, Celeste continued her venture, expertly pulling my zipper down and revealing the hardness straining against the fabric of my boxers. I bit my lip, resisting a gasp, but couldn't quite contain a soft grunt.

Leigh looked back over her shoulder, the glint in her blue eyes full of playful secrets. "Shh… let's not spoil their fishing," she murmured, nodding at

Diane and Yeska.

Celeste proceeded, her deft fingers slipping my manhood free from its confinement. The sensation of her bare skin against mine was a fierce jolt of pleasure, and my hand snaked over to her to squeeze one of her pretty butt cheeks.

"That's it, Celeste," I groaned, my voice thick with desire. The potent combination of Leigh's squirming hips and Celeste's tantalizing grip had entirely disarmed me, my protests drowning in a silent sea of pleasure.

Celeste gave a playful little wiggle that made her breasts and butt bounce before she reached around and undid her top, letting her ample bosom bounce free — a sight to make my mouth water.

"You know," Celeste whispered, her voice barely audible above the wind rustling the leaves around the lake. "Leigh has told me about a particular place she likes to… feel you."

Her blank canvas bikini top now abandoned, Celeste's full breasts were boldly presented, their pertness echoed in her mischievous eyes. Her nipples, colored the hue of ripe peaches, tipped upwards towards the sky as if seeking a kiss from the sun.

"Is that so?" I groaned, my hand still kneading her soft butt cheek.

"Hm-hm," Celeste purred.

"And what place is that?" I asked.

But Celeste gave a bashful giggle and looked away. Still, her hand remained wrapped around my hungry cock. The soft rhythmic stroking made the heat rise inside me.

Meanwhile, Leigh moaned lustfully, pushing her round and oiled-up ass against me. I responded by slipping my hand gently inside the fabric of Leigh's thong, finding her soft and wet.

"Oh, David," she moaned. "That's sooo good…"

Celeste watched us, her hand speeding up on my pulsing length, maintaining a tempo that tantalizingly danced around release. With her other hand, Celeste traced her own full bosom, her slender fingers teasing erect nipples, mirroring my desire.

Leigh's body tensed with anticipation as I began to pleasure her. Her back arched, pushing against my touch, presenting even more of her delicious form to my admiring gaze.

Celeste bit her lip as she gathered her courage once more and looked at me. "Leigh told me about the... behind," she confessed, her luscious lips quirked up in a suggestive smirk. "About the pleasure you gave there."

"Behind?" I grunted, my voice merely an echo as I was lost in touching Leigh's warm womanhood with one hand and Celeste's bountiful ass with the other.

"She's talking about a good ass-fucking, baby," Leigh said, bringing clarity as she shot me a naughty look over her shoulder. "She wants to see… She's curious."

Celeste gave a playful giggle at that, but she did not avert her eyes.

A possessive growl rumbled deep within my chest, my lust rising at this dirty suggestion. Clenching my hand, I grasped Leigh's fuller cheek, digging my fingers into the supple flesh.

Leigh let out a startled yelp before it transformed into a giggle, the sound carrying a note of naughty delight. Pinned beneath my weight, her body writhed and squirmed, creating an enticing movement that called forth an even more primal lust within me.

"You want to see?" I asked Celeste, my words barely a growl as her hand worked me faster. I held Leigh's butt cheek, kneading with rhythmic pulses in time with Celeste's orchestrated rhythm.

Celeste nodded, her magnificent bosom as captivating as the innocent submission in her eyes. "Yes, David. Show me."

Pursuing the wicked path towards satisfying Celeste's curiosity, I pulled Leigh's thong aside to reveal her tight and ready little rose. The thin piece of fabric yielded, a barely-there barrier between my fingers and my intended course.

"Show her, baby," Leigh purred. "Come lie next to me and show her…"

"Yes," I ground out, breathless and teetering on the brink of forbidden desire as I shot a look at Celeste. "Watch closely." I sighed deeply with pleasure as I leaned in, ready to plunge us deeper into wicked delight…

In between the easy rhythm of our breathing, I turned on my side, shifting Leigh to match my movement. With a playful caress, her curvaceous bottom met the hardness that throbbed against the thin fabric of my pants.

"Are you ready, baby?" Leigh's low, sensual drawl cut through the afternoon air, her teasing invitation swirling with the scent of lotion on her skin. "Because I need it!"

I responded to her impish challenge with a slow, circular probe, the pads of my fingers moving against her tight little rose in a way that made her moan lazily, ready for the pleasure soon to come.

Celeste, visibly entranced, moved to the other side of Leigh and lay down on her side, allowing their breasts to brush against each other – a teasing scene that spiked my arousal further.

Breathing deeply, my fingers explored Leigh's tender backdoor, preparing her for my intimate intrusion. As my fingers circled, easing the tension, the anticipation surged, filling the space between us with a dull, electric hum. Then, I playfully pulled up the strap of her thong and let it slap hard back in place.

"Ow!" Leigh yelped before she giggled and playfully swatted her hand at me. "Don't tease me, baby," she urged, her husky whisper catching on the gentle breeze.

Seeing the curiosity shining in Celeste's eyes, I smiled at her. "Ready, Celeste?"

The elven beauty bit her lip and nodded, her eyes wide in fascination at the display.

With a quick tug, I shifted the flimsy fabric aside, closing my eyes momentarily to brace myself for the sensations that awaited. I lay behind Leigh, running my tip over her oiled-up cheek as I slowly made my way toward her ready rose.

Leigh looked at me over her shoulder, biting her lip as she brought one hand around to part her cheeks for me. With a lustful grunt, I moved in.

The slow plunge was met with a tight, silky, and intense heat that sent waves of pleasure through me.

Leigh moaned melodiously, her body undulating with each gentle thrust. She encouraged me, her words lucid despite the tremors of delight rippling through her. "Oh, David, it feels heavenly. I feel so full!"

Clearly fascinated by our intimate display, Celeste slid her fingers under her thong, her light gasp mingling with Leigh's heavenly croons.

Emboldened by Leigh's response, I increased my rhythm, each thrust deeper into her rose followed by a soft exhalation from both women. The heat between the three of us was a living entity, wrapping us into its warmth.

Between sporadic gasps, Leigh managed, "Baby, faster!" Her eyes sparkled with wild delight as she nestled a hand between her thighs.

Hitting the right tempo, I moved faster, our pleasure intertwined like silk threads. Leigh moved in tandem, her body rhythmically accommodating me. Our skin slapped together as I plunged deeper into her ass, and a ripple passed down her delicious cheeks every time I pounded her.

Celeste, fingers dancing between her thighs, watched wide-eyed as Leigh squirmed under my pacing, her breathing uneven as her impending climax hung in the balance.

"Uhn, fuck," Leigh moaned. "David... You're makin' me cum."

I growled as I plunged in deeper, and Leigh picked up her own rhythm, touching herself. By the hazy veil draping over Celeste's eyes and the slight opening of her plump and moist lips, I could tell our little show was making her ready, too.

"Yeah... Uhnn... Yes, David... Oh... Oh, I'm cumming!"

"Yes!" Celeste hummed. "I'm... ooooh..."

Announcing their climaxes almost simultaneously, their gasping pleas hung in the air. The raw lust spiked my own arousal, pushing me closer to the edge as my two women tensed up.

Then, Celeste, her body flush with release, trembled as I continued to thrust into Leigh. Her eyes, reflecting flickers of sunlight, depicted a world of rapturous delight and pure, unadulterated pleasure. Leigh, under the spell of our intimate dance, convulsed gently against me as she moaned my name over and over while I plunged into her ass.

Driven by their responding pleasure, I felt the white-hot wave of release inching closer, my rhythm unrelenting yet tender against Leigh's behind.

"C-cum!" Leigh pleaded, still trembling. "Cum on us!"

Celeste mewled and leaned over, her soft breasts resting on Leigh's oiled-up ass cheek, and that was a sight I could not resist. With a desperate release, I pulled out just in time, aimed my cock, and shot my load over Celeste's breasts and Leigh's curvy ass, stacked together and ready to receive.

"Oh, baby, that's a big load!" Celeste crooned as I released another rope, covering my two beautiful women. Celeste giggled, eyes wide in amazement as she saw how I coated her and her harem sister.

Then, with a broad smile on my lips, I collapsed beside Leigh. The three of us lay there, panting, chest and bosoms heaving, in the sunlight, the tussocks teasing our bare skin.

Leigh snuggled close, fitting perfectly in the crook of my arm while Celeste gingerly lay on her other side. Their soft exchange of breaths, mixed with the tranquil sounds of Pakauley Lake, enveloped us in a peaceful cocoon.

Celeste broke the silence, her tone as whimsical as the breeze rustling the nearby leaves, "I'd love to try this sometime — the intense pleasure you both experienced."

Laughing softly, I reached over to kiss her sun-touched shoulder, "We will," I said. "It's a pleasure I'd love to share with you."

Celeste grinned; her green eyes sparked with anticipation, a promise of more shared secrets. She quickly hopped to her feet, then lay down on my other side, nuzzling against me.

Surrendering to exhaustion, I felt them slip away into a quiet nap against me, their breaths steady, their bodies relaxing against mine. In the background, Yeska and Diane shared a laugh.

Soon enough, the sweet serenade of the lake softly lulled us into a gentle nap.

Chapter 16

My nap had only been brief, but even as I lay there with the afternoon sun warming my skin, I felt refreshed. The soft sound of gentle waves whispered in the background, lulling me further into a state of tranquility.

With this serene soundtrack to my rest, I opened

my eyes to find Celeste and Leigh still napping beside me, seemingly without a care in the world and both of them thoroughly satisfied. A smile tugged at my lips at the picture they made.

I propped myself up on one elbow, leaning over to plant a soft kiss on Leigh's shoulder, feeling the heat of the sun on her skin. She stirred slightly, a contented murmur escaping her lips. Turning to Celeste, I kissed her cheek, and she smiled without opening her eyes, a gesture so full of peace it could have melted the heart of any man.

With a light breeze playing across my face, I rose, brushing off grains of sand that clung to my arms. The lake lay before me, placid and inviting, but my thoughts had shifted to Diane and Yeska. They were still at the edge of the water with their fishing gear, hopeful for a catch.

My steps toward them were unhurried. As the distance closed, I took note of their postures, relaxed but engaged, as if the fishing rods they held were lines connecting them not just to the fish below but to one another.

Their laughter reached me before I was within

earshot of their words, a sign of blossoming friendship that delighted me. There was a rhythm to their conversation, an ease that seemed to have bloomed effortlessly between them, grounded in the shared experience of the day's adventure.

Stepping closer, I heard fragments of their exchange — Diane's recount of older fishing tales and Yeska's descriptions of the methods she had learned in catkin territories. It was a dialogue rich in the textures of their individual pasts, brought together by the quiet of nature and the joy of spending time outdoors together.

"And then, just as I was about to give up and accept that I'd end my day hungry, the biggest fish you've ever seen leapt straight onto the bank. Like it was surrendering to me!" Diane was saying, gesticulation adding animation to the tale.

Yeska chuckled, this present catkin woman who, hours before, had seemed like an outsider. Now, she appeared as one who had found an unexpected comfort in our company.

"I love those little unexpected moments when fishing," she confessed, her eyes fixed on the water.

"Surprise and joy of the catch like that combine with time to unwind and relax."

"Well, you're doing great," Diane assured her, gesturing to the bucket between them. It was brimming with the evidence of their success — a collection of fish that spoke of a productive day.

"Well done, both of you," I said, bending to inspect the bucket. The fish, some still gently flapping, were magnificent specimens — their scales catching the light in a display I knew would impress anyone in Gladdenfield.

Diane looked up, her smile one of sincere satisfaction. "We make a good team, don't we?" she said, a spark of pride evident in her voice.

Yeska's nod was firm, her usual feisty manner softening. "Your intuition about this spot was correct." The respect in her tone was palpable, coloring the air with newfound appreciation.

The sight of them — both competent, both beaming with the day's triumph — filled me with a deep sense of joy. There are few things more rewarding than witnessing bonds strengthen and friendships deepen.

"How about we pack up and head to Gladdenfield?" I asked the girls. "We can sell these fish and spend the night at Leigh's." I was already calculating the time it would take us to get there before darkness set in. "Provided we can wake those two lazy bones up," I added with a chuckle, nodding in the direction where Leigh and Celeste were sunbathing.

"Lazy?" Yeska said, arching a graceful eyebrow. "*Something* must've exhausted those poor girls, I'd say..."

I grinned, understanding the meaning behind her words. With no comment, I smiled at Diane. "What do you say, Diane?"

Diane stood, wiping her hands on her pants before addressing Yeska. "Sounds good to me. What do you think, Yeska? Up for a trip to Gladdenfield?"

"Count me in," Yeska replied without missing a beat, her gaze lingering on the bucket before turning back to the lake one last time, as if saying farewell to the still water.

"I'll get started packing up camp," Diane said,

and she headed off after shooting me and Yeska a quick smile.

As I prepared to call to Celeste and Leigh, Yeska placed a hand on my arm, stopping me momentarily. “Thank you,” she said, her intensity returning like a turning tide, “for this day. For the lake, the laughter, and... well, the fishing.” It was a simple statement, but the depth of feeling behind it was unexpected, captivating.

“You’re very welcome, Yeska,” I said. “It’s nice to see you girls getting along.”

Then, I called out to Leigh, who turned out to be awake already. Her voice came from the other side of the beach, already on her feet and securing the last of the picnic gear. “Ready in a minute!” she shouted.

Celeste joined her, her movements all grace and softness, as the two of them quickly changed out of their bikinis and into their hiking gear. There was not a note of bashfulness to them, and I caught Yeska shooting them an appreciative and intrigued glance.

As we gathered our belongings and started

towards the path that would lead to Gladdenfield, the lake lingered in my peripheral vision, and I found that coming here had been a great decision indeed.

The girls had bonded, and I had explored my pleasures with Celeste and Leigh even more, enticing the elven maiden to try and experience new things.

Chapter 17

We gathered our fishing gear and the day's catch, ready to leave the placid embrace of Pakauley Lake. I slung my pack over my shoulder, feeling the weight of our gear inside. Diane, with her keen Scout instincts, naturally led the way, her strides confident as she navigated us back under the roof of leaves and branches that Springfield Forest provided.

As we walked, the conversation wove gently through the group. Leigh's laughter punctuated the air now and then, a light rhythm to the muffled sounds of our footsteps on the forest floor. Celeste hummed a melody in Elvish that seemed to belong to the trees and the shadows, an echo of the peaceful environment.

The afternoon light dappled through the leaves, painting patterns on the ground that danced with each soft breeze. I watched as the sunlight played off Yeska's dark hair, occasionally catching glimpses of the wildness that seemed to be settling down, domesticated by the camaraderie of the day.

"Diane knows these woods like the back of her hand," I remarked, admiring the way she avoided roots and low branches with an ease borne of familiarity. Yeska nodded, her eyes following Diane's movements with an appreciative gaze.

Leigh piped up with her tone casual yet curious. "So, Yeska, you and Diane seem to be getting on alright now, huh? Haven't seen any cat fights yet," she said, a teasing lilt to her words that invited a light-hearted reply.

Yeska responded with a small chuckle, and though it didn't carry any edge, I could sense a thoughtful undertone to her laughter. "We've found some common ground," she admitted, the lines around her eyes softening. "Diane's quite skilled, and I respect that."

I knew this conversation was important. It mattered to me that Yeska felt welcome, that she and Diane could find harmony. "And Diane?" I prodded gently. "Do you feel she's warming up to you?"

Yeska's reply came with a subtle pause, hinting at the complexity behind the simple words. "She's... cautious, I think. Maybe not entirely happy with my presence, but she's civil. She is protective of you — of her family. I cannot blame her for that."

Diane, a few paces ahead, didn't hear our exchange, focused as she was on leading us through the woods. Celeste glanced back at us, her eyes registering the conversation, and nodded her agreement with Yeska's assessment.

"Diane will come around," I assured Yeska. "She's protective of what we have here, of our peace. But she's also fair. She'll see the good you're bringing to us."

Celeste chimed in with quiet support, "Time helps us all adjust. And today has been good for everyone." Her tone held the unshakable optimism that was part of her charm.

Leigh nudged my arm, her grin speaking volumes. "Trust us, Yeska. Our little family here? We're a tight bunch, but we've got room for one more."

The forest seemed to watch our passage, the old trees bearing witness to the bonds forming and strengthening among us. Birds called above, and somewhere, not too far off, the river accompanied our journey with its soothing burble.

As we emerged onto the dirt road that bordered the woods, I felt the shift beneath my boots, the texture of ground changing from the soft earth to pebbles and packed dirt. It was a familiar transition, one that always signaled the return to more populated realms.

The sun hung lower now, beginning its measured descent toward the horizon as evening would soon come on. Shadows lengthened, and the air held the promise of evening chill, prompting us to pull jackets tighter and quicken our steps.

Conversation turned to plans for our arrival in Gladdenfield, Leigh and Celeste speculating about the town's reactions to our impressive catch, while Yeska listened with the attentiveness that seemed part of her nature.

"Think Darny will give us a good price today?" Diane called over her shoulder, knowing full well the proprietor of the Wild Outrider was always fair in his dealings.

"He'd better," I replied with a grin. "After all, we've brought him some of the best fish the Silverthread has to offer."

The dirt road curved gently, and ahead, the outlines of Gladdenfield Outpost began to take shape. The wooden palisades stood tall and reassuring in the fading light; a man-made stalwart defense nestled amidst natural splendor.

Yeska's gaze followed mine, lingering on the sight for a moment longer than necessary. "Almost there," she said, a note of something akin to reverence in her voice. Or perhaps it was anticipation, a newcomer's eagerness to witness the heartbeat of a community.

We walked the final stretch toward the outpost, the sturdy wooden structures growing more distinct with each step. Thoughts of warm beds and a night spent within the town's cozy embrace rose unbidden in my mind.

Our group moved with an easy flow, each lost in their own thoughts yet bound by the shared experiences of the day. The closeness I felt towards these ladies — my family — sparked a warmth that echoed the satisfaction of a day well-lived.

As we neared the entry to Gladdenfield, the sounds of out chatter fell away, replaced by a collective intake of breath. What lay before us was familiar, and we would easily make it inside before nightfall.

Chapter 18

As we stepped through the wooden gates of Gladdenfield Outpost, the evening air carried the sounds and scents of a town alive with the close of day. Smoke curled from chimneys, and the murmur of voices blended with the clop of horseshoes on the dirt road. Children played between the stalls, and their laughter was a bright and merry thing that brought a smile to my lips.

A soft pink hue spread across the western sky as the sun made its slow descent, washing the palisade and rooftops with a gentle glow. The townsfolk were busy with their evening routines, some closing up shop while others were just starting their night.

We followed the main street, making our way toward the heart of the outpost. Alongside me, Diane walked with an air of familiarity, nodding greetings to passersby who called out to her with smiles and warm hellos.

Leigh's buoyant mood seemed to permeate the air around us, her spirited presence drawing looks from those we passed. Her hand gestured grandly as if introducing Yeska to the vibrant life of Gladdenfield, pointing out the quaint details of shops as we walked.

Celeste kept pace, her eyes taking in the scenes of commerce and community with the grace of an observer quietly making notes on the human condition. Every so often, she'd lean in to whisper a comment or question to Leigh or Diane.

As for Yeska, she took it all in with an appreciative gaze, her head turning this way and that to catch the sights and sounds. The hum of the outpost, the aroma of fresh bread from a nearby bakery, the gentle neighing of horses at the hitching posts — it all seemed to captivate her.

The warmth of recognition bloomed in my chest with each nod and wave directed my way. The people of Gladdenfield knew me, not just as a resident, but as someone who had brought honor to their home, from the victories at the Aquana Festival to the protection I had offered Clara and her party of adventurers at Hrothgar's Hope.

A group of dwarves took notice of our approach, their bearded faces breaking into broad grins as they called out to me, "Hail, Dragon-Slayer!"

The title, a rare honor bestowed upon me by Lord Vartlebeck after I bested the dragon at Hrothgar's Hope, caused me to straighten a bit taller, acknowledging the respect they offered with a grateful nod. The dwarves stood to the side as we passed, their murmured words of reverence a reminder of the shared history that linked me to this place and its people through acts of bravery and unity.

"Dragon-Slayer, eh?" Yeska mused, glancing up at me with an expression that seemed just a touch more respectful than before. "Quite the title you've earned, David."

"It wasn't something I set out to achieve," I replied. "But these things have a way of finding you, I suppose." The pride was there, yes, but mingled with the humbling knowledge of what that title had cost.

Down the crowded street, the Wild Outrider came into view, its inviting weather-worn sign swaying slightly in the evening air. The tavern, a staple of Gladdenfield's social life, was already alight with the promise of food, drink, and company as night drew near.

The windows of the tavern glowed, a beacon to weary travelers and those looking to unwind after a day's work. The sound of a fiddle drifted on the air, the plaintive notes intertwining with the general bustle of the outpost.

The Wild Outrider's door swung open as someone exited, letting out a brief burst of laughter and conversation that beckoned us to enter and partake in the establishment's offerings.

"Ready for a well-earned rest?" I asked my companions, gesturing toward the tavern with a smile. "Darny always knows how to make everyone feel at home."

Diane's steps quickened slightly, her longing for a moment of relaxation evident, while Leigh practically bounced on her toes, her irrepressible spirit undimmed by the day's activities.

Celeste glanced through the window, her gentle disposition finding solace in the idea of the cozy interior that awaited us. "It sounds wonderful," she said, her voice quiet but pleased. "It's been a while since I enjoyed Darny's hospitality. I am still grateful for the lodgings he offered."

I smiled and nodded, remembering how I had intervened on Celeste's behalf to get her a gig at the Wild Outrider and a temporary place to stay after she could no longer afford the rent of the place Waelin had set her up with. "Well," I said, "let's head on in."

Yeska, ever the adaptable one, nodded her readiness, her gaze moving from building to building as we walked, cataloging this new part of her experience with us. "Lead the way," she encouraged.

We reached the Wild Outrider's threshold, the wooden planks echoing under our boots. The scent of roasting meat and the warmth that spilled from within was an invitation we were all eager to accept.

As we entered, the familiar atmosphere of the tavern enveloped us: the soft glow of lantern light against dark wood, the murmur of conversations layered over the clink of mugs and plates.

Regular patrons glanced up from their tables, recognition lighting their faces as they took in our group, the day's fatigue replaced by smiles and welcoming gestures.

Darny, the proprietor, stood behind the bar, his robust frame a familiar sight. A friendly man who was sharper than he'd let on; his keen eyes missed nothing. He stood still for a moment watching us walk further into the room.

The patrons continued their meals and conversations, yet there was a subtle shift in focus as many acknowledged our presence, the murmurs mingling with the soft music to create a backdrop that felt inviting, felt like home.

Darny's eyes met mine across the room. His broad smile stretched beneath his gray mustache, his hand lifting in a silent greeting. His greeting held the promise of a warm welcome and perhaps, the beginning of a long evening spent in good company and tales exchanged as we entered the Wild Outrider tavern.

The Wild Outrider tavern's interior was wrapped in the warm glow of lanterns as we approached the bar, the burnished wood and the comforting din of evening chatter bringing an immediate sense of belonging. Darny, with his customary apron cinched around his waist and rough hands planted firmly on the countertop, awaited our approach with the open interest of a host ready to cater to familiar patrons.

"Caught yourself a nice bunch today, David?" Darny's deep voice rumbled, his eyes moving briefly to the fish we were carrying. Over the many visits and shared experiences of living in Gladdenfield, we had formed a rapport that didn't require much by way of explanation.

"We did indeed," I answered, the pride evident even in the weariness of my voice. "We were thinking..."

But before I could finish, Darny was already nodding, reaching over the counter to take the covered bucket.

"Say no more! Let me have a look then," he said, his fingers deftly unlatching the wrapper to peer at the day's catch. An appreciative whistle escaped him, the sound making its way over the low hum of the tavern. "You'll have the best fish dinner my wife can put together."

"Thanks, Darny! Serve the rest to your customers," I said. "Or have some yourself!"

"Ha!" he boomed. "We'll eat this ourselves. We love a fresh catch! Now, come — sit, have a drink! The wife'll get cooking for you!"

The exchange was amiable, the easy familiarity of it was comforting, making me once again realize I was at home here in Gladdenfield. With dinner secured, Darny gestured towards an empty table in the corner.

"Go on! Settle down, and I'll send over a round of whatever you're having," he said, already moving to get our drinks.

We took our places at the table, the weave of the chairs conforming to our shapes as if remembering us from times before. The expectation of rest after a fulfilling day had us leaning back, shoulders dropping tension by degrees.

I stretched my legs under the table, the solid feel of the chair and floor grounding me in the moment. Diane's chuckles mixed with Leigh's brighter tones, drawing a smile from Celeste as she settled into her seat beside me.

Yeska seemed to melt into the surroundings, her posture relaxing in a way that suggested

Gladdenfield was working its magic on her. She watched the table being set with undisguised interest, the setting becoming more comfortable with each passing minute.

The drinks arrived, steaming mugs and chilled glasses placed before us with Darny's efficient care. "This one's on the house," he said with a wink before leaving us to enjoy the libations.

We raised our glasses in a small toast, the clink of glass to glass a tangible marker of shared time and blossoming friendship. The first sips were like seals on the day, honoring the work and the company equally.

Time stretched out like a pleasant yawn, our conversation ranging from memories of the day to plans for the future, light topics that didn't stray too far into weighty thoughts. Leigh took the lead in entertaining Yeska, sharing stories of her upbringing and her coming to Gladdenfield after the Upheaval.

Yeska listened with a tilt of her head, her mouth curling up at the edges with each humorous anecdote. It was heartening to see the developing bond, the lines of communication growing stronger as they exchanged tales. I once again admired how effortlessly Leigh connected with Yeska. She had such a powerful and disarming personality — I supposed it was difficult for anyone to dislike Leigh.

The fish dinner arrived then; an aromatic vision of culinary promise set before us by Darny's capable hands. The flaky white flesh steamed beside a medley of root vegetables; each piece cooked to tender perfection by Darny's wife.

The first forkfuls were greeted with appreciative noises, the savory flavors and delicate textures melting on our tongues. It was a fitting end to the day's fruitful endeavors.

Yeska sampled the fish with fervor. "This is exquisite," she said, and I knew she meant it.

Diane's sigh of satisfaction matched the expressions around the table, a collective sense of indulging in something crafted with care and shared with warmth.

Leigh's eyes shone brightly as she glanced around the table, her enjoyment a palpable thing, infecting us all with its charm. "Who knew fishing could lead to such a feast?" she quipped, laughter bubbling up like a spring.

Celeste sipped at her water between bites, her movements deliberate and measured, each taste an experience to be savored. "A day on the lake followed by this," she mused, "truly makes one appreciate the simple things."

We ate with relish after that, and it took a while before conversation picked up again with the worst of our appetites sated. Then, as the meal wound down, our conversations quieted while the fullness settled comfortably in our stomachs.

Darny, ever the attentive host, watched from his vantage, ensuring our needs were met without fuss or fanfare. The tavern's ambiance was perfect — the murmurs and drifting melodies from the other patrons a fine background to our contented sighs.

Leigh leaned back, her chair creaking slightly as she eyed Yeska, seeking to get to know the cat girl better. "So," she said, folding her hands in her lap, "How did you enjoy the day with us? And how do you like Gladdenfield?"

Yeska's response was a languid stretch, arms reaching toward the ceiling before settling back down. She then purred happily. "I enjoyed it very much," she said. "And while I've been to Gladdenfield often enough, I've rarely lingered. It's a charming place, and I'm happy to see it now in the company of people who know it well."

With that, the conversation continued, the voices of my beloved women a gentle ebb and flow around the table. But as the evening stretched on, I realized it was time to take the next step.

Chapter 19

After our fulfilling dinner, I leaned back in my chair, a contented sigh escaping me. The warmth of the Wild Outrider tavern was comforting, its familiar creaks and murmurs a reminder of many evenings spent here with the locals and travelers passing through.

But tonight, my thoughts turned toward the adventure that beckoned us, the quests that could lead us into unknown dangers and hopefully bring us closer as a group.

I excused myself from the table, promising I'd be back shortly, and strode toward the bar where Darny was at work. The wooden planks beneath my boots felt solid, bearing me steadily to the counter, where the smell of aged wood and spilt ale greeted me like an old friend.

"David, back to stir up trouble?" Darny called out as I approached, his voice deep and rich with mirth. A smile was already stretching across my face, knowing well the kind of 'trouble' he joked about.

"You know I'm the picture of innocence, Darny," I replied with a mock-serious tone, resting my elbows on the well-worn bar top. "I wouldn't dare disrupt your fine establishment."

Darny chuckled, wiping down a glass with a clean rag, his movements practiced and sure. "So you say," he said with a good-natured grin. "But ever since you carried Celeste away to your homestead, my patrons have been nagging me for her songs! She has a voice that could tame a griffin!"

I laughed, understanding the tease buried in his words. "Well, it can't be helped," I teased back, "a girl like her can't spend her days singing for a bunch of grubby dwarves, now, can she?"

His hearty guffaw rolled through the room, and a few heads turned, glancing curiously in our direction. "Grubby dwarves, he says!" Darny thundered, setting down the polished glass. "Now, you didn't come over just for my delightful banter. What do you need?"

"Actually," I began, leaning in a bit closer, "I wanted to ask if there's word of any good quests around. Something that might suit a party of our level — about level 7. Heard anything like that?"

Darny paused, tapping a thoughtful finger against his chin. His eyes roamed the room for a moment before focusing back on me. "Come to think of it, there was something... An elven mage looking to fetch a magical staff from a cursed barrow-type Dungeon or something. The undead are involved, and he pegged it for level 6-7 adventurers."

My interest was immediately piqued at the mention of the quest. "Sounds intriguing," I said. "Something we might be able to handle. You think I could talk to this mage?"

"Upstairs," he replied, jerking a thumb in the direction of the stairs leading to the rooms above. "He's renting for the week while he looks for help. Third door on the left. You want me to send up word you're coming?"

I considered his offer for a beat. "No need, I'll go introduce myself. Thanks, Darny."

As I made my way back to our table, the girls' curious gazes followed my progress. "Got a lead on a quest," I told them. "I'll be back in a sec to fill you in — just need to have a quick word with the one who posted it."

Diane nodded, her eyes flicking toward the staircase where I was headed. Leigh raised her glass as if in a toast to my endeavor, and Celeste gave a small wave, the gesture supportive.

Yeska's intrigued eyes met mine, a trace of that

same intensity from earlier seeming to ask silent questions. "Good luck," she said.

I gave them a confident smile before I ascended the stairs, the weight of the quest already forming within my mind. The corridor above was dim, the lanterns casting pools of gold on the floorboards.

I passed the first and second doors, listening to the soft sounds of life from behind them — faint conversations, the rustle of pages, the hush of Gladdenfield at dusk. As I walked, I wondered what kind of challenge this new quest would pose.

So far, not all of the estimates regarding level and challenge had been accurate, but that was a risk of this world — a Dungeon could grow more dangerous over time.

Approaching the third door on the left, I raised my hand and knocked firmly. The wood felt cool and solid beneath my knuckles, the echo a sharp punctuation in the stillness.

A moment of silence followed, the waiting a small void between what was and what might be. Then, the latch clicked, and the door creaked open, spilling more amber light into the hallway.

Chapter 20

The door creaked open, revealing an elder male elf, his long silver hair flowing like rivulets of moonlight down his back. His eyes, though rheumy, regarded me with an intensity that belied his age. They spoke of wisdom and of years spent in pursuit of knowledge. The lines on his face suggested a lifetime of concentration and study, and yet, there was a softness there too, a hint of kindness in the downward curve of his mouth.

"May I help you?" he inquired, his voice carrying the faint trace of a distant luxuriance, as if his words were accustomed to echoing through the halls of a grand institution rather than the simplicity of a tavern room.

"Good evening," I responded, extending my hand in greeting. "I'm David Wilson. I heard about a quest you posted — I believe it involves retrieving a magical staff?"

The elf's hand met mine, his grip surprisingly firm, and a smile lifted the corners of his mouth ever so slightly. "Ah, you're the Dragon-Slayer. I heard of you! Good, good! Step in, please. I am Lernoval of Thelluan," he said, gesturing for me to enter the room, which was as uncluttered and solemn as a library corner, with only the necessary furnishings for a traveler and the unmistakable insignia of the Academy of Thelluan on his robe.

Once inside, the quiet of the room enfolded us, its sparse decoration a reflection of the man before me — utilitarian and without unnecessary embellishments. Lernoval moved to the window and beckoned me to take a seat in one of the two chairs by a modest wooden table.

"I apologize for the accommodations; they are rather austere for a conversation of this nature," Lernoval commented, sitting across from me, his posture erect, every inch the scholar I had perceived him to be.

"Think nothing of it," I assured him, eager to learn about the quest. "What can you tell me about this staff you seek?"

Lernoval's gaze drifted toward the window, his voice a shade softer as he began to recount the tale. "It's a family heirloom, passed down through generations. My ancestors understood its power and protected it. But during the Upheaval, it was lost to us… That is, until now. My studies have revealed it to me, and I wish to have it returned for my family's benefit."

The evening sun cast golden streaks over the room as Lernoval described the challenge: "The staff rests now in a cursed barrow Dungeon, deep within the forested area known as Copperwinde. The undead guard it. They were once the guardians of the staff — an elven mercenary company hired to transport it. However, they never completed their quest. Something happened — I never learned what — and they died. The power of the staff made their oath to guard it transcend their deaths, and a barrow-like Dungeon formed around it due to the innate pull and weight of the staff's magic."

I listened intently, absorbing every detail Lernoval provided. "What can you tell me about this barrow, and the undead who guard it?" I asked, my thoughts already racing through the implications of what he'd shared.

Lernoval leaned forward, his features sharpened by the gravity of his words. "The barrow is an ancient place of power, long before the elven academies rose, when mages practiced their arts without rule. The undead... they are not to be trifled with. Perversions of life's natural course, they are bound to that staff as their last charge in life, which serves as a focal point for their restless spirits."

Every sentence he uttered helped paint an elaborate picture of the potential dangers we might face, and the intricate dance between life and death that the quest appeared to involve.

"It's about three-day march south from here into Copperwinde," Lernoval continued, "through terrain that can be treacherous as it is beautiful. If you make good time, you'll get there on the third day easily."

I already felt the pull of the adventure, the call to arms that always resonated within me. "You have an exact location for this barrow?" I asked, my eyes not leaving his.

"I have maps, and I can provide you with the necessary references," Lernoval assured me. "However, retrieving the staff will require more than knowing the way. It'll demand bravery... and subtlety."

The mage's earnest tone revealed the value he placed on this quest, and in that moment, I understood that helping him is about more than just another adventure — it's about restoring a sense of heritage and pride. The urgency burning in his eyes revealed to me that this was of great importance to him.

"The reward will be appropriate," he said, taking a pouch from the table and tossing it over to me.

It was heavy, the jangle of gold easy to feel. I quickly inspected the contents, and Lernoval was generous.

"As I said," he muttered. "It is a dangerous Dungeon. Level 7, I would say, and there aren't many adventurers in this area who can take on such a challenge. Accordingly, the reward is high. It should be satisfactory.

"It is. And I appreciate your candor," I said, my determination solidifying. I replaced the pouch on the table with an audible cling. "My companions and I — we have faced our fair share of dangers. I believe we can take on this quest."

Lernoval's eyes lit up, a youthful spark ignited in their depths. "Indeed? That's heartening to hear," he said. "It would mean a great deal to recover what was once a defining symbol of my family."

I rose from my chair, offering Lernoval my hand

once more. "Then consider us at your service. We'll depart in the morning, taking a short detour to my homestead to get our supplies. Can you come down in an hour or so and talk to me and my Scout, so we know the way? I need some time to explain the quest to my party members."

He clasped my hand, sealing the agreement between us. "Excellent," Lernoval replied, a genuine sense of relief evident in the release of his breath. "And of course, I shall come down and tell you what I know of the way there."

"See you in an hour, then," I said, and he replied with a gracious nod before getting up and opening the door for me.

As I left, I felt the mage's gaze on my back. This exchange had been more profound than a simple hiring for a quest — it's as if I was giving him hope for something thought irretrievable.

The door closed behind me with a soft click, the sounds of the tavern rushing back to greet me. I headed back downstairs to my companions, my stride purposeful, thoughts of the quest filling my mind and the sense of excitement growing once more.

Chapter 21

I navigated my way back through the jovial crowd at the Wild Outrider, the hearty sounds of conversation and laughter acting as my guideposts. The evening had settled into that comfortable cadence found only in places like these, where the worries of the day give way to the easier rhythms of night.

At our table, my women greeted me with happy smiles. Slipping back into my chair with a grateful sigh, the eyes of Diane, Leigh, Celeste, and Yeska were fixed on me, each of their faces reflecting a mixture of curiosity and anticipation.

"So, any luck with the quest?" Diane's voice cut through the surrounding noise; her eyes bright with an eager spark.

Leigh leaned in, her attention honed in on my every word, while Celeste's gentle demeanor seemed to soften even further with interest.

"Lernoval, an elven mage, has lost a family heirloom — a magical staff," I began, my voice low so as not to roam too far from the circle of our group. "He believes it's fallen into a cursed barrow guarded by the undead. It's a dangerous quest, suited for adventurers around level 7, and he's offering generous compensation for its return."

The information sank into the space between us, hovering like the first note of a long-awaited melody. Their faces remained still, absorbing the gravity of the quest I was proposing, understanding that this entailed more than the usual foray into the wilderness.

"Undead, huh?" Leigh's tone betrayed no fear, only the thrill of the challenge. "We've handled worse, right?"

"We have," I affirmed, meeting her gaze. "Lernoval seems to think highly of our capabilities. And, well, I've agreed to take on his quest."

Yeska perked up, her earlier quiet supplanted by the intrigue I had come to associate with her. "When do we leave?" she asked, her voice a clear note among the tavern's murmured harmonies.

"Tomorrow," I replied, already feeling a surge of excitement at the prospect ahead. "We'll return to the homestead after fetching some supplies here at market in the morning. Then, we'll make the homestead ready for our absence and be on our way. It's a three-day trip, so we should be back within a week."

Diane gave a decisive nod, her determined mien showing her readiness. "Then we best prepare tonight. We'll need to leave at dawn if we want to make good time."

The table's enthusiasm was palpable, a fervor that quickened the heart and solidified intent. Their nods and affirmations felt like a pact sealed in the quiet understanding of the danger we were about to face.

Celeste folded her hands atop the table, her serenity never once faltering. "I'm looking forward to it," she said, a whisper heard clear across the wooden surface. "There's much to do, but the thought of adventure stirs something deep within me."

"Me too," Yeska agreed, her green eyes vivid in the tavern light. "I haven't had an outing like what you're describing in... well, a long while."

I could see in their faces the different tides of emotions — Leigh's unshakeable cheer, Diane's protective streak, Celeste's poetic calm — all converging into a single stream of collective resolve.

Before we could delve deeper into the conversation, Darny ambled over, two pitchers in hand. "Another round of drinks," he announced, setting them down with a practiced ease. "Seeing as you're back and smiling, I'm thinking you got yourselves a quest."

We each leaned forward to refill our own cups, the rich amber of the ale mirroring the lingering glow of the setting sun outside. Darny stood with a smile, eyes scanning over the glasses.

"Thanks!" I said. "And we did! We're going to retrieve his staff from the undead."

"Good!" Darny said, a note of caution threading through his otherwise convivial tone. "But the undead are no easy foes."

"We know," I reassured him, catching his eye. "We'll be careful, Darny. We've always managed before, haven't we?"

Indeed, the ambiance around us seemed to punctuate the truth of my words — the clinks of cups, the quiet strumming from a weathered lute near the hearth, the safe haven we were all part of.

"Just be sure you're prepared," Darny insisted, his gaze sweeping over each of us. "No heroics that'll land you in trouble, alright?"

We raised our cups in a silent promise to the barkeep, our collective nod as solemn as any oath given in the more formal settings of courts and councils.

An hour passed with genial chatter, as our growing excitement for the journey pieced together plans for a meticulous departure. Darny made his rounds, leaving us to talk, laugh, and steel ourselves for the uncertain path ahead.

After that, Lernoval came down, and I introduced him to my women. He seemed impressed by the party, and he sat down with me and Diane and his collections of maps, explaining everything he knew about the route to Diane, who absorbed the information with care. It turned out the foxkin Scout had ventured into Copperwinde before, and she knew the way better than Lernoval.

When the signs and landmarks that would point us to the barrow had been explained, Lernoval bade us good luck and rose to leave.

"Expect us back within ten days," I told him, already picturing us marching southward to the mysteries Copperwinde forest holds.

"I'll be waiting for your triumphant return," Lernoval said, the formality of his manner slipping into something warmly anticipatory.

After that, he returned to his chambers, obviously not a man for taverns.

Eventually, I glanced at the nearby clock and sighed. "I think it's about time we headed to the apartment above the general store. We all need some rest for the early start tomorrow."

My suggestion was met with reluctant agreement, the day's pleasantries winding down as the night drew its dark curtain around Gladdenfield, the hour growing late.

"We'll head back, then," Diane said, standing up first, ready as ever to lead us.

We filed out of the Wild Outrider, satisfaction warming us from within as we ventured through the quiet streets of the frontier night, each of us looking forward to the adventure that was soon to begin.

Chapter 22

As dawn crept into the room, a soft light broke through the curtains and spread across the floor, touching the edge of the bed where I lay entwined among my companions. Diane's breathing was steady and even, Leigh's a gentle murmur, and Celeste's a quiet whisper.

I slipped from the bed, taking care not to disturb the quiet scene, and tiptoed across the room. The floorboards were cool beneath my feet, the crisp morning air nipped at my skin as I made my way to the kitchen of Leigh's old apartment. It was a space once familiar for daily routines, now a waypoint for new beginnings.

Yeska was already there, her silhouette outlined by the dim glow of the stove. She was the picture of solitude, early morning light casting soft shadows across her face. We exchanged quiet greetings, a mutual understanding between early risers, as we moved about the cozy kitchen to prepare breakfast.

The silence between us was companionable as Yeska placed a kettle on the stove, its soft hiss soon filling the room. I busied myself with setting out bread and jam, the simple act of breaking bread together an intimacy that life on the frontier afforded.

Yeska reached for plates from an overhead shelf, her movements fluid and graceful even in a task as mundane as this. "Did you sleep well?" she asked, as if our earlier acknowledgment needed reaffirmation now that the day was truly upon us.

"*Very* well," I replied, turning my attention to the eggs I had started to scramble. The sizzle of the butter as it hit the pan melded with the sharp crack of the eggshells, the aroma soon wafting throughout the small kitchen. "And you?"

She smiled broadly as she watched me, and I felt my heart swell under her gaze. "I did," she said. "Although the walls are thin…"

She let the last remark linger in a teasing way, and I knew full well what she meant. Last night, I and my women had indulged a little, and a little soon turned into a lot. No doubt she had heard us.

I just smiled, choosing not to say anything right now.

Leigh was the first to join us, rubbing sleep from her eyes with the back of her hand, a half-smile playing on her lips as she sniffed the air. "Smells like someone's been productive," she mused, taking a seat at the table.

Celeste followed, a touch more awake, her hair a tousled cascade of amber as she tied it back in a loose knot that revealed her elegant, pointed ears. "Everything looks wonderful," she said, her voice clear and bright as morning itself.

Diane came last, stretching as she entered, each limb extended with a languidness that spoke of good rest. "I could get used to waking up to this every day," she chimed, taking her seat and eyeing the food with appreciation.

Together we ate, the act of sharing a meal binding us in ways words often could not. Conversation flowed easily, snippets of laughter and soft replies drifting as we got ready for a long day ahead.

Yeska became more animated with each bite, her initial reservation melting away amid the chatter. Leigh recounted a humorous encounter from the day before at the lake, and I watched Yeska's face light up with genuine amusement.

After breakfast, the four of us lingered at the table, cups of coffee warming our hands. Leigh stretched, a spark of energy already igniting her gaze as she said, "We should get moving. Supplies won't buy themselves."

I nodded in agreement, setting down my cup with a decisive clink. "An hour should be enough time," I added. "Why don't you accompany me, Leigh? The rest of you can get our stuff ready here."

"Sounds good," Diane said.

"Meet us downstairs in an hour," I instructed, and the girls all acknowledged with nods, the routine of setting out familiar to each of us by now.

Leigh and I exited the apartment, making our way downstairs to the general store, which Randal was already tending to. The early birds of Gladdenfield had begun to stir, their own routines intersecting with ours.

As we entered the store, Randal looked up from his ledger with a warm smile. "Morning, you two," he greeted, his eyes sharp and alive with the day's promise. "Nice to see y'all in Gladdenfield once more!"

"Morning, Randal," I replied. "How's the store holding up?"

"Doing just fine, thanks to you," Randal said, his tone rich with gratitude. "You keep bringin' in the goods, and folks keep buyin'. It's a good thing you set up this place when ya did, Leigh."

Leigh beamed, proud and pleased by his words. "The store was the best decision," she agreed, her eyes scanning the shelves she had once stocked herself. She then eyed me sideways and grinned. "Well, the *second-best* decision."

I chuckled before turning to Randal again. "Any unusual requests or needs from the townsfolk lately?" I inquired, aware that Randal was often privy to the needs and wants of Gladdenfield's inhabitants.

Randal shook his head, a chuckle escaping him. "Nope, nothin' the store can't handle. But I'll let y'all know if anythin' comes up."

As Leigh and I rummaged through the supplies, selecting ammunition and odds and ends for the trip, conversation ebbed and flowed between us. The importance of each item was discussed, Leigh's knowledge of the store's inventory proving invaluable.

With supplies in hand, Leigh and I made our way back toward the front of the store, where

Randal was just finishing a transaction with a customer. "If that's all you need, I'll tally up your total," he said, a practiced smile guiding his actions.

We thanked Randal and, with goodbyes exchanged, stepped out into the brightening morning. Gladdenfield was coming to life around us, but now we had our sights set on a different sort of day ahead. With everything we needed for the expedition packed away, we were ready to return to the homestead and make the final preparations before setting out on our adventure.

Soft light spread its gentle fingers over Gladdenfield Outpost, brushing the wooden gates with a warm, golden hue. We had assembled there, our little group of travelers, taking in the stillness of the morning before setting off. It was that still-on-the-edge quiet time when the world seemed to hold its breath, waiting for life to stir.

With our supplies strapped securely to our backs, we began our trek through the Springfield Forest. The path was well-trodden, wide enough to allow homesteaders and traders alike to journey to and from Gladdenfield. The air was crisp, filled with the scent of pine and earth, the kind of aroma that wakes you up and fills you with energy.

We weren't alone on the path for long. Soon we came across other walkers, each engaged in their own early endeavors. A family of homesteaders came from the opposite direction, a sturdy wagon pulled by a pair of oxen creaking under the weight of freshly harvested produce destined for the market stalls. They waved cheerily at us, and we waved back.

Tradesmen with their carts full of goods traveled in the opposite direction, eager to set up their wares before the outpost fully awoke. Their faces were etched with the light of anticipation, hoping that they would do good business in the little frontier settlement.

We continued down the path, flanked by trees that stood like silent sentinels. As the forest canopy thickened above us, spears of sunlight darted through the leaves, creating a mosaic of light and shadow on the forest floor. The sounds of the forest accompanied us, the soft rustle of leaves and the distant calls of birds serenading our passage.

After a brisk walk, we reached the old cottonwood tree that marked where the larger path gave way to a narrower one, less frequented, that led to my homestead. It stood towering and broad, its bark gnarled with age and its boughs stretching wide like the welcoming arms of an old friend.

As we turned onto the smaller pathway, the ambiance of the forest grew denser, more alive with the secrets it held so close. Our steps became more deliberate as we navigated the roots and rocks, the earth beneath our feet speaking a language only known to those who frequent it.

We walked in a comfortable silence, each lost in thoughts about the upcoming journey. Diane's hand brushed against the greenery lining the path, a connection to this place that was etched deep in her heart. Celeste moved with soundless grace, her gaze lingering on the gentle sway of ferns caressed by the wind. Even Yeska, the outsider among us, seemed drawn into the quiet rhythm of this place.

Then, the stillness of the woods was broken by a familiar hulking shape ambling toward us. It was Leigh's pet larroling, lumbering out of the underbrush, its massive frame moving with surprising gentleness.

"There's my boy!" Leigh exclaimed, her voice infused with warmth as she went to greet the creature, reaching up to scratch the place behind its tusks that she knew it loved. The larroling's grunt of contentment rumbled through the air, a low and reassuring sound.

Celeste and Diane came forward to join her, their hands reaching out to the larroling's shaggy fur, exchanging a look of affection with the beast. Even Yeska, who had watched with measured curiosity, stepped closer, offering a tentative stroke to the larroling's side.

With our beastly companion content, we started moving again, the homestead drawing ever nearer. Leaves crunched underfoot, and small creatures darted away from our approach, the whole forest teeming with life just out of sight.

Then, ahead of us, another guardian of the homestead appeared. It was Mr. Drizzles, hovering in place, its form crackling with elemental power. I nodded to the storm elemental, signaling our peaceful intentions and familiarity.

Beside Mr. Drizzles floated the second storm elemental, the one I had summoned for yesterday's departure. They both gave off low, deep thrums, the sounds of their innate power pulsating gently like a silent warning to any who dared to trespass.

We passed the elementals with nods, and I felt a surge of pride for the security they provided. Yeska glanced back at them with intrigue, her eyes reflecting the fading light like twin green lanterns in the growing shade of the forest.

The homestead came into view, its outline a comforting sight against the backdrop of the forest. The large front porch where many evenings had been spent was now bathed in a soft light that seemed to beckon us home.

Leigh was the first to step onto the porch, her boots thumping against the wooden planks in a triumphant return from our day's journey. Celeste followed, her steps lighter, carrying the serene satisfaction of arriving back to familiar surroundings.

Diane joined her, setting down the cooler with a chuckle that spoke of both fatigue and fulfillment. Yeska, still taking it all in, stepped up beside me, a curious look crossing her face as if registering every detail of our home.

I felt a gentle relief wash over me, the comfort of returning home, even if it was temporary. The nostalgia mingled with the certainty of the challenges we would soon face.

Leigh turned, leaning against the railing of the porch, her gaze sweeping over the property. The land we had worked hard to cultivate, to tame and make our own, stretched out before us in the afternoon light, the fruit of our labors here.

Celeste moved to stand by her side, their shoulders brushing as they both took in the sight of the homestead. The corners of Diane's mouth turned up in a knowing smile, understanding the depth of emotion this return stirred in each of us.

Yeska remained quiet, her composure holding back whatever thoughts might be swirling within her.

Leigh's gaze lingered on the horizon, her quiet remarks drifting toward us. "They say every journey begins with a single step. But it's returning home that measures the distance we've traveled."

I couldn't help agreeing as I looked at the home we'd leave behind come first light. Preparing for the morrow's journey, for the quest that Lernoval had entrusted us with, would be the task of the day. There was much to do, still, before dusk would creep in, and the homestead awaited to grant us a night's reprieve.

Luckily, it was still morning; most of the day remained ahead of us.

"Let's grab an early lunch, girls," I said. "After that, we'll get to work."

Chapter 23

The bustle in the homestead kitchen had begun with the slicing of bread and the soft bubbling of a pot on the stove. Diane, Leigh, Celeste, Yeska, and I moved about in a synchronized dance of cooking and serving, almost practiced in our movements as each of us contributed to the early lunch.

As the food came together piece by piece, platters and bowls filled with simple, hearty fare covered the sturdy oak kitchen table. The rich aroma of a stew, thickened with root vegetables and tender chunks of meat, mingled with freshly baked bread.

"Looks like we have enough food here to feed an army," Diane commented as she came up to the table, filling her plate with a generous helping.

Leigh chuckled as she slathered butter on a slice of warm bread before passing it to me. Her lively spirit was as infectious as always, "Better too much than too little, considering the work we have ahead!"

I nodded in agreement, aware of the tasks that lay before us. "Eat well, because after lunch it's back to chores," I reminded them gently, my mind already turning to the fields and the tasks that would ensure the homestead could manage our short absence.

We sat down, making quick work of the meal, the conversation drifting to the chores at hand. Yeska listened attentively, her learning curve on the homestead still steep, but her willingness evident in the set of her shoulders and the note-taking gaze.

Celeste spoke up, her tone matter-of-fact, "I'll start by checking the domesticants, making sure they're all right." Her affection for the little creatures brought a soft smile to my face. "After that, I'll start preparing our supplies for tomorrow."

"I'll head to the workshop," I said, finishing my slice of bread. "I need to make sure everything is in order and that the tools are cleaned and stored away."

Leigh stood, plates already in hand, "And I'll see to the larroling and the domesticants to make sure they're all set with their tasks while we're out. I'll help Celeste with tomorrow's supplies once I'm done."

Yeska finished eating and pushed her plate aside, eager to offer her assistance. "Point me to where I can best be helpful," she offered, a new side of her coming to light — the side that wanted to contribute and belong.

Diane nodded at Yeska. "I could use your help with the fences — they always need checking, and an extra pair of hands would be most welcome. I'll check on the crops myself."

Lunch wrapped up, and the plates were cleared away with a shared sense of purpose driving us. Yeska and Diane headed outside, each picking up the necessary tools as they went.

Celeste moved with a quiet grace to where the domesticants — Ghostie and Sir Boozles — hovered, waiting for her instructions. Her gentle words seemed to settle the creatures, their eager chirps showing their readiness to work.

I made my way into the workshop, the scent of sawdust and the tang of metal greeting me. Methodically, I began to arrange everything, cleaning saw blades and sorting through screws and nails, placing them back into their respective jars and bins.

The alchemy laboratory was mostly untouched as I had done no alchemy these past few days, and I was looking forward to getting back into it once this quest was finished. The reward would allow me to purchase many new ingredients, perhaps even seeds to grow some of my own.

Leigh's voice traveled to me through an open window, a soft melody carried by the breeze as she issued quiet commands to the larroling and Mr. Drizzles. Their deep thrums in response assured me they understood the importance of their tasks.

Time passed, marked by the sun's glare as late afternoon came around. The domesticants flitted back and forth from the garden plots to the well, tending to Magebread flowers and Wispsilk leaves before the day's end.

It was in the golden hour of the late afternoon that we reconvened on the porch, everyone's skin glistening with the sheen of honest toil. Yeska and Diane returned from the fence line, the latter describing how Yeska caught on quickly to the work, while she had observed as Diane inspected the crops.

"The fences should hold up nicely now," Diane said, and Yeska's cheeks flushed slightly with what I took to be pride at accomplishing something so outside her usual expertise.

Celeste and the domesticants completed their rounds as well, the tiny creatures whirring happily around her, their part in the day's chores done efficiently.

Leigh stooped to pat the larroling on the snout, murmuring words of thanks before nodding at Mr. Drizzles, who crackled softly in response, towards his usual patrolling track.

With the day's work behind us, supper was a quiet affair — a simple meal to end the work-filled day. Our plates filled with greens from our garden and the last of the bread and butter we had brought from Gladdenfield, we ate mostly in silence, the fatigue settling into our bones.

"Feels good though," Leigh mused as she leaned back, "accomplishing so much in one day."

I couldn't help agreeing with her sentiment. The work had been fulfilling, and each chore was a step closer to ensuring the homestead would be fine without us.

The meals were cleared away, and the evening waned. The kitchen's warmth held us a moment longer before we all began to feel the pull of our beds beckoning for a night's rest.

As I lay down, the day's efforts weighed heavy on my eyelids. Rest came easy, a welcome friend in the quiet cocoon of the homestead. Despite the exhaustion of the day, I was happy to get some sleep and looking forward to the expedition tomorrow.

Chapter 24

The next morning, we gathered around the table where our supplies lay, each of us with a cup of coffee in hand, ready to take stock of what we'd carry into the forest and beyond. I cleared my throat, encouraging my companions to tuck into the quick breakfast of porridge that lay before us.

Diane, her brow furrowed with concentration, checked off items from a list she'd written the night before. "Two tents, got them here," she announced, patting the canvas bundles that were neatly rolled and tied. They were compact and easy to carry, vital for our journey.

Leigh, unrolling a sleeping bag to ensure it was dry and free of tears, flashed me a cheeky grin. "And don't forget the bedrolls. Wouldn't want to sleep on hard ground, would we?" She winked, her good humor a constant even in the midst of preparation.

"Got the torches," Celeste piped up, pressing the button on one to test its beam. The light cut sharply through the morning shadows, a beacon that promised safety when night would fall on us along the trail.

I reached for the cooking gear, a compact set that included a small pot, pan, and a portable stove that would serve us well when we made camp. "This should see us through," I said, ensuring everything was accounted for and in working condition.

Yeska hefted the water containers, her eyes

sweeping over the labeled jugs that held our drinking water. "Plenty to keep us hydrated," she confirmed, the muscles in her forearms standing out slightly as she judged their heft.

Diane continued through the inventory, her voice steadily calling out each item. "Ropes, check. Foldable shovel's here too," she disclosed, ensuring the essentials wouldn't be left behind.

Leigh handled the ammunition, her fingers deft as they counted the rounds for her revolver. Diane did the same for her crossbow bolts, her attention meticulous, while I made sure my rifle's magazines were fully loaded.

Celeste went through our food supplies, checking the sealed packs of preserved meals we had purchased in Gladdenfield. High-calorie and nourishing, they'd sustain us through the physical demands of the upcoming days. "We won't go hungry," she said lightly, a small smile reassuring me.

Satisfied with the state of our gear, I looked around at the expectant faces of my companions. "Looks like we're all set," I encouraged them, receiving nods of consent as we all felt the gravity of the expedition before us.

Leaving the dishes to the domesticants, we each grabbed our packs, feeling their weight as a tangible reminder of the adventure we were embarking on. Yeska lingered by the table, taking one last look at the map Lernoval had provided. "Alright," she said, clutching her now packed bag, "time to go."

I called upon Ghostie and Sir Boozles, the domesticants who had been buzzing about, eager for their instructions. "Keep an eye on the homestead, alright?" Their chirps were like affirmations, their eyes glowing a steady blue. "Tend to the crops as well."

Mr. Drizzles and his fellow storm elemental hovered in their usual places, their presence a silent promise of vigilance. I addressed them with a nod, appreciative of my summons' unwavering loyalty to our home's safety.

The larroling grunted softly as we loaded it with some of the heavier supplies, mainly the drinking water. Its large frame was built for such burdens, and it shifted under the weight with reliable grace.

Distributing the remaining supplies among our packs, we each shared the load. The balance of weight against our shoulders was a familiar comfort, the snug straps a sign that we were ready for the journey ahead.

With everything secured, I glanced back towards the homestead, its sturdy walls standing as a haven for our return. "Let's head out," I said, motioning towards the treeline that marked the beginning of our journey.

Diane stepped forward at my request, her Scout Class skills coming to the forefront. She examined the forest ahead, her keen eyes scanning for the subtle signs that would lead us through the underbrush and towards our destination.

"This way," Diane directed, her confident stride carrying her into the greenery, a pathfinder in her element. We followed her lead; the forest's embrace a welcome constant as we ventured into its depths.

The sun climbed higher as we walked, the light slipping through the leaves in a dappling of golden spots on the forest floor. Our footsteps were in sync, a rustling symphony complemented by the occasional calls of birds overhead.

Leigh remained beside me, her pace light and assured. Whether it was the comfort of companionship or the thrill of the quest, her bright spirit lent an energy to the group that was irreplaceable.

Celeste moved with a hush of motion, her steps seeming almost to respect the silence of our surroundings. She left no trace as she walked, her presence among us as natural as the woodland itself.

Yeska took up the rear, her gaze sweeping over her new companions in contemplation. I sensed the beginning of a deep kinship taking root, her place among us becoming clearer with each shared mile.

The forest around us was alive, a hidden audience to our passing. The crisp air filled our lungs, the uneven terrain tested our steps, and the destination called to us with the promise of untold challenges.

Our conversation was minimal, words spoken

softly against the backdrop of nature's chorus. It felt good to be on the road again, the path unrolling before us like a ribbon of possibility.

The shadows grew shorter as the morning wore on, our progress gradual from the known to the unknown. And with the homestead behind us and the promise of the quest ahead, there was a sense of rightness to our endeavor — a fitting quest for the bonds we shared, and the future we were building together.

The forest around us was a living thing. Each step we took set off a small flurry of birds or squirrels that then settled back into the invisible weave of their everyday lives.

The Springfield Forest was familiar to us, an often-traveled space around the homestead — a stretch of green between New Springfield and Gladdenfield Outpost, yet it never ceased to offer tiny surprises — a flower I hadn't noticed before, a footpath barely visible beneath the brush.

As the morning wore on, the sun climbed higher, and the light filtered through the leaves in a pattern that painted the forest floor. This part of the journey was comfortably familiar, a preamble to the unknowns we would soon face as we drew closer to the Copperwinde Forest.

Diane, Leigh, Celeste, Yeska, the larroling, and I walked in an easy silence, communication more about companionship than words. The larroling had taken well to its burden, the jugs of water now familiar weights upon its already massive frame, plodding along with a steadfast certainty.

We took our lunch break on a fallen log, using it as a makeshift bench. Pulling the food from our packs, we set up a simple meal of bread, cheese, and dried meat. "We should hit the Red River by tomorrow," I said, breaking off a piece of bread, "after which the real journey begins through the magical lands of Copperwinde."

"Copperwinde is a different beast," Diane replied as she took a bite of her cheese. "It's touched by Tannoris, and it is certainly different from the forests of Earth." She smiled softly. "It is more like home. It holds magic... more magic than we see in Springfield. More creatures, too, and not all of them friendly."

I nodded, taking her words seriously. Copperwinde sounded like a place awaiting our mark — a new chapter to write, and potentially a more dangerous one. "I trust we'll manage," I said with reassuring confidence. "We're prepared, and we have each other."

Lunch continued pleasantly, with talks of what lay ahead filling the space between bites. Leigh told another chapter of her life before the homestead; each anecdote laced with laughs and the rolling cadence of fond memory. Celeste shared her meal with Yeska, each girl picking things they liked best first.

Yeska seemed to have settled into this new rhythm. The earlier hint of a cat-like readiness to pounce had been replaced with a deliberate calmness, as if she had found her footing among us. Her eyes flicked from face to face, a quiet observer soaking in the tales and the bonds between us.

After lunch, we picked our way back onto the path, the remainder of our day marked by steady hiking. The forest seemed to change as we moved — subtly, almost shyly offering up its less familiar aspects as if it were assisting us on our journey.

Late afternoon came, wrapping the forest in a pre-evening glow. We found a clearing and decided to camp for the night. We divided the tasks; Diane and Yeska went to collect firewood while Leigh, Celeste, and I unpacked the tents from the larroling's load.

I started a fire, working until its flames were just robust enough to cook our meal using the supplies we had packed — smoked fish. Diane and Yeska returned with enough wood to last the night and then some, their faces flushed with exertion.

Meanwhile, Celeste and Leigh set up the tents with practiced ease. Yeska watched and helped where she could, still the newcomer learning our ways but engaging with an earnestness that bridged any gaps from her inexperience.

We sat around the fire, eating once again, this

time with the forest as our dining room. The crackling of the flames provided a backdrop to our meal, the snapping and popping a counterpoint to the softer sounds of the night beginning to settle around us.

As darkness seeped through the trees, more stars than I could count began to appear, a symbol of the purity of the wilderness we were lucky enough to call our temporary home. Celeste pointed out a few constellations that had carried over from Tannoris after the Upheaval, their histories woven into the fabric of her elven heritage.

Leigh plucked a small harmonica from her pack and played a few bluesy notes, a touch of music to end our day. It wasn't a song so much as a series of sounds that somehow matched perfectly with the evening. Celeste leaned back, gazing on the skies, while Yeska watched Leigh, taking interest in the soothing notes the blonde produced.

After dinner, I sent Yeska and the others to rest in the tents while I took first watch over the camp. "I'll wake you for the next shift," I promised Diane as I saw them off, eyes already heavy with sleep.

The forest at night was a wholly different world, each shadow was thicker, and the silence was filled with the nuanced noise of nocturnal life. The firelight threw everything beyond it into obscure relief, and I felt the weight of our safety on my shoulders.

I kept the fire steady, adding wood every so often to keep the darkness at bay. My thoughts hovered between the protective warmth of the flames and the unknowns held beyond. Would the creatures of the night keep their distance, I wondered, or would curiosity draw them closer?

With each log I placed on the fire, I considered the strength of the group sleeping behind me. They were more than a collection of wanderers; they were my family, each bound by something stronger than the road beneath us.

The sky continued its slow revolution, unaware of the small band of travelers nested beneath it. Celeste had described the stars as the eyes of the gods, and I couldn't help but feel, perhaps, they were watching over us.

I occasionally glanced back at the tents, the

rhythm of deep, peaceful breathing reaching me from within. It was late, and the chill of the evening air hinted at the approach of deep night.

Time passed, the night deepening, the forest around us hushed and dark. A few clouds drifted lazily across the sky, occasionally obscuring the brightest stars — a veil of mystery over the night's clarity.

Ensuring the fire was strong enough to last, I stood and stretched the stiffness from my limbs. I walked the perimeter of our camp, alert and ready, a final check before I would wake Diane for her turn at watch.

Shouldering my rifle, I patrolled the camp to make sure the women would get in a good night's sleep. After that, it would be my turn.

Chapter 25

The stirrings of dawn ushered a soft chill through the trees as we rose from our rest. Shafts of light pierced the canvas of our tents, and within the tangle of sleep-warmed bodies, silence lingered. The world outside beckoned us to begin anew, the next leg of our journey ready to unfurl beneath the weight of our footsteps.

As I emerged, raking fingers through my hair, I found the others stirring, their movements slow but determined against the breath of the morning. Diane was the first to join me around the fire with the cooking supplies we had arranged the night before. Together, we began the ritual of breakfast preparation.

The air warmed as the porridge bubbled in the pot, a simple fare that would sustain us for the hours to come. I watched the steam rise in thin wisps, dissipating into the canopy above. Leigh yawned her way into wakefulness, rubbing at eyes that held the remnants of dreams as she took her place beside us.

Celeste's sleepy smile bloomed as she shuffled from the tent, draping a soft blanket over her shoulders. The serenity of the forest dawn seemed to find a reflection in her, its hushed symphony a match for her muted grace. Yeska followed, her catkin alertness cut through by a thread of weariness, yet the anticipation of the day's journey appeared to shore her up.

We gathered around the pot, ladling the steamy porridge into bowls. The breakfast was consumed with few words, each spoonful chased down with sips of strong coffee that Diane had brewed. The meal was quiet, yet the silence felt like the calm before the song, the intake of breath before the first note is played.

Once our bellies were filled, we set to breaking camp with the practiced ease of those familiar with the wilderness. The larroling eyed our progress, snuffling softly as it awaited the weight of packs and provisions. Diane folded tents with mechanical precision; her motions fluid as the forest breeze.

Leigh checked every knot and tie, ensuring our supplies were secured against the long day's march. She hummed, a habit she had on mornings filled with purpose and destination. The sound was a soft thread pulled from the heart of contentment, soothing the fold and spindle of fabric and rope.

Celeste folded bedrolls with delicate fingers, each crease and tuck betraying the care that underpinned even the most mundane tasks. The motions were folded into the lore of our companionship, the fabric telling stories of past travels and shared dawns. We had gone on several trips now — first just me, Diane, and Leigh. Later with Celeste, and now with Yeska.

Yeska observed and learned, her hands slowly gaining the memory of tasks such as snuffing out the fire and dispersing its cooled ashes. Each instruction was absorbed; her previous life's formalities eased away by the tactile truth of life under the open sky.

With everything packed, we shouldered our burdens, the larroling obediently waiting to be laden with gear. The weight felt familiar across my shoulders, a solid comfort that rooted me to the road we would travel.

Diane led us away from the clearing, her strides finding rhythm with the heartbeat of the forest. I followed, watching as her form blended with the shifting patterns of shade and sun, a Scout in her element.

Leigh's steps formed punctuations in the quiet, her boots a soft staccato against the dirt. She had an energy about her that defied the early hour, a readiness that fed the very air we breathed.

Celeste walked lightly, the whisper of leaves and the murmur of distant water a song tailored to her step. The trees seemed to acknowledge her passing with a nod of branch and bow of bough — something magical about her wood-elven nature that made her seem so in tune with every aspect of the outdoors.

Soon, the Red River appeared as a ribbon of silver cutting through the land. Its banks were embraced by reeds and willows that swayed in the gentle current. The sound of its flow was a persistent whisper, a reminder of the fluidity of our own journey.

Diane navigated us to an old bridge, its timbers worn but holding strong against time and weather. "This'll see us across safely," she assured, her eyes scanning the structure's span.

One by one, we tread its width, the creak of aged wood beneath us mingling with the river's song.

On the other side, the Copperwinde Forest revealed itself, its thresholds marked by the curling tendrils of mists that wound themselves around the trunks of trees. Hues of green were deeper here, splashes of Tannorian blue bees darting amidst the foliage, a sight unseen in the lands we'd left behind.

The first steps into Copperwinde were like entering a realm set apart from our own. There was a tang of magic to the air, a vibrancy that pulsed beneath the leaf and loam. Bovine rofthuari loomed in the distance, their six-legged bodies wholly alien to this Earth.

In addition, we caught the occasional glimpse of larrolings in this wood, shaggy and wild. They reminded us that we were not astray from the familiar, yet their presence seemed accentuated here. Our own larroling grunted whenever it caught scent of one of its own kind.

We walked on, the forest embracing us in a fold of shadows and secrets. At its edge, where the day neared its close, Diane found the perfect spot for our next camp — a nestled cove surrounded by protective thicket and overlooking a misty vale cradling our destination.

A fire was kindled, its light a beacon against the

coming of night. Tents rose amidst murmurs and soft laughter as once again, the domesticity of our troop spun warmth into the evening chill.

Dinner was a contented event, simple rations of dried foods mixed with the occasional sweet berry foraged from the forest's bounty. Our conversations deepened, braided with the threads of shared endeavor and the yarns only twilight could tease from memory.

As the stars appeared one by one above the reaching hands of Copperwinde's trees, I found myself looking towards the vale enshrouded in mist, knowing that soon we would step into a legend older than many of the songs that Celeste sang so sweetly. An elven barrow Dungeon was a new challenge altogether, and I was excited for it, but I knew we would have to be on our guards.

The others retired to their beds, each in turn softly wishing me goodnight as I took the first watch. With a nod, I accepted their trust, my gaze lingering on each tent flap that fell closed, sheltering my sleeping family.

Night fell upon us, and the Copperwinde held its

secrets close. But together, we understood that we would venture into the Dungeon tomorrow, and as I settled in for my vigil, that knowledge was both a weight and a wing, tethering us as surely as the embers that glowed before me.

Chapter 26

Morning arrived with a hush, the early light weaving through the branches above and brushing against the fabric of our tents. I woke up to the serene sound of our surroundings, feeling the sense of a new day filled with unexplored possibilities. There was a slight chill in the air — a crisp reminder of the dew that settled overnight.

The camp began to stir, wakened by Celeste who had drawn the last watch. She glanced around, her eyes taking in the pale mist that shrouded the vale beyond our campsite. As she stood like that, I realized she was a creature of silent beauty, her presence blending seamlessly with the natural world she so revered.

Diane stretched as she exited her tent, a look of determination already set upon her features. "We should break camp quickly; we have plenty to uncover today," she said, her voice clear in the misty air.

Leigh was soon by our side, her energy undimmed despite the early hour. She pulled on her boots and rolled up her sleeping bag with efficient swiftness, mirroring the purpose that drove all of us.

Yeska's gaze swept across the camp, her eyes reflecting the subdued tones of dawn as she helped Celeste gather and pack our gear. They moved together quietly, bonded by the shared tasks of the morning.

The larroling grunted softly, waiting for us to load it up. Its large body seemed ready and capable, as much a part of our journey as any of us.

With breakfast a quick affair of leftover bread and dried fruit, we did not linger. The early meal was sustenance for the path ahead, the flavors barely registering as we readied ourselves to leave.

Once the final checks were made and the last straps tightened on our packs, I signaled to the group. "Let's head out," I said, my eyes already on the vale that awaited us, cloaked in mystery and mist.

Diane took the lead, guiding us with secure steps through the thick fog that began to envelop us as we left the sanctuary of our camp behind. The mist seemed to be a living thing, caressing our skin and hair, leaving tiny droplets in its wake.

As we walked deeper into the misty vale, Celeste broke the silence. "This place," she murmured, almost to herself, "It's like walking through one of the ancient burial grounds on Tannoris."

Her observation resonated with us, lending an ethereal quality to our march. The deep mist seemed to hold secrets, and the standing stones that dotted the landscape were sentinels to a time long past.

"These monuments," Celeste continued, gently brushing her hand against a stone adorned with Elvish script, "mark the place as sacred — a resting place for those who once walked among us."

Diane regarded the inscriptions with admiration, a reverence for the history they represented. "They're a reminder of what stood before the Upheaval," she said thoughtfully.

Leigh watched us interact with the monuments, her natural curiosity kindling. "To think these stood in another world — a world linked to ours through events we still don't fully understand," she mused.

Yeska listened closely, an appreciative nod to the words shared. "There's an undeniable power to this land," she agreed, the mist swirling around her.

As we descended deeper into the valley, the number of standing stones increased, larger and more intricately inscribed. Celeste's translations touched on themes of honor and remembrance, bringing depth to our expedition.

The mist began to thin as we approached the heart of the vale, revealing the startling sight of a vast stone barrow, its entrance a dark maw in the pale morning.

"This must be it," Diane commented, taking a step closer. "It matches the description Lernoval gave us."

I nodded in response, my gaze fixed on the ancient structure. "He said the staff lies within, along with the remnants of those who once sought to claim its powers."

"The Undead," Yeska hummed, and I gave her a nod.

Leigh squinted into the shadows of the entrance. "We'll need to be cautious," she said evenly. "Dungeons are rarely as straightforward as they appear."

Celeste's eyes scanned the stonework, catching glimpses of further inscriptions that wove around the entrance. "The elven text speaks of guardianship and eternal wakefulness," she relayed to us, voicing a silent prayer in her native tongue. "That does seem to imply the undead roam here."

It was a sight that brought introspection to us all — the balance of light against dark, the weight of history against the pulse of our own lives.

Yeska peered into the dimness beyond, the notion of exploration and discovery evident in her stance. "We're about to step into a tale," she said, her voice barely above a whisper. "I can feel it."

I looked at each of them, feeling a unity in our shared resolve. "We'll eat an early lunch, discuss our approach, and gather ourselves before entering," I decided, the echo of my words hanging in the balance between anticipation and apprehension.

We settled on a grassy knoll strewn with boulders just a stone's throw from the barrow entrance, where the cold damp of the misty vale seemed less intent on reaching our bones. The larroling positioned itself beside us, its hulking presence both familiar and comforting in this strange part of the forest. Leaves clung to its shaggy coat, remnants of our trek through the Copperwinde.

Diane laid the cloth out before us, a makeshift tablecloth that spread across the grass. Onto it, she placed dried venison, nuts, hard cheese, and a loaf of crusty bread that had survived the journey well enough. The simple meal spoke to our need for practicality over luxury on expeditions such as these.

Leigh uncorked a thermos, the scent of strong tea wafting towards us as she poured into tin cups. "Warmth from within as we plan for the venture ahead," she said, handing out the tea.

Celeste passed around slices of apple, their freshness a sweet reminder of the comfort and care of our homestead. Yeska accepted her share with a small, grateful nod, one that acknowledged the thought behind each picked item.

We chewed in the companionable silence that shared hardships often birth, finding solace in the rhythm of bite and chew, the warmth of tea in our throats, and the closeness of trusted companions around us.

"Once inside," I said, breaking the calm, "Diane should scout ahead a little. Or take point at the very least." The mist wrapped around us like a shawl as I spoke, my breath visible in the cold air.

Diane nodded; her sharp features set with determination. "I can manage that. I'll look for signs, traps, anything out of place."

"I'll follow close behind," I continued, "The larroling can flank us."

The larroling snuffled, its large nostrils flaring as if understanding its role in our plans. Its loyalty was unfaltering, a fact that brought me immeasurable peace as we faced unknown challenges ahead.

Leigh and Yeska elected to bring up the rear, a position from which Leigh could watch our backs with sharp eyes and quickdraw if need be. "Don't you worry," she said, "we'll have no problem keeping pace."

Yeska, looking over to the shadowed barrow

entrance, her expression one of focus rather than the carefree mannerisms from days spent idle in the sun. "When necessary, I can provide a buff. It will cost the recipient some Health, but it might be just what we need in a pinch."

"And those curses?" I prompted, remembering the power Yeska possessed that was unlike anything I had encountered before. "A means to weaken our enemies?"

"Just so," she confirmed. "Especially if they carry a strong Bloodline. Most bosses do. It could be crucial in a Dungeon such as this."

As we conversed, Celeste kept one eye on the entrance, the elvish runes whispering forgotten tales to her senses. Her connection to the arcane was undeniable, a silent commitment to the world's older magics at play around us.

The meal was soon finished, and the leftovers carefully stowed away. I brushed crumbs from my hands onto the ground, where the world would reclaim them in time.

Diane checked her crossbow, her fingers familiar with each curve and notch of the weapon as she examined the string and stock. Her readiness was like a stone in a running stream, unmovable and sure.

Leigh checked her revolver. She tested the release and gave me a slight nod. "All set."

Celeste arranged her satchel, ensuring her sword and supplies were secure and within easy reach. Despite her shapely and womanly frame, Celeste was an impressive swordfighter, her Stellar Maiden Class a boon in any Dungeon.

Yeska's loadout was the lightest, a testament to her role that relied more on skill and less on material aid. A dagger hung at her side, a simple blade that held more purpose than it let on.

The larroling was prepared, its broad back ready to shield us from harm should the need arise. Its patient wait felt like the breath held between two notes of music, necessary in the melody of our venture.

As the sun climbed higher, the chill of the vale's mist began to dissipate, replaced by a tempered warmth that felt like encouragement from the world itself. I rolled my shoulders to ease the slight tension, readying for what was to come.

I took one last look around the clearing, ensuring we had left nothing behind that we would need in the dungeon. The camp itself we left as it is.

Diane scanned the landscape, her gaze lingering on the rise and fall of the land, her mind already mapping our path before she turned to the others. "We should get moving," she said, "the day won't wait on us."

I nodded. "We don't want to be in a Dungeon when it's night, and we're getting tired. Let's move out."

We gathered our courage like we had our packs, slinging it over our shoulders with an acceptance that bore the weight of the responsibility we carried — to one another, to Lernoval, to the greater order of the world we fought to protect.

And with our strategy laid out and weapons checked, we stood before the Dungeon's yawning entrance. The mist had now completely lifted, revealing the barrow's promise of peril and possibility.

Chapter 27

The barrow's entrance loomed before us, raised by the errant magical energies of the staff itself. It had to be a powerful artifact indeed to be able to create such a Dungeon.

Yeska bore the torch, and it cast flickering shadows that danced across the elaborate carvings adorning the doorway. She hesitated just a moment before crossing the threshold after me, her eyes catching mine with firming resolve.

With a nod from me, she followed us. Before us, the first chamber unfolded.

The air was still, the silence deafening, as if the barrow was holding its breath with our intrusion. The walls were covered in elegant bas-reliefs, depicting scenes of elven majesty — the rise and fall of kingdoms, the passing of wizards whose wisdom seemed almost palpable.

The chamber stretched out, grand and stoic, with a high ceiling that vaulted into obscurity above, shrouded in darkness that the light from Yeska's torch could not pierce. The ground underfoot was smooth, stones fitted so perfectly together that no sound betrayed our steps. It was cold here, the kind of cold that whispered through layers of armor and clothes and nipped at your bones.

Large statues — maiden figures with serene faces, hands clasped in eternal prayer — flanked a path leading towards the center, where a solitary dais stood, empty but clearly once a resting place for something revered. The air was rich with the quiet power of histories untold, woven into the very fabric of this sacred space.

"What were they like, do you think?" Celeste pondered aloud, her voice a ghostly echo. "The ones who walked these halls before us?" She reached out tentatively, touching the base of one statue, as if half-expecting it to impart some ancient wisdom.

Leigh gave a low whistle, her eyes wide as she scanned the room. "Elves sure knew how to impress," she remarked, only half-joking. "Imagine the kinda gatherings this place must've seen."

Yeska held the torch higher, the flame's quiver sending erratic patterns against the walls. "It's impressive, yes," she agreed, "But also... there's a sadness here, don't you think? The kind that weighs on you."

I felt it, too, a heaviness in the air that bore down on us with the echo of loss — of glory days faded and wisdom lost. The chamber seemed to tell its tale with every notch and sweep of the carvings, a silent narration of a grandeur absent.

"Let's be careful," I cautioned, instinctually lowering my voice. "Diane, would you scout ahead? There's a hallway there," I gestured towards the only exit from the room, a dark passageway that promised both secrets and dangers unseen.

Diane nodded; her features set in determined lines. Trust shone clear in her eyes — trust in her skills, in us, in the unspoken bond among our little group.

"I'll be quick and quiet," she promised before slipping into the shadows of the hall, her form soon swallowed by the darkness.

As she vanished from sight, I felt the trust settle over me like a mantle — a weight and a privilege. She was our eyes and ears now in the ancient solidity of the barrow, and I stood at the ready, waiting with a patience born from necessity and faith.

Leigh and Celeste held their breaths with me, a mutual tension holding us still. Yeska remained a silent sentinel, her presence a sturdy reassurance as we lingered in the chamber, allowing Diane to scout the path ahead.

The minutes stretched, marked only by the crackling of the torch and the soft sound of our breathing. Time here seemed a concept devoid of meaning, untethered from the world outside.

And then Diane was back, emerging from the shadowy corridor. Her expression was taut, the lines around her eyes pronounced with unease. "There's a large chamber beyond," she reported, her voice a touch higher than usual. "Lots of sarcophagi, either side of the hall."

A chill shot through me at her words, the sharp twist in my stomach betraying my own concern. "Anything else?" I probed, hoping for a detail that might lessen the weight of foreboding her report carried.

Diane nodded gravely. "There's... *something* there. A force, dark and oppressive. It felt like it was watching me, waiting." She shook her head, her decision explicit in her firm stance. "I wouldn't go in there alone."

I took in her words, each one shaping the picture of what awaited us. "We'll go together then," I said. "Whatever this force is, facing it as a team is our strength."

Diane seemed relieved, the affirmation of our support a visible balm to her nerves. "Together," she echoed, her resolve steadying in the shared commitment of our group.

I took a deep breath, feeling the air of the chamber fill my lungs. This was it, the moment before the plunge into depths unseen, where the history of the barrow would unfold before us on terms not our own.

We fell into a ready formation, a line of heartbeats synced with a singular purpose. With Diane taking point, the torch in Yeska's hand casting light upon our path, and Leigh's steady hand at the rear, we advanced to the chamber Diane described.

Each step echoed in the hall, the sound of our collective courage reverberating off the cold stone walls. The anticipation was a living thing amongst us, heightening our senses as we approached the darkness that waited beyond.

We paused at the threshold; the air was thick

with the tangible possibility of encounters unknown. The chamber with the sarcophagi beckoned; its secrets hidden by the shadows.

We stood at the entrance to the chamber, the stillness of the barrow wrapping around us like an unseen cloak. An uneasy quiet reached out from the open maw of the doorway, as if the shadows themselves were listening.

"Something feels off," Diane hummed, peering into the darkness. "I think there might be a trap here. Let's not move."

I nodded, trusting in her Scout abilities as we all looked around, cautious and immobile.

I peered closer at the threshold, my eyes tracing over the edge where stone met stone, and that's when I saw it — a small, cleverly concealed groove that ran along the lintel.

"Look here." I pointed to the groove, its purpose clear to me: a trap that would seal us inside once activated.

Diane's gaze followed where I pointed, a frown creasing her brow. "Good catch! And you think... once we're in, it'll close on us?" she asked. She moved closer, her Scout's instincts kicking in, analyzing the trap's design with a critical eye.

Yeska leaned in, squinting to make out the detail I had highlighted. "Clever," she muttered, a note of respect in her voice. "Designed to seal intruders with whatever lies beyond."

Leigh nudged my shoulder, her eyes wide with curiosity. "So, what's the plan then, baby? How do we outsmart this age-old security system?" Her voice was light, but I caught the undercurrent of tension.

I glanced back at the sunlit forest visible through the barrow's entrance, an idea forming in my mind. "We're going to block it," I said. "We can use boulders from outside to keep the mechanism from fully engaging. It'll be hard work, but it'll create a narrow opening, allowing us a way out and a bottleneck to fight, should creatures come once the trap is sprung." My finger jabbed toward the chamber, where shadows hinted at the dormant sarcophagi. "Considering the undead theme of this Dungeon, I expect those sarcophagi will open."

Celeste nodded, her understanding immediate. "Smart," she affirmed, her voice steady despite the gravity of our situation.

With our course of action decided, I summoned two domesticants to help with the heavy lifting, their playful energy a stark contrast to our focused intent.

"You're going to help us," I told the domesticants, and the creatures darted around in expressive chirps, ready to follow my commands.

The domesticants, the larroling, and Leigh followed me outside. We scanned the woods, searching for stones sizable enough to serve our purpose, yet small enough to be moved.

Yeska stayed by the entrance, keeping an eye on the chamber. Diane knelt by her side with her crossbow ready. An air of concentration surrounded them, a shared silence that bespoke their dedication. Celeste was there as well, massive two-handed sword drawn and ready.

It didn't take long to find what we needed: large, irregular boulders that had been tossed aside by time and the elements. The larroling and the domesticants gripped the edges of one, while Leigh and I grabbed another. The rocky surface felt rough against our hands, and we hauled with all the strength we could muster.

The boulder's weight was oppressive, each push and pull a test of our resolve. Together we grunted and heaved, inching the stones toward the barrow's entrance.

"That should do," I panted, as we positioned the first boulder by the doorway. It stood like a sentry, its bulk partially blocking the mechanism I had spotted earlier. I nodded at the domesticants. "Get a few smaller ones to make it fit nice and snug."

One of the domesticants gave a happy chirp and began zooming back and forth, its form a blur of motion as it assisted by nudging smaller stones into place, filling the gaps to ensure the doorway would not close. The others followed its lead.

Soon enough, the work was done, and I dismissed the domesticants — they would be of no use if battle followed, and they would fade when the spell ended anyway.

The sweat on my brow was cold as I surveyed our handiwork. The opening remained accessible, but now it was narrow, restricted. We had turned a potential trap into a strategic choke point.

Diane wiped her hands on her trousers, stepping back to judge the makeshift barrier. "Looks sturdy," she said.

Yeska, who had been watching our progress intently, gave a small nod. "A bottleneck," she said. "A way to control the flow of battle."

Leigh bounced slightly on her toes, the energy never quite leaving her. "Now we'll have 'em right where we want 'em," she said with a confident grin. "Provided there are indeed some nasties waitin' to hop out of those stone boxes."

With the women in position, I felt a readiness settle over me. My gaze met each of theirs in turn, an unspoken pledge passing between us, a commitment to face whatever emerged from the sarcophagi.

Diane clasped her crossbow a little tighter, her

instincts as a scout telling her that vigilance was our best defense. Leigh's hand rested on the grip of her revolver, a small comfort against the unknown.

I turned back to the entrance, my palms itching for the grip of my rifle. Confidence surged within me, a feeling both familiar and exhilarating. The trap was set, our preparations complete.

I was ready to trigger the trap and see what would come out of the sarcophagi.

Chapter 28

Stepping into the chamber alone, the torch in my hand carved a circle of light against the pressing darkness. I studied the sarcophagi lining the walls, each one carved from dark stone that seemed to absorb the flickering flames, rendering them almost ineffective. Their lids were etched with intricate designs that spoke of nobility and long-lost power.

My heart hammered in my chest as my next step triggered the trap, a simple step onto a concealed plate within the floor's mosaic. A grating sound erupted as the massive stone door behind me began its descent, intent on sealing me within this chamber of the dead.

But as the door met the boulders we had placed, it ground to a halt, leaving a narrow opening back into the hallway. I felt a rush of relief, knowing our plan had worked.

The moment I retreated into the hall; the sarcophagi creaked open. From within, ghouls emerged, crawling out with grotesque slowness. Their sharp teeth and elongated claws glistened under the torchlight, their movements quick and agile despite the confines of their stone prisons.

"Let's light 'em up!" I called out to the others, my voice a steely calm as I backed through the narrow doorway, leaving the bottleneck to the undead monstrosities.

I raised my rifle, aiming carefully, and I let loose.

Leigh and Diane followed my example, thinning their numbers before they even got to the bottleneck.

At once they came, shrieking and clawing, eager to taste the flesh of the living. But the opening was narrow, and it forced the frontmost ghoul to slow down to a crawl.

More ghouls emerged, each one attempting to break through our bottleneck. But they could only come one by one, and with grim precision, we confronted each threat as it appeared.

Leigh's aim was unwavering, each shot punctuating the silence with its finality. Diane, beside us, readied her crossbow, her bolts finding their mark with deadly accuracy in the narrow space we had created.

The ghouls came in a relentless wave, but our fortress of stones, and the skilled hands that wielded weapon and bolt, held firm against the tide. They had to squeeze through, and they got stuck. And we would just shoot them.

With every ghoul that collapsed before us, the next ones who would enter shrieked in frustration as they pulled and clawed until the remnants of their fallen compatriot were gone and another could try to climb through. We didn't even have to clear the bottleneck ourselves thanks to the ghouls' mindless bloodlust and willingness to throw themselves at our weapons.

Still, the chamber beyond the bottleneck was alive with movement, but the narrow opening disrupted their advance, turning their number from advantage to downfall.

Ghoul after ghoul was met with the bark of Leigh's revolver, the sharp report of my rifle, and Diane's bolts, each one felled before it could so much as set foot into the light. Diane was unyielding, her crossbow a harbinger of swift ends.

Yeska watched; her readiness untouched by the fray. Beside her, the larroling growled lowly in its throat, eager for a command from Leigh, its body a barrier should the ghouls break through despite our best efforts.

Like the larroling, Celeste stood in reserve, her countenance serene amidst the chaos. Her sword hung silent at her side.

One by one, the ghouls continued to come, and one by one, they fell. At last, twenty-four ghouls lay dispatched before us, each delivering a message of what lay within the barrow's heart — a cautionary tale written in blood and malice.

The last ghoul gave a final shudder before going still, its claws scratching the stones in its dying spasms. Silence descended once more, heavy and absolute.

We caught our breaths as the reality of our victory settled around us. Diane leaned against the wall, her eyes alight with the triumph of our success. "Well done," she said, her voice rich with pride.

Leigh holstered her revolver with a flourish, her face aglow. "That's how we handle things at the Wilson Homestead," she declared, her joy a reflection of our shared sentiment.

Yeska approached the opening, her gaze lingering on the stone door that had failed to imprison us. "Resourceful," she whispered as she glanced at me, and there was admiration in the quiet certainty of her words. "Very good."

Celeste's smile was one of quiet satisfaction. "The music this time," she observed, "was in our coordination and planning."

As I surveyed the scene, the resolve within me hardened. We had faced the first of the barrow's challenges and emerged the victors, but I felt certain more tests awaited us before we found the staff. The ghouls were only the beginning.

Chapter 29

"Let's keep moving," I said to my women, my voice steady as we collected ourselves for the next phase of our descent into the barrow's heart.

The passage ahead was carved with the same care as the rest of the barrow, though the walls appeared closer here, the weight of the earth pressing in around us. Our steps echoed in the confined space, a quiet drumbeat to accompany the steady thrum of blood in my veins. With each step, the air grew cooler, the stone beneath our feet firmer, as if leading us toward a place untouched by time.

The corridor opened up as we journeyed deeper, expanding into an underground chamber that stretched out before us. It was small, but that didn't mean it was safe. The only thing here was the staircase.

"Let's keep our eyes open for more traps and nasty surprises," I whispered, eyeing the emptiness that seemed to swallow the torch's light whole.

Diane agreed with a nod, her eyes scanning the chamber's edges. The light from the torch played across her face, emphasizing the resolve etched into her features.

Finding no traps or hidden enemies, we descended deeper into darkness. The staircase invited us with a silent promise of discovery and hidden things below. We did not falter, and we went down in order, ready for anything.

The stairwell twisted downward, a helix that wrapped around itself. My hand trailed along the wall, the cool surface reassuring under my touch. The descent was slow, measured — each step taken with the deliberateness of those who know that haste can be a misstep's or a cunning trap's invitation.

At the bottom, the air felt even colder, a chill that suggested the depth of our venture. There was a smell, too — old, like damp earth and stone. It brought to mind images of hidden places and the secrets they kept shrouded within.

We emerged onto a landing that bordered a wide chasm, the space opening into a cavernous void that my instincts told me was dangerous. Yeska's torchlight faltered at the edge, unable to penetrate the abyss that yawned before us.

A bridge spanned the chasm, a narrow arch of ancient stones fitted together with an architectural grace that defied their utilitarian purpose. I eyed the bridge, the way the shadows seemed to clutch at its sides.

"Wait," I cautioned, holding an arm out to stop

the women as they approached the bridge. My gaze settled on the stonework, seeking out the tell-tale signs that had saved us before. In the wavering torchlight, I spotted them — small, indistinct shapes etched into the stone surface.

Diane leaned in beside me, her eyes sharp. "Pressure plates," she confirmed, pointing to the patches on the bridge in front of us. "Another good spot! Definitely traps." Her voice echoed softly, undercutting the quiet.

I focused on the nearest patch. "It's like the doorway — step on these, and I bet something unpleasant happens." My eyes lingered on the first plate, its outline now clear against the rest of the stone.

Yeska's hand was steady as she handed me a small rock from the ground. "Let's see what we're dealing with," she said, her tone a mix of curiosity and caution.

I tossed the rock onto the pressure plate, the thud of its landing punctuated by sudden movement. Bolts shot out of hidden recesses in the walls, their flight swift and deadly. They sliced through the air where a body would have stood, clattering with sharp clanks on the far wall of the canyon.

The women watched with their eyes wide. "Good call," Leigh murmured, her brows raised at the array of traps now revealed. "Even if we'd survive those bolts, they're goin' fast enough to make a body lose their balance on that nasty old bridge."

I nodded, agreeing with her comment, picked up another rock, and lobbed it onto the next pressure plate. This time, swinging blades emerged from the walls, mimicking a deadly dance designed to cut and maim. Then, I tried the bolts again and found that they had been depleted.

"Alright," I said. "They look to be single use. But let's triple-tap each of them to make sure."

One by one, I triggered each plate from a safe distance, the subsequent traps springing to life and then falling silent. Spears, darts, flames — each presented a new terror that would have awaited an unwary traveler.

As the last trap spent its fury and did not reactivate on the second or third toss, the women exhaled in unison, a collective relief washing over us.

"You have a sharp eye for these things," Diane said, a touch of pride warming her voice. "Even I didn't spot them. You would've made an excellent Scout!"

"You would've seen them before you stepped on them," I assured her.

Yeska nodded in agreement. "I think so too." Diane shot her a warm smile at that.

The bridge was now seemingly safe with its surface laid bare, and all hidden dangers revealed or triggered. I crossed first, feeling the smooth stone beneath my boots, the chasm's emptiness yawning below.

Celeste followed, and Leigh and Yeska came next, their steps less wary now that the way appeared clear. Yeska looked back at the cavern after she had crossed the bridge, her green eyes reflecting the torchlight.

"This place keeps you on your toes," she remarked, and I could only nod in response. We needed to remain sharp.

Diane brought up the rear this time, her eyes lingering on the mechanisms of the traps, the way they had been cleverly hidden within the architecture. "Makes you appreciate the minds that built this, traps and all," she said.

On the other side of the bridge, I allowed myself a small smile of victory. We had so far managed to avoid injury or risky confrontation, but the journey was far from over.

As we delved deeper into the barrow, the hush of ancient stone surrounded us. Our progression was marked by the soft padding of our boots and the careful breathing that mingled with the air of long-kept secrets.

With Yeska's torch leading the way, we encountered a room that spread wide and high with statues of exalted elves, noble figures emanating a once-lived regality, now immortalized in stone.

The statues stood tall with their faces carved with quiet honors and their pedestals inscribed with the flowing script of Elvish. Eyes upon them, I spoke in a near-whisper, respecting the sanctity of this chamber.

"Look at these," I urged Leigh and Celeste, who approached with intrigue, their fingers already tracing the archaic symbols etched into the bases.

While Leigh admittedly knew only bits and pieces of Elvish, Celeste, on the other hand, was fluent and began to translate the writings. Her voice was filled with an awe that paid homage to the times long past, recounting stories carried by the lines. They were tales of the major families of Thelluan, the feats of their kin during times the wars waged, and the peace cherished. The Dungeon that the staff had created around itself was filled with the memories of the family it had served.

Leigh hung on every word, the few Elvish terms she knew springing to mind, aiding her in piecing together the historical puzzle. "This one's from the house of Eäron," she guessed correctly on occasion, a fire of discovery aglow in her eyes.

Yeska stood beside me, less invested in history but no less caught in the gravity of the moment. "You have an impressive heritage, Celeste," she observed, her tone suggesting that she, too, felt the weight of the legacy before us.

We lingered, our tour becoming a silent study, taking the time to honor the memories of a people whose bloodlines wove through the elves that still populated the world today, where Tannoris and Earth had met.

After a respectful pause, we moved on, the stillness broken by the sound of our steps echoing softly in the chamber. I led the group, with Diane by my side, vigilant for any signs of hidden dangers that might lurk among these relics of a proud lineage.

It wasn't long before we stood before another obstacle: a door, closed and formidable in its sturdy construction. Its entire face was covered in a riddle, peculiar lettering that invited not just to be read, but to be understood. The letters curled and arched across the stone, composed yet enigmatic.

Celeste leaned forward, squinting at the script. "It asks what begins but has no end and is the key to hearts and home," she recited, the torchlight flickering over the words, highlighting their intricacy. "And we must speak the answer aloud, or the door shan't open!"

"Now that's a riddle if I ever saw one," Leigh remarked, her head tilted as she tried to decipher the puzzle. The lines were crafted in an older style of Elvish, deep and complex, full of traditions that predated even the tale-filled chamber we had left behind.

"Hmm," Yeska pondered, bringing a slender finger to her plump lip. "Can we force it open?"

"Good question," Diane said as her gaze followed along the carved words. "But this is no simple lock; it is magical. It'll take more than a blade or bolt to open this."

The women began discussing the riddle, and Celeste's expertise in Elvish was invaluable now as they pondered the riddle together. She murmured the words, again and again, giving them space to breathe, to be more than mere inscriptions on stone.

"What begins but has no end and is the key to hearts and home?" I muttered, contemplating the answer.

We settled into a thoughtful silence, each of us weighing the words, their possible meaning. The trick wasn't in outwitting the riddle's author but in reaching into the depths of its truth.

"Love," I finally uttered, that singular point of clarity piercing through the conundrum. The word felt right, evoking the endless quality of the most profound of feelings.

Yeska's green eyes widened, reflecting the triumph the answer sparked. "Yes, of course," she agreed. "Love is endless."

Leigh nodded. "And only through love can you win hearts and open doors."

"Exactly," I said.

Diane nodded with an approving smile. "That sounds about right."

I turned to Celeste. "The Elvish word for 'love,' do you know it?"

"Of course, my love," she said with a smile

before taking position before the door and spreading her arms. She spoke the word aloud, and the sound of fair Elvish speech reverberated throughout the hall.

The door responded with a slow and heavy grind of shifting stone.

"That was it!" Diane said, clapping her hands as she gave a happy hop.

Yeska grinned, joining Diane in her exuberance. "Well done, David!" she purred.

The others watched with expectant gazes as the door inched open, revealing darkness beyond. I stepped forward while the others took up their defensive positions beside me. We braced for what we might find, our anticipation palpable in the cool air of the dungeon.

Leigh crouched slightly, her eyes darting swiftly from shadow to shadow, watching for any sign of movement. Her readiness was the complement to my own, and the larroling flanked her, ready to rend and tear if anything hostile came out.

Yeska scrutinized the widening gap of the door, her analytical mind likely racing infinitely faster than the door's arduous opening. Diane remained close, her crossbow loaded and ready, though I knew she hoped for a moment's respite on the other side — a break in our vigilance more welcomed than another fight.

Celeste took a discrete step back, allowing the fighters to advance. Her trust in us mirrored in her steady posture, her art to soothe rather than to attack.

The door's opening reached its utmost, enough space for us to pass through single file. We paused for the span of a heartbeat, for the breadth of hope intertwined with trepidation.

At my signal, Diane took the lead and stepped through the open door. Beyond was a corridor, we fell in behind Diane as we advanced.

Chapter 30

Diane paused at the entrance to the next chamber, her hand raised in a silent command that halted us all in our tracks. She had gone ahead to scout, and her signal told us she wanted a little more space between her and us to scout farther ahead.

I watched as she eased forward, each step

deliberate and poised as she melded into the shadows stretched out before us. The faintest rustle of her clothing against the stone floor was the only sound that betrayed her movement as the others and I waited, holding our collective breath.

Yeska clutched her torch close, the light flickering uncertainly at the edge of the dark expanse that spread beyond the doorway. Leigh shifted weightlessly beside her, her gaze darting with barely suppressed restlessness while Celeste's fingers grazed the hilt of her sword, a comforting presence that belied the tension of the moment.

In the stillness, our whispers felt too loud, too jarring, as we speculated in hushed tones. "What do you think she saw?" Leigh's voice was barely audible, her hand resting on the grip of her revolver with an unreadable anticipation.

"Could be anything," I murmured back, my finger on the trigger guard of my rifle, ready for whatever might come. "Trust Diane. She'll know if there's danger."

The larroling let out a low, rumbling sound — a subdued note of vigilance as it sensed our unease. I glanced at it, reassured by its solid presence at my side, a constant ally amid the uncertainty.

Time seemed to twist and stretch, a waiting game played in the arena of echoes and half-lights. And then, just as my heart threatened to beat out of my chest, Diane reappeared, her form coalescing from the shadows.

She slipped back into the light of Yeska's torch, her face etched with something like awe. "There's a skeleton," she announced, her voice low but firm. "Floating, in a robe — keeps muttering to itself in Elvish as it reads a book."

A chill tiptoed down my spine at the description — a being existing between the realm of the living and the dead, a keeper of ancient rituals and forgotten lore.

"A lich," Yeska breathed, her catkin eyes wide with both fear and fascination. "A powerful undead mage."

The word 'lich' piqued my interest — so *that* was the being guarding this place. I nodded, processing Yeska's explanation. "If it's a lich, we'll need to be extra careful. Their magic is old and potent."

"What's the strategy?" Diane's gaze went from face to face, waiting for my lead. I admired her courage, her willingness to face what was before us with unyielding resolve.

"First, we'll buff up," I said, remembering the collective strength that lay within us, the raw potential of magic and bravery. "We'll use your passive buffs, Yeska, even if it costs us a little Health."

"Celeste, you'll go in with the larroling," I instructed, grateful for the versatility of our small yet capable group. "You two are the melee fighters, and my summons can support you."

Celeste nodded, acknowledging her part to play as the spearhead.

"And I'll keep up my fire," Diane said, "and aim for whatever will stop the lich from focusing on its spells."

Leigh cracked a quick grin, the tension dissipating slightly with her humor. "Sounds like a fitting dance for us," she said, her revolver already in her hand.

Yeska exhaled softly, the weight of her mana-heavy role settling upon her. "I'll start with the buffs then," she said, her confidence an anchor amid the swirling doubts.

"And I'll get some summons up first," I finalized the plan, feeling the steely thread of leadership winding tight. "Aquana's avatar and a storm elemental. And a guardian to shield the others." Every part of me was alert, primed for what had to be done.

The plan was in place, each knowing their role within the intricate beats of the combat that lay in wait. Leigh had her revolver aimed down the passage. Yeska began incantations for our buffs. Diane prepared her bolts for quick firing. Celeste clutched her sword. And finally, the larroling, was ready to flank or charge on command.

It was there, in the silent accord of our shared determination, that I reached into my pack and drew forth a small vial. A mana potion — vibrant and swirling with captured potential. I needed to restore my mana to ensure I could cast as many spells as were necessary for this confrontation.

As I uncorked the vial and drank deeply, the

potion's magic surged through me, a resurgence of power that tingled in my veins. It restored the mana I had expended to summon domesticants.

"Time to go," I said, holding the empty vial loosely in my hand.

Yeska cast her spell on each of us. Receiving the buff was a strange sensation — a pang of pain, not altogether unpleasant in a strange way, followed by a rush of power and adrenaline. Heightened senses, increased mana and damage.

"Wow," I hummed, clenching my fists as they thrummed with power. "This feels amazing."

Yeska gave a smile. "It does, doesn't it?" she agreed before buffing my other women.

As she did so, I set up my summons, calling forth Aquana's avatar, a storm elemental, and a guardian. I also cast my Evolve Summon spell on each, and watched with a satisfied smile as their forms grew more powerful — muscles became more pronounced, colors more vibrant, and the crackling energy more intense. When I was done, I drank another potion to restore some of the 38 Mana spent casting my array of spells.

Yeska finished her incantations, her own aura flaring with magical readiness, while Diane and Leigh gave sharp nods, their eyes narrowing with fierce intent.

And as the others readied themselves, the larroling took its place, a grounding force amid the bubbling currents of magic and adrenaline.

We stood, a force of combined might, each of us poised on the precipice of action, the moment before the storm. With roles assigned and hearts aligned, we faced the shadowed corridor ahead.

With everyone knowing their duty, we were ready to confront the lich.

Chapter 31

The chamber where the lich lingered was cast in shadows with only the faintest glow from Yeska's torch to guide us. We paused just outside its reach, huddled in the semi-darkness of the barrow's hallway. The air was thick with the musty scent of undisturbed stone and the faint echoes of the lich's droning incantations.

My heart raced, adrenaline pumping through my veins as I reached for the comforting weight of my rifle, feeling the solid stock against my palm as my summons got into position. Diane's poised silhouette beside me was reassuring; her crossbow ready in her hands as we prepared for the ambush.

Leigh's steady breathing was audible in the silent chamber, revolver at the ready while her gaze fixed on the lich's form — a mere wraith among the more substantial outlines of the barrow.

Celeste stood a step behind, sword ready. The serene expression on her face belied the intensity of the moment and of the battle we would soon join.

Yeska's voice was barely above a whisper, "Ready."

In one fluid motion, I signaled to Diane, and like a whisper of wind, she slipped into the chamber. The lich remained oblivious, floating pensively with its book; it was now or never. I swiftly cast my Aura of Protection, bolstering the defenses of my allies and my summons.

My fingers tightened on the trigger as the lich

continued to mutter, a drone of sound that vibrated through the ancient stone and into my bones. This was it — the moment between breaths, between heartbeats, where everything would change.

With a nod to Leigh, I stepped into the chamber, rifle aimed at the floating figure. The lich's empty sockets turned toward me, a silent recognition of my presence breaking its vigil.

Leigh's revolver cracked loudly beside me, the sound a harsh punctuation to the previous silence. The bullet found its mark, disrupting the lich's woven spells with a flash of impact.

Diane's crossbow twanged as she fired a bolt. The magical water damage and her Mark Foe ability combined to greatly increase her damage output. And the lich twitched as the bolt struck it.

Yeska's voice rose in a chant, and a glow enveloped the figure. Blood Pox — a curse that sent pulsing waves through the air, wrapping around the lich like a virulent shroud.

Then came Celeste, the larroling, and my bolstered summons. Before the lich could lay down a web of defensive spells or pelt us with a fireball, they were there. The lich shrieked and clawed, but the guardian was there to catch bony claws on its stone-like shield.

Then, Celeste, the larroling, and my two other summons were upon it. The battle raged, each attack from Leigh and Diane met with shadowy spells from the lich as it fought fiercely, summoning skeletal minions from the ground with outstretched claws.

The skeletons joined the melee, trying to divert our fighters so the lich could focus on its more complex spells, but I commanded my storm elemental to intervene. It darted forth, blasting the lich with lightning that disrupted its more complex shadow spells as the guardian shielded Celeste from the horde of skeletons that seemed to grow by the second.

"Focus on the lich!" I called out to the ranged attackers. "It can summon more skeletons than we can handle, so we need to take it out."

Diane nodded as she reloaded her crossbow, her movements a blur of efficiency even as one of the lich's spells sent a shadow dart her way, narrowly ricocheting off her shoulder thanks to my aura of protection.

After reloading Leigh's revolver continued its song, each shot a note of defiance against the deathly magic that threatened us. Her aim never faltered, her eyes alight with the thrill of the battle.

Meanwhile, Celeste's dervish of death continued, the sword a streak of metal as it shattered bones and skulls to each corner of the chamber. But the web of skeletal warriors was too thick for her to reach the lich now, and I knew we needed to rely on ranged damage. Even as I understood this, the storm elemental went down, having exposed itself to many attacks to follow my order to disrupt the lich's spells.

But Yeska followed my command as well. Her hands weaved intricate patterns in the air as she cast Boil Blood on the lich, a scorching spell that sent tendrils of heat snaking around the malevolent mage.

The lich, though formidable, began to falter under our assault and the stacking damage over time from Yeska's blood magic. Its incantations grew desperate, the skeletal minions falling before us one by one, decimated by our strategic offense.

I focused my fire on it, my rounds shattering bones and taking a chip out of its skull. Leigh followed suit, and with a final, resounding shot from her revolver, the lich stumbled in its hovering dance, sparks of dark energy erupting from its bony fingers as another malicious spell was disrupted.

Diane was relentless, Yeska's buff granting her even more accuracy and damage at the cost of a slight wince as her Health had dipped from the spell's price like mine.

"Keep it up!" I encouraged them, seeing that the lich's skeleton was damaged. "Just a little longer!"

I pulled the trigger of my rifle once more, the shot echoing through the barrow. A direct hit — the lich's form convulsed before it began to dissipate, the robes emptying as its skeletal frame disintegrated.

"That's it!" Diane shouted. "You got it!"

And as the lich disintegrated, its skeletal minions followed suit and faded. Celeste struck one apart even as it shimmered, and then they were gone. It was a good thing, too, for my guardian had fallen as well, leaving only the slightly battered larroling and Aquana's avatar at Celeste's side.

"Well done, everyone," I said, and the girls all beamed with pride.

Battle-bred brotherhood, or — in this case — sisterhood; there was no substitute for it. I noticed my women throwing impressed looks at Yeska, whose blood magic had borne a large part in this battle, both in terms of buffs as well as in terms of damage dealt. I was happy to see these signs of acceptance.

And now, we stood among the remnants of shadow and bone, catching our breaths as the realization of victory washed over us.

As my breath steadied, a notification blinked at the edge of my vision. I focused on it and saw the words in the air before me: I had leveled up.

Chapter 32

Breathless from the fight, I gazed around at my companions, the torchlight flickering over our faces, still etched with the tension from combat.

"I've leveled up," I announced, a satisfied smile on my lips despite the exhaustion.

Diane brushed away a stray lock of hair, her blue

eyes reflecting a mixture of relief and excitement. "So have I," she said.

Leigh and Yeska shared similar sentiments; they too had gained a new level. Celeste, usually more reserved, exhaled softly as she relayed her own progress.

They had all grown in strength — Diane, Leigh, and Yeska reached level 7, and Celeste level 5.

Yeska leaned heavily against the wall; her gaze fixed on me with newfound respect. "Such quick advancement," she murmured, more to herself than to us. "It wasn't too long ago that I attained level 6, and many never reach that level or stay there for years. I've never advanced this rapidly."

The thought seemed to perplex her, the mysteries of power and advancement suddenly deepened with the unknown factors at play.

"It might be my Bloodline," I speculated, recalling the conversations I had with Caldwell. "Caldwell believed it could influence the growth of those around me." My eyes met Yeska's, trying to convey the complexity and the gravity of what we were discovering together.

Yeska nodded with her green eyes sharp with an analytical glint unique to her Bloodmage sensibilities. "There's definitely something extraordinary about your lineage," she agreed. "I can sense it even now, pulsing around us. Unraveling it will be... fascinating."

As the implications of my Bloodline and its effects hung between us, the group proposed we take a moment to apply our advancements. I looked to each of them in turn, considering their suggestion. They insisted I should go first.

Turning my attention inward, I felt along the channels of my own power, now more pronounced with the leveling up. With clarity, I realized I had gained 10 Health and 5 Mana, a clear indication of my growth as a Frontier Summoner.

Three spells materialized in my mind, clear options for me to choose from. Call Vapors offered concealment with its promise of mist. Summon Duergar could bring forth a skilled dwarven crafter from another realm. And Summon Pest, the ability to plague foes with a swarm. Weighing the choices, I considered our needs and what would benefit us most.

The choice seemed clear. The potential utility of a dwarven craftsman would be a valuable asset, and I already had several good combat summons. A craftsman would be useful. I chose Summon Duergar, intrigued by the skills it could bring to our quest. Though now was not the time to test the spell, its presence in my arsenal was a comfort.

Another notification flickered into my awareness — I had one more slot to bind a familiar. Deciding quickly, I extended my power further, summoning a new storm elemental and binding it to myself — at least for the dungeon's duration — bolstering our strength with another ally.

Satisfied with the options and my choices, I gave my character sheet a once-over, noticing that Summon Storm Elemental had advanced beyond level 15, meaning the Mana cost had been reduced by 1.

Name: David Wilson

Class: Frontier Summoner

Level: 10

Health: 110/110

Mana: 55/55 (+10 from Hearth Treasures)

Skills:

Summon Minor Spirit — Level 25 (3 mana)

Summon Domesticant — Level 29 (5 mana)

Summon Guardian — Level 23 (7 mana)

Summon Aquana's Avatar — Level 17 (9 mana)

Summon Storm Elemental — Level 16 (9 mana)

Bind Familiar — Level 9 (15 mana)

Aura of Protection — Level 3 (6 mana)

Banish — Level 1 (6 mana)

Evolve Summon — Level 3 (4 mana)

Summon Duergar — Level 1 (8 mana)

Identify Plants — Level 19 (1 mana)

Foraging — Level 21 (1 mana)

Trapping — Level 24 (1 mana)

Alchemy — Level 23 (1 mana)

Farming — Level 12 (1 mana)

Ranching — Level 1 (1 mana)

As I emerged from the focus of my level up, I informed the others, "Your turn now." Trusting in their ability to manage while I stood guard, I stepped away, allowing each of them space and quiet needed to discover their new abilities.

Diane went first, focused and precise. She closed her eyes, delving into the essence of her Scout class. The faintest of smiles touched her lips as she finished, a silent acknowledgment of the newfound strength she now commanded.

Leigh followed suit; her enthusiasm barely contained as she embraced the energy coursing through her. She seemed to draw on it as naturally as one would draw on a deep breath, ready and willing to explore its extent.

Celeste approached her advancement with a soft reverence. She too felt the surge within, allowing it to wash over her. Her gentle nature seemed to absorb the change, weaving it into the fabric of her being.

Lastly, Yeska closed her eyes, a concentrated frown gracing her brow as she reached out to the power of her level up. Her presence took up more space somehow, as the increase in her strength became a tangible part of her Bloodmage essence.

As I watched them, a sense of pride surged within me, mixed with the readiness that was beginning to buzz through my veins. Each of them showed signs of fatigue, but also clear signs of strength and capability.

Diane's figure straightened as she opened her eyes. No words were needed to express the success of her level up. Leigh practically glowed with her usual vibrancy with her grin as wide as the day is long.

Celeste sighed, a sound so content and peaceful that it spread calm throughout the chamber. Yeska's determination had only grown. She met my gaze with a nod that spoke volumes of her readiness to continue.

"Well now," I said to my women. "We shouldn't linger too long, but let's quickly take turns to explain the benefits of our new level. That is, after all, valuable knowledge of our own capabilities since we're in the middle of a Dungeon."

As the adrenaline from the fight began to ebb away, I explained in a few short words what abilities I had gained. The duergar wouldn't be very useful in this Dungeon, so I wrapped up swiftly, then nodded to Diane.

Diane's focused gaze met mine as she explained her Shroud ability, which would cloak her presence and make scouting ahead even more effective. "It's like I can weave the shadows around me," she explained. The notion of her becoming even more adept at moving unseen piqued my interest. I nodded in approval, eager to see it in action.

Leigh was next, her ever-present energy tinged with excitement as she described her newly acquired ability to heal her pets. The larroling grunted nearby, almost as if understanding that Leigh's care for it would now extend beyond just physical attention.

"I can mend their wounds with just a touch," she said, eyes sparkling with the joy of this newfound skill.

She then demonstrated her new ability at once, healing her larroling's minor wounds sustained in the combat with the lich. I couldn't suppress a smile. This was not only useful but fit Leigh's nurturing spirit perfectly. Plus, it would make the larroling an even more valuable ally.

Celeste detailed the Stunning attack she had gained, an ability that could momentarily incapacitate enemies with its potency. "It'll give us the upper hand when we need a moment to breathe," she said softly.

Yeska, having observed us all, held herself with quiet confidence. Her intensity had only sharpened with her advancement, and she spoke of intensifying her Heat Blood spell.

"The buff it brings now could turn the tide of battle," she stated, a hint of pride in her feline eyes. I felt reassured knowing her abilities would bolster our strength further, making us a formidable force.

The mood was high, our collective morale boosted by the progress we had each made. "These are great advancements," I said, "We're stronger, more capable. Let's keep this momentum going."

Encouraged by the developments, we all felt ready, maybe even eager, to move forward and face whatever the deeper parts of the Dungeon might hold. And it was certain there was more in store for us.

Once we regrouped and readjusted our packs, we decided it was time to continue our exploration of the barrow. The larroling took its position beside us once more, and we ventured on. The torchlight bobbed ahead as I led the way, the flickering flames casting a soft glow on the age-old architecture surrounding us.

Walking in step with the others, I felt the weight of my rifle on my shoulder and the comforting presence of the familiar faces moving in front of me. Each step took us farther into the ancient structure, the hushed sounds of our movement a counterpoint to the quiet majesty of the barrow.

Our path wound through silent corridors, the craftsmanship of the stonework speaking to a history of meticulous care and reverence. I ran my fingertips along the carved walls, feeling the cool touch of the stone. The very earth around us held stories, the whispers of which seemed to linger in the air, and I wondered what secrets it still kept.

We eventually came upon another staircase, its spiraling descent beckoning us to realms untold. I glanced at Diane, who nodded back at me — a silent confirmation that we would continue down with caution, minds alert for any hint of danger.

The staircase itself was a marvel, age-worn stones smoothed by centuries of use, dark shadows clinging to each step leading to the unseen depths below. Diane took point, her lithe form descending with a scout's grace.

I followed closely behind, the grip of my rifle firm in my hands, senses sharply tuning into the encompassing gloom. Each step seemed to take us deeper not only into the earth but also into the mystery of the place we were intruding upon.

Yeska's torch cast a precarious circle of light in the dense dark, revealing glimpses of walls that felt close enough to touch. The muted shuffle of our group's passage was the only sound that filled the descent, a cadence to the silent song of exploration.

I saw Leigh pause for a moment to study an engraved passage, a curious glint in her expressive eyes. She was interested in elven culture, in a way that would likely surprise many that didn't know the bubbly blonde.

"Let's stay alert," I urged the others. "Deeper is usually more dangerous."

The women nodded their assent as we reached the bottom of the stairway, and the Dungeon opened further to us...

Chapter 33

As we reached the third level of the barrow Dungeon, a sharp chill enveloped us, biting through our layers and nipping at any exposed skin. I wrapped my jacket tighter around me, casting an inquisitive glance toward Yeska, whose torch did little to warm the frigid air.

"I think this cold isn't just from being underground," I murmured, my breath visible in a cloud of condensation.

Yeska nodded, holding the torch before her like a talisman against the creeping cold. "I agree. The chill is… unnerving. Too uniform, too persistent. It doesn't fluctuate like natural cold would — it's almost as if it is being sustained," she said, her words measured and thoughtful.

Leigh hugged herself, shivering visibly as she stepped closer to Diane. "Feels like it's seeping into my bones," she said with a forced chuckle, trying to lighten the mood despite the oppressive cold.

Diane seemed less bothered by the temperature, her focus on the task ahead. "All the more reason to be cautious," she cautioned, her gaze sweeping the dark passage that stretched out before us. "There could be some sort of ice magic at work here — maybe even a guardian creature that uses it."

Celeste, who had been quiet, spoke with a soft certainty that drew our attention. "The cold might be an elemental barrier — like those that protect ancient tombs in Elvish lore." Her eyes met mine, and I could tell she was piecing together bits of knowledge gleaned from her heritage.

With the consensus that the cold had a magical origin, we agreed to move forward with increased vigilance. Diane, with her newly acquired Shroud ability, would scout ahead. "I'll be as quiet as a shadow," she promised, disappearing into the dim corridor with an almost spectral grace.

Leigh turned to us with a wry smile that didn't quite reach her eyes. "Guess all we can do now is wait," she said, sitting down with her back against the cold stone wall.

As minutes ticked by slowly, the sense of anticipation was palpable. I found myself rubbing my hands together for warmth, my thoughts drifting to the potential threats we might face.

An ice creature, perhaps, or some ancient Elvish construct set to guard its secrets against intruders like us. Or maybe it was just an atmospheric magical effect because of the undead — they were traditionally associated with cold.

I pushed away the considerations and focused on

my surroundings, my gaze drifting to Yeska. The pretty cat girl's eyes remained fixed on the path Diane had taken, her expression unreadable. The flickering torchlight threw her sharp features into relief, casting dancing shadows across her face. Leigh gave a barely audible sigh, her gaze following the subtle movement of Celeste's fingers as they tapped on the hilt of her blade.

I glanced back the way we had come, the darkness of the staircase looming behind us. The thought of something coming down from those shadows, following us, made me uneasy, my hand instinctively reaching for the trigger guard of my rifle.

Our breaths hung in the still air, a testament to the cold that seemed to swallow all warmth. I shuffled my feet, trying to maintain circulation, while the larroling beside us was stoic and unmoving, unaffected by the chill.

Suddenly, a faint noise echoed down the corridor — the sound of Diane's return. We all stood, our eyes turning toward the sound as she emerged back into the dim light cast by Yeska's torch.

Diane's face was drawn, her eyes wide with what she had seen. "There's a chamber ahead," she began, her voice hinting at the awe she felt. "A vast underground lake, completely frozen over and eerily blue. Beneath the ice are... Well…the ice is thick — unnaturally so. And within it, the remains of various creatures are encased. As if they were... preserved," she continued, her tone filled with disbelief.

"Creatures?" I prompted her, eyebrow raised.

"Yes. Elves, dwarves, even catkin and foxkin," she said, the list causing a collective intake of breath. "There must be a couple of dozen, at least, frozen within it. Some look recent. They look like adventurers who met an ill fate."

"That sounds like the work of an ice elemental or maybe even a frost spirit," Yeska whispered, her expertise on magical creatures lending credibility to her words.

I processed her theory as we all huddled closer to discuss our next move. "Or another trap. But whatever it is," I deduced, "it must be the source of this cold. If these remains are recent, it means it's still active, and we might be next."

Leigh nodded, her hands tightening around her revolver. "If we have to cross that lake, we'd better be on our guard," she said. "Shadows beneath the ice or not, we've got no choice but to face it."

"Can we avoid the lake?" I asked Diane.

She shook her head slowly. "I tried to look for a way around it, but there are none. We must cross it."

"That settles it, then," I said. "Let's go and see what we can see."

The weight of the decision hung over us like the chill in the air. We gathered our gear, each of us carrying the silent acknowledgment of the danger we would soon confront — whatever lay ahead had power over cold and death.

"We move slowly," I advised. "Stay sharp and together. Diane, keep scouting ahead, but no more than a few paces."

Diane's nod was firm, a promise of her continual vigilance and skill. "I'll lead the way," she replied, her confidence a beacon in the surrounding chill.

Celeste's grip on her sword was steadier, her

preparation evident. Yeska's expression was serene, her readiness apparent despite the unnerving discovery.

Resolved, we made our way toward the chilling sight Diane had described. With every step, an awareness grew within me — the certainty that the frozen lake held a hidden threat we were bound to face. It now lay ahead of us, a glacial barrier we must cross, the undeniable obstacle between us and our quest's end.

The otherworldly chamber revealed itself slowly, arcing overhead and around until even the light from Yeska's torch seemed swallowed by its breadth. Our mere presence in this expanse felt like intruding on a sacred slumber, the chamber's air undisturbed until our breaths fanned it into subtle, swirling eddies.

My gaze fell upon the ice that blanketed the lake, its surface a reflection of ghostly azure against the torch's fire. A frozen mirror to the world above; I saw shapes encased within like macabre sculptures; a gallery of tragedy held in frigid stasis. There were humans, elves, dwarves, catkin, and foxkin – some formidable warriors and mages, others mere commoners.

"Careful," I cautioned, the word a sharp exhale that crystallized before my eyes. "Spread out and move slow. Keep to the surface – if it's solid enough to trap them, it should hold our weight." My voice carried, rebounding in low echoes that lingered long after I'd turned to test the ice with cautious steps.

Diane followed, her footfalls measured as she navigated onto the quivering surface. Tendrils of frost snaked out, creeping over her boots, each step a pilgrimage across the lake's crystalline sheath.

Yeska gripped her torch tighter, brightening its light as though urging it to push back the cold. "I'll be right beside you," she affirmed, stepping onto the ice with the same mindful poise she'd carried throughout this journey.

Leigh flexed her fingers, fighting against the chill

that sought to pry into her bones. She moved to flank Diane, revolver glinting dully in the pale light — a ready ward against any uncertainty that lurked beneath us.

Celeste's breaths came in soft clouds; she hesitated before venturing forth, her eyes bright with an inner resolve that contrasted with the creeping trepidation shadowing her features.

The larroling grunted, its fearsome claws biting into the ice. It led the way with ponderous strides, more surefooted than any of us could hope to be on the slippery surface thanks to its clawed feet.

I watched as Diane tread farther out, a spread hand and whispered words keeping us tied together — visible threads that connected us across the perilous terrain.

The encased remains were grotesquely magnificent, and my heart twinged at the sight. Would-be explorers, mages, warriors — each one captured in a moment of despair, their final struggles eternally stilled by cold's unforgiving grip.

"They were like us," I murmured, so that even

my closest companions had to strain to hear. "Adventurers, drawn to the whispers and promises of the Dungeon. Victims of the ice now."

Leigh cast a glance downward, her expression a silent question at the sight of a frozen foxkin, jaws opened in airborne protest. I shook my head gently, acknowledging the shared fate we sought to avoid with each delicate pace we maintained.

Yeska's brow knitted at the realization. "To freeze in such a manner," she whispered, "is to become a monument to caution. We'll heed their silent warning."

Celeste caught my eye, a glint that spoke of the unsaid kinship felt towards those entombed in cold's embrace. "Their journey has ended here, but ours must continue," she voiced, a mix of empathy and determination in her soft words.

As we reached the center of the lake, the ice behind us cracked, barring our way back unless we would go around. It was sudden and unexpected, not preluded by cracking or groaning. I had seen ice in nature and I realized at once this cracking was fueled by magic.

I paused, ashen breath held within my lungs, the torch's flame now a timorous dance amid the cavern's breath. A sign, a portent — something within the very earth had stirred against our passing.

Diane, stepping lightly, turned her head over her shoulder, a wisp of worry darkening her eyes. "Don't like that," she said, her usual fervor dulled by the deep, fathomless cold.

"It... It's getting worse," Yeska muttered.

She was right; the vibrations beneath us heightened, subtle at first, then more assertive, as if the chamber awoke from an eon-long slumber with an ire that geared towards unwelcome guests.

Leigh's fingers tightened on her revolver; her balance unerring even as the tremors sought to contest her. A flurry of silent curses danced on her lips — a silent portrayal of her innermost thoughts.

I noticed a minor crack threading out under my feet. "Stand still," I commanded, the order a grainy rasp that betrayed my disquiet. It whispered out but echoed back a thunderous sound.

But it didn't help. The ice was cracking, and it

was not because of our weight or movement.

It was a trap.

Chapter 34

The chamber resounded with the alarming crescendo of ice giving way underfoot. In the cold clarity of imminent danger, my eyes darted around, seeking something, anything, to offer refuge. Amidst the chorus of cracking, a shape solid against the sliding world caught my attention

— a rock outcropping that jutted from the ice like a lifeline.

"There!" I pointed to the salvation within our slippery grasp. The urgency in my voice cut through the fear, rallying our group into action. "Make for that rock! Now!"

I watched as Diane took the lead, her steps a careful sprint across the treacherous expanse. Leigh and Celeste followed, their movements swift, with the larroling and my storm elemental coming up behind them. Their dash mirrored the desperation for their lives that I felt.

Yeska, however, hesitated, her eyes wide with alarm as the ice groaned doom, a symphony of potential endings.

"Move, Yeska!" I shouted over the sounds of destruction, propelled by worry fueling my words.

With instincts kicking in, Yeska pushed off, a burst of speed carrying her toward safety. I covered the rear, my steps a syncopated beat against the ice's rhythm, rifle clutched firmly, ready for hazards yet unseen.

As the stability of the world shifted with each

step, the rock outcropping stood as a beacon amidst the chaos. Each of the girls reached it, grasping at the stone, pulling themselves up and away from the fracturing plane.

I lunged for safety, closing the final distance with an adrenaline-fueled jump. My hands scrambled over the rough surface of the rock — solid, real, and wonderfully motionless.

Together, we huddled on the narrow perch as the ice splintered in a grand orchestration, the water beneath revealed in a rush of cold air and violent waves, the nightmare ballet complete as our frozen path vanished.

The waters churned, each wave an animal movement in this sudden sea. Then, without warning, shapes emerged — long, sleek, and deadly — leaping from the freezing depths from between the drifting shards of ice and eager for our flesh. They were shark-like fish, only a little smaller and much more aggressive.

I saw Leigh's muscles tense, her Beastmaster instincts identifying the creatures with instant recognition. "Thimmerfish!" she hissed, dread lacing her acknowledgment.

Without hesitation, I raised my rifle as one of the predatory shapes launched itself toward Yeska, its jaws wide in a violent promise. The shot I fired rang true, sending the Thimmerfish back into the icy embrace from which it came.

Yeska, who had just been gathering her composure, shot me a thankful look, knowing I had saved her from injury — or worse. "Thank you, David," she said.

I smiled at her despite everything, then turned to Leigh. "Thimmerfish?" I prompted her. "Not friendly little fellows like we see in the Silverthread, right?"

Leigh's expression turned grave as she locked eyes with me and shook her head. "They're aggressive, and there are more surfacing. They thrive in the cold."

The Thimmerfish circled our little rock outcropping. Each leap and snap of their maws was a sharpening of their intent while the rocky outcropping remained an island in a desperate ocean.

Diane held her crossbow at the ready with her focus narrowed to the threat below. Celeste stayed close to me, her sword a silent companion to her courage, her eyes calculating our scant options.

"You're the Beastmaster, Leigh," I said. "Any ideas?"

As I took the moment to unload my rifle and push some new rounds into the magazine, Leigh's mind worked rapidly, her knowledge of water creatures a potential key to our survival. "You're right. They're animals after all — even if they are vicious ones," she muttered, her eyes tracing the patterns of their assaults.

Yet, in the confrontation of elements — water, air, and the intrusions of the cold — my thoughts began to churn, possibilities crafting scenarios within my mind.

Celeste leaned into me. "The water is too cold," she said. "Even if Leigh could tame them all, we can't swim for it. We need to think of something fast, David." Her breath was a puff of anxious white, a cloud against the severity of our circumstance.

Leigh's focus intensified, her gaze now going past the immediate, to the far shore, the breadth of the frozen lake, and the confines of the chamber. "My Calm Waters ability might just stop the Thimmerfish, but the crossing — how?"

I recalled the ability she had learned on one of our adventures — shortly after we crossed the Blighted Land and our encounter with the grapplejaws. It would allow her to tame the creatures in the water for a short time, and we might cross during that window of opportunity.

But how indeed?

A shiver shook my frame, not from the cold, but from the rapid whir of ideas. The solution danced on the edge of understanding, a peripheral hint at an unconventional exit.

My lips tugged into a broad grin, the action surprising even me, juxtaposed against the bleakness of our outlook. "I might...," I started, glancing at the girls, the challenge igniting a small fire. "I might have an idea."

They exchanged hopeful looks, but I gestured for silence as I scanned the treacherous waters. The

Thimmerfish continued their circling, each jump near our rock a reminder of their deadly potential.

The girls watched me, hope layered within their stares. "Well, now would be a really good time for one of your plans, David," Leigh joked, the undercurrent of unease unmistakable.

I smiled and nodded, the idea solidifying in my mind. "Alright," I said. "Listen up..."

Chapter 35

Standing on the frostbitten outcrop, enveloped by the darkness of the chamber and the biting chill, thoughts rushed through my head — ideas intertwining with the necessity of survival. My voice broke the tense silence, clear and confident, "Here's the plan."

Yeska's torchlight sputtered against the icy air as my companions shifted their gaze toward me, anticipation mirrored in their stances — like actors awaiting their cue. "I can try to use my Summon Aquana's Avatar spell," I proposed, "creating a water elemental that can tread upon water and carry each of us to safety."

Acknowledgment unfurled across their faces as I laid out the notion of summoning the elemental individually for each of them. They knew the inherent risks; our safety net was the measure of my magic's reliability. Yet their trust in me held steadfast as they nodded in approval, words unnecessary for the promise we all felt.

Leigh's eyes glinted as she chimed in, "And what about our sturdy larroling here?" Her usual mirth was threaded with the gravity of the moment. "He should manage the swim with your help as he's used to cold biomes, and my Calm Waters spell can keep those Thimmerfish at bay while we cross."

I agreed, grateful for her quick mind and her Beastmaster's connection to our companion creature. "That's the plan," I said, the foundation of our plan solidifying with each contribution. "And I'll go first to see if it works."

A collective spirit of resolve bolstered us as we prepared for this unconventional crossing. Leigh voiced her faith, stem-winding with a hint of her old vigor amidst the cold, "David, if anyone can get us through this, it's you."

Celeste's gentle expression bore the soft glow of admiration. "I agree," she said, a serene smile lifting her spirits against the chamber's despair. "And this is a fine plan! The best we can do."

Diane's nod came firm and sure, an implicit agreement that was as robust as her armament. "Let's do it," she put in. "It is the only chance we have."

Yeska, typically self-assured and untamed, seemed touched by my willingness to risk myself first. She regarded me with a new depth of respect, the sentiment lacing her features. "It is a fine plan," she said. "And you are a brave man, David."

I grinned and gave a little shrug. "Wouldn't be much of a plan if I didn't trust in it myself," I quipped, winning a smile from the girls to take the edge off a little bit.

With the affirmation of my makeshift family, I turned to face the elemental plane that lay ahead. Hands steady yet apprehensive, I began the incantation of the Summon Aquana's Avatar spell.

A blue light bloomed in the darkness as I called forth the avatar. It emerged — a watery silhouette against the stark backdrop of the chamber, taking shape with a fluid grace that could belong only to a being of pure elemental power.

Leigh, on cue, activated her Calm Waters ability. The surface of the water stilled under her command, the circling Thimmerfish suspended in a temporary reprieve of their predatory circling, like dancers in the wings awaiting the orchestra's command. In this state, they were less harmful than goldfish.

"There ya go, baby," she said. "Should be all good!"

I gave her a thankful nod and, with the scene set, stepped toward the water elemental. It was a formidable form of shifting waves, majestic and poised, as it waited for my approach — an ally bound to my will and ready to serve.

I motioned for it to do a test round of the water, to demonstrate to me that it could indeed move on the surface and that the Thimmerfish would not accost it. The elemental glided across the water with a sureness borne of a creature at one with the element, and I smiled with satisfaction as the plan took its initial breath — the beginning of an escape from our dire straits. The Thimmerfish left the elemental alone as well, content to simply swim and do nothing.

"Looking good," I remarked, and my women gave hopeful nods. I mentally commanded Aquana's avatar to return to me. "Now, for the real test..."

The water elemental reached our rocky perch, the blue of its form deep and rich against the starkness that enveloped us. Like a lantern in the dark, it caused shadows to flee, if only for a moment.

I gave the women a reassuring look and instructed the elemental to carry me first. No futile bravado, only the intrinsic need to ensure their safety above my own — the weight of responsibility I could not, would not, shrug off.

It extended what I could only think of as its arms — columns of swirling water that promised the buoyancy of hope. I took in a deep breath and gripped them, the chill from the elemental a stark contrast to the surrounding cold that I had become accustomed to.

The water elemental lifted me without falter, and it placed me on its shoulders as easily as I would a child. When I sat, I flashed a grin and a thumbs up at my women, who stood wringing their hands with worry on the rocky outcropping. They answered my gesture with nervous smiles, concerned for my safety, but I remained confident.

"Let's go," I said softly to the elemental.

And it moved. With each passing second, the elemental tread upon the lake's surface, carrying me effortlessly. The water lapped around us, an icy void that awaited any misstep.

Though droplets splashed upward, soaking through my layers, the mere discomfort could not overshadow the emerging hope that I harbored deep within. I held fast as the elemental drew closer to the safety of the far shore.

The others watched from the outcrop, their forms a line of steadfastness against the uncaring cold. Celeste clutched her harp close, Leigh's hand never straying far from her holster, Yeska's torch a guiding beacon.

The elemental set me down upon solid ground; the feeling of firm rock beneath my boots was as invigorating as a new dawn. I turned, motioning to the others that the plan was effective.

Their gazes met mine across the intervening space, each pair of eyes alight with relief as the realization settled in that we had found our passage, our way across the desolate span of frozen lake and hungry fish.

With my plan proven, the water elemental could now proceed to move the women from the precarious perch to my side, one by one, with the storm elemental and the larroling crossing on their own.

The chill of the underground lake receded as if yielding to our collective determination, and we watched as one by one, Diane, Leigh, Celeste, and finally Yeska made their way across the icy expanse cradled by the water elemental's grasp.

Leigh, with the larroling swimming alongside her, managed a grin despite the cold, her Beastmaster's instincts keeping the Thimmerfish calm as they glided over the treacherous surface.

Diane reached solid ground, her Scout's poise never wavering as she stepped off the elemental and onto the frost-kissed stone. "Well, that was one way to make an entrance," she said, a light laugh betraying the residual adrenaline from our crossing.

Leigh, with a relieved exhale, complimented our strategic planning, patting the larroling's wet hide. "That was a proper bit of thinking, using the elemental like that."

"And your Calm Waters ability kept those Thimmerfish in check," I said. "It's a great ability."

"We couldn't have asked for a smoother ride," Diane said, nodding to both me and Leigh appreciatively.

Celeste, her expression serene as ever, added her own note of gratitude. "The way you orchestrated our escape was nothing short of masterful. It speaks volumes of your leadership, David," she said.

Yeska, last to step off the elemental, shook off the cold as if shrugging away a mere inconvenience. "This was well contrived," she told me, her green eyes sharp with newfound respect that seemed to pierce the lingering shadows of the chamber.

With our group now safely reunited on the other side, we shared a moment of quiet celebration, the relief palpable in our collective breath. "Let's move on," I urged, "Time is still against us, and we've got a staff to locate."

Diane once again took point, her silhouette slipping through the dim corridor, alert for any unseen dangers. We huddled closer, following her into the heart of the barrow, each shadow holding the potential for mystery or menace.

Our progress was slow, as if the weight of the barrow pressed down on us with each step we took. The black stone underfoot was slick with an unseen frost, and the dark sigils etched along the walls seemed to watch us with ancient, unblinking eyes.

Suddenly, the corridor opened into a vast, pillared chamber. Our torches flickered, casting long, dancing shadows across the pillars that stood like silent watchers. At the back of the chamber, an altar rested, and upon it lay a staff that caught the dim light in a peculiar way.

I motioned for the group to halt, my hand instinctively reaching for the rifle. "Hold on," I said, eyeing the mysterious staff. "This feels too easy. There might be guardians or traps we haven't triggered yet."

Diane stepped back, her instincts as a Scout affirming the caution I had advised. "It does look suspiciously unguarded," she agreed, bowing her head as she examined the floor for any telltale signs of traps.

Leigh stood by; her grip on the revolver still firm, ready for any movement that might spring from the shadows. "It ain't ever straightforward with these ancient places," she murmured, echoing my sentiment.

Celeste stood still like a statue, but her sword was at the ready. "We should take the time to study the chamber more closely," she suggested, her gaze lingering on the icy glow of the staff.

Yeska stepped forward, her bright eyes scanning the chamber with a hunter's precision. "The light plays oddly in here, bouncing among the pillars," she observed, tilting her head slightly as she pinpointed the source of her intrigue.

We all took notice of the strange shimmer that Yeska had pointed out, the torchlight refracting in ways that defied natural law. The columns held more than just shadows — they concealed something else, something unseen.

"Invisible creatures, maybe?" I voiced aloud, the thought chilling despite the already cold air that encompassed us. "That would explain the eerie feeling this place gives off."

Yeska's eyebrows drew together, her lips pressed into a thin line as she pondered the notion. "There is one way to be sure," she said, her voice laced with determination.

With a swift incantation, her hands weaving through the air, Yeska cast her Bloodsight spell. The room became illuminated by an otherworldly glow, bathing everything in a spectral light that revealed the previously unseen.

"Specters," she confirmed, her eyes now seeing through the veil of invisibility that the creatures had hidden behind. "And there's the spectral mage, an elven mage — right at the far end of the chamber, guarding the staff."

The revelation sent a shiver down my spine, and I tightened my grip on the rifle. Specters were not to be taken lightly, and a spectral mage, that apex of undead mages, even less so.

We stayed silent with our eyes trained on the shimmerings that betrayed spectral figures that Yeska could now clearly see. Their transparent forms drifted among the pillars.

"There are more than I initially thought," Yeska said, her voice betraying a hint of unease. "They float through the columns, guardians of the barrow, but they do not seem to have noticed us."

Diane's hand edged toward the bolts of her crossbow once more, her mind already calculating the distances and potential trajectories necessary to pierce the ethereal beings. Meanwhile, Leigh tightened her jaw, her resolve firm as she weighed our odds.

With the invisible specters unveiled to Yeska's spell and the aim of our weapons uncertain, this was a new kind of challenge. I knew we couldn't do this without having a clear line of sight, and the vague shimmerings were not enough.

Chapter 36

The barrow's chilled breath clung to our clothes, a coldness that seemed to seep into our very bones as we huddled together near the entrance of the vast frozen chamber. Yeska held her torch steady, its light pushing weakly against the encroaching darkness. The spectral figures flowed between the pillars; their presence revealed only to Yeska.

I drew my rifle close, eyes fixated on the peculiar dance of light around the silhouettes that only Yeska could see. "We need a way to reveal them," I said quietly, "to even the playing field."

Celeste tilted her head, considering the torch's battle against the cold chamber's gloom. "If light bends around these specters, they must have substance — physical forms that are touched by this world."

Diane's lips pursed in thought as she contemplated the riddle before us. "A form that bends light — it must be like a glass lens." Her pragmatic approach to the mystery at hand was reassuring in its simplicity. "What if we could make them visible somehow?"

At the same time, Yeska and I spoke the same words, "Perhaps if we covered them in some sort of liquid..." Our voices mingled in the darkness, proposing the same strategy in an almost comical synchrony.

A shared chuckle rippled through our small group, a light moment amidst the tension that brought a warmth that even the barrow's frost seemed to honor. Such brief respite reminded us of the bond we shared — the kind of unity forged in the quiet moments.

With a more focused gaze, I detailed my strategy for the non-visible opponents. "I can have my Aquana's Avatar advance and start spraying water around," I offered, the thought of watery outlines revealing the specters a plan both rudimentary and ingenious in design.

The women wore expressions of agreement, their acquiescence to the role my elemental would play as obvious as our shared breaths in the icy air.

"It's a sound plan, David," Diane said.

"It will cost us the element of surprise, though," I added, acutely aware of the delicate nature of the situation.

"That's acceptable," Celeste replied with a measure of resolve. "To see our foes is to be one step ahead, regardless of the surprise we forgo."

I gave a curt nod, feeling the mantle of leadership settle around my shoulders as I issued my summons. Aquana's Avatar and two water spirits emerged from the mystic veil at my calling, their forms rippling with elemental power.

I glanced back at the women, each one poised and braced for the next inevitable confrontation. "Are you ready for this?" My voice was hardly more than a whisper, but I knew my words would carry clearly to them.

"Ready," they each confirmed, the singular word a mesh of assurance and apprehension.

With an unwavering stare, I gestured for the water elemental and its lesser siblings to enter the chamber. I commanded them to move swiftly, knowing that just spraying foes with water and not defending or fighting meant they would not last long.

At my command, the three water-based beings glided forward, light dancing off their liquid forms in a display that, had the situation been any different, would have been mesmerizing.

"The specters will see them soon," Yeska hummed, still seeing through her spell. "Should they engage?"

I nodded. And at my command, they fanned out.

At once, their aquatic streams arched through the air. The projected liquid was as a quill upon parchment, poised to write revelation across the darkness. I watched the water cascade and the expectant faces of my companions, each one mirroring my own hope that this plan would shed light on our ghostly adversaries.

And it worked! Water's touch began to articulate forms. Invisible became visible, the droplets clinging to the specters. They were still not as visible as I wanted them to be, but their shapes were outlined by water — good enough for us to target them.

"It's working," Yeska hissed in an excited voice. "It's really working!"

In a barely audible murmur, Celeste whispered a soft prayer to the elven gods. Her lips moved in the silent incantation that spilled forth to curl around us as we witnessed the birth of clarity in the water's wake.

"Get ready," I commanded.

Diane let out a controlled breath, steadying her crossbow as the revealing specters took shape before us. "Solid targets to aim at," she noted, her practicality a welcome companion in the burgeoning urgency.

Leigh's hand twitched reflexively near her revolver as her gaze fixed on the shapes now visible in the chamber before us. A nod passed between us, affirming our readiness to confront whatever challenge awaited.

The elementals' work complete, the chamber now home to discernible threats, the moment came — a pause that stretched into an eternity before the specters' awareness of our presence would ignite our battle.

And just as the final specter was revealed — the spectral mage itself — that undead conjurer turned, and the time of hiding was over. Our plan had worked, but the elementals had drawn attention.

They converged on the elementals, and they would make quick work of them.

"Let's go!" I called out. "Spread out and keep up the fire!"

Chapter 37

The spectral mage hovered near the altar at the chamber's rear. It raised a hand, and with a swift incantation, a torrent of flame burst forth, enveloping my elementals in a consuming inferno.

The perfect timing of Yeska's observation cut through the shock of the fiery explosion. "They're all doused. The plan can proceed," she noted, her voice steady despite the fury that had just transpired.

With her assurance, I signaled to charge, relying on the strategy we had hatched in the safety of light and reason. The women followed my command, readying weapons as I called forth a guardian and bolstered it with my Evolve Summon spell, bracing for the encounter with these dripping adversaries. I followed up with Aura of Protection.

We advanced as one, a solid phalanx pushing into the heart of spectral resistance. My rifle crackled as I called out my command to Celeste, the larroling, the storm elemental, and the guardian to advance. The report of my firearm rang sharp in the confined space as it sought the soaked entities that lunged at us from their shimmering concealment.

Diane's form melded into the shadows, her newfound ability cloaking her advance. She moved unseen, her crossbow singing a silent song of death. With every bolt released, a specter faltered, its wet outline scattering in tendrils of dissipating mist.

Leigh's revolver punctuated the chamber's quiet with explosive echoes, her shots ringing clear. She stood her ground near the entrance, picking off specters that aimed to close in, her aim true and protective.

Celeste's bright call rose above the commotion, her voice calling on the gods as she engaged and sought to carve a path to the spectral mage. Her sword whirled and danced with the Stellar Maiden's grace, and the specters fell before her.

Beside me, Yeska radiated a calm fury, her hands weaving through the air as she cast her spells. Blood Pox sprouted among the specters, a curse that bound them in a vicious thrall of damage over time as they attempted to press forward — the seed for their destruction.

The larroling, a creature of formidable strength, advanced with Celeste. At Leigh's command, it barreled into the fray, its mass a testament to the Beastmaster's influence as it scattered enemies with primal ferocity. It did not need the liquid outlining because it could sense the unnatural undead as clearly as I could see my own hands.

But there were many specters.

"There's a lot of 'em," Leigh called out, echoing my own thoughts.

I gave a grim smile. "And they're all wet," I muttered, hardly loud enough for any to hear me as a new plan surfaced in my mind.

As the specters converged, their numbers now visible and constrained, I reached out with my will, summoning another storm elemental to join the battle beside the first. Its form crackled into existence, a gathering of thunderous energy at my side.

The elemental flexed its growing form, its essence forged of tempests and sky's wrath. Then, at my command, dual bolts of lightning streaked across the room, aimed at the heart of the specters – figures still dripping from their exposure to elemental water.

And water and lightning don't mix…

The electrical discharge danced across the wet outlines of our enemies, the lightning finding eager conduits in their moistened forms and amplifying the damage. Each hit was a burst of light, a thunderclap of victory as the specters faltered under the elemental's assault.

"Brilliant!" Leigh called out, recognizing this relatively old trick in the book.

I grinned and called forth another storm elemental, setting up a battery of the summons to blast lightning at our dripping enemies, although I bade them take care not to hit Celeste, the larroling, or the guardian keeping Celeste safe.

The electrified onslaught proved devastating, the specters reeling and sparking as the currents unraveled their existence. One by one, they crackled into nothingness, their howls of departure a fading echo in the vastness of the chamber.

Through the elementals' relentless fury, we pressed on, closing the distance between us and the spectral mage that still loomed near the altar. It seemed uncertain now with its fiery offense dampened by the demise of its allies.

My rifle's muzzle flashed repeatedly as I moved up, a steady rhythm that marked the decline of the spectral warriors. I quickly renewed Aura of

Protection as I advanced, but my Mana was running dry.

Diane's form flickered into visibility as she dispatched specters with precise shots, her presence a shadow amongst shadows. The specters were undone by her skill, their numbers dwindling beneath her crossbow's whisper.

Leigh's laughter mingled with the reverberating gunfire with her spirit undampened even as the spectral mage launched another desperate incantation. Her bullets tore through the conjured flames, disrupting the mage's deadly spellcraft.

Celeste's swordplay reached a crescendo as she hacked her way to the boss. She did so with trust in my bolstered guardian and aura of protection, and many of the specters' life-draining attacks were deflected by both, although my guardian was worse for the wear and would not last much longer.

Meanwhile, Yeska's curses wove through the chamber, a weave of sorcery that entangled the remaining specters. Her spells were a chorus to the elemental's arcs of power, the specters caught in a perilous symphony of our creation.

The larroling, encouraged by Leigh's calls, tore through the ranks of the spectral figures with an animalistic fervor. Each strike sent chills through their essence, a corporeal testament to the beast's might.

The spectral mage, now faced with the full brunt of our assault, unleashed a last wave of fire in a bid to halt our advance. The guardian threw himself in front of Celeste and perished protecting her, but the path was clear now. She advanced with a fierce and clear cry; two-handed sword ready to destroy the creature.

With a mental command, I forced my storm elementals to focus fire on the spectral mage. Bolts of lightning struck true even as Celeste swung her blade. The power of it was overwhelming, and the specter wailed before the attacks scattered its form like ashes in the wind.

And as the spectral mage fell, its allies howled dolorously as they withered and faded, the spell that had bound them to this world now finally broken.

We stood victorious...

As the last of the spectral forms scattered like smoke, a jubilant feeling coursed through the chamber. Diane let out a whoop of delight before joining Leigh and Celeste in engulfing me with hugs. They clung to me with love and enthusiasm, and their voices formed a chorus of joy that rang as true as the songs Celeste often played.

Smiling as I held my women, my eyes found Yeska's, who stood with a broad grin, her cat ears upright. "We did it!" she exclaimed, her eyes shining brightly in the torchlight. There was genuine admiration in her voice.

"The lightning idea was great, baby!" Leigh purred before planting a kiss on my lips, and the other women joined in with words of agreement and praise.

I felt a flush of warmth at their praises, though my own thoughts were more tempered. "It was really everyone's efforts," I said, deflecting the compliment with a modesty that felt more comfortable than basking in any limelight.

In the shared silence that followed, I turned to each of my companions in turn. Observing Yeska's reaction out of the corner of my eye, I noted the slight blush coloring her cheeks as she watched me plant a grateful kiss on the forehead of Diane, Leigh, and Celeste.

Yeska's gaze lingered with a curiosity I found endearing, her usual composure tinged with what appeared to be a mixture of bewilderment and fascination. It was evident that she still tread unfamiliar ground amidst the intimate bond we all shared, which had grown stronger still in this adventure.

"Let's not dally here," I suggested after a moment, the weight of our mission refocusing my mind. "We should quickly search the chamber. The day is likely waning, and crossing back over the lake, leaving the barrow will take some time."

The women sprang into action, their movements methodical as they combed the chamber. I watched as Diane investigated the recessed niches along the walls, Leigh examined the grounds, and Celeste perused the remaining contents of the altar.

Yeska, her torch now set aside, aided in the search, her fingers tracing along the cold stone in search of hidden compartments or overlooked treasures that might have been secreted away.

The chamber, though grand in scale and rich in history, held no further secrets, no other treasures to claim. And so, I focused on the staff. Approaching the altar where it lay, I felt a sense of completion as my hands closed around the intricate artifact. It was heavier than it appeared, a solid heft that hinted at power dormant within its craftsmanship.

With careful motions, I turned the staff in my grasp, the dim torchlight catching along the inlaid runes that spiraled down its length. The markings were familiar — echoes of the same Elvish script that adorned the walls around us.

I caught my reflection in a polished segment of the altar's surface, the staff held before me like a new piece of my history now touching the legacy of this place. The sense of responsibility that came with such a relic was not lost on me, a weight beyond its physical presence.

After a lingering examination, I stowed the staff securely in my pack, ensuring it was wrapped tightly to prevent any damage during our return journey. The others watched, understanding its significance and the need for care.

A steady resolve settled around our shoulders as we turned back toward the entrance of the chamber. Our mission had been successful. The retrieval of the staff marked the completion of Lernoval's quest, though our return to the surface remained.

We retraced our steps, the silent shadows of the barrow whispering farewells as we left the grand chamber behind. Celeste's light tread led the way, her ease amidst the dark a beacon for us all to follow.

Leigh's quiet hum filled the spaces between our footfalls, a sound more contemplative than her usual boisterous tones. Her contemplation mirrored my own thoughts on the journey's end that lay ahead.

Yeska walked beside me. In its absence, her presence provided a different sort of illumination, that of a mind still turning with the thoughts of an enigma unraveled.

Diane's vigilance never waned, her gaze moving like a lighthouse beam, cutting through the cavern's shadows. The inherent danger had not diminished, yet we moved with a confidence earned through trials faced and overcome.

The ascent to the surface was, of course, shorter than our descent — except for crossing the treacherous underground lake. The traps were disarmed or overcome, the riddles solved, and each step was confident, although we remained careful and watchful. The chill of the barrow's depths lightened with every level we climbed, a subtle warmth returning to our limbs.

Soft whispered conversations began to fill the air as we navigated the spiraling staircase, our voices low but filled with the warmth of a shared experience ending. As we approached the threshold between barrow and world, the soft glow of daylight appeared, inviting us back into life and light and warmth.

Each of us emerged from the barrow's grasp with a shared sigh of relief, the open sky a welcomed sight. We paused for a moment, taking in the sun's rays as they caressed our faces, erasing the cold from our bones.

The larroling stretched its massive form under the sunlight, shaking off the remnants of the barrow's chill. I smiled at the sight, then followed suit.

Standing at the entrance to the barrow, we all shared one final glance back into the descending dark — a farewell to a challenge met and overcome, a chapter in our history that would remain etched in stone and memory.

With the barrow Dungeon behind us, our eyes could turn to the path home.

Chapter 38

Evening descended upon Copperwinde Forest like a sigh of relief, the sky painted in shades of soft pinks and deepening blues as we emerged from the dank bowels of the barrow.

As the group stepped out into the fresh forest air, taking in deep, grateful breaths, there was a chorus of pleased murmurs. The earthy scent of pine and the undercurrent of flowering thyme were a welcome contrast to the musty chill of the dungeon we had left behind.

I led us away from the stone mouth of the barrow, the forest floor springing gently beneath our boots. The canopy above rustled with the last whispers of the day's breeze, and the fading light dappled the ground through gaps between the leaves. It felt good to be out in the open, to feel the space around us, the limitless sky overhead.

I turned to Diane, who was pulling on her jacket against the evening chill. "Would you mind scouting around to make sure we've found a safe spot for the night?" I asked, confident in her exceptional skills to safeguard our temporary haven.

Without a word, she gave a smile and a short nod before she slipped into the shadowy embrace of the forest's edge. Her form seemed to blend with the trunks and underbrush, something about her quieter and more at one with the woods since her leveling up.

The rest of us gathered our supplies from the larroling's back, unloading the tents and our cooking gear. Yeska and I grabbed one of the tents, its fabric sturdy and familiar in our hands as we began to lay it out on the relatively flat ground we had chosen.

Working side by side, the two of us unfolded the shelter, coordinating effortlessly as we slotted the collapsible rods into their fabric loops. It was a routine task, one we had done before, yet there was an undercurrent of a new depth to our relationship that made it exciting somehow.

As we stretched the tent's base and began to stake it into the ground, our hands occasionally brushed — one 'accidental' touch following another. Each contact sent a jolt, electrifying in its own right.

The flirtatious energy built with every smile we exchanged, with every quiet chuckle at our 'mistakes.' There was something about the way Yeska moved, agile and close, that hinted at stories untold and latent tension waiting to be explored.

In the midst of our work, I couldn't resist the pull

of curiosity that had been nagging me since our rapid advancements earlier that day in the Dungeon. "Yeska, have you had any revelations about my Bloodline yet?" I ventured; my voice casual as I met her eyes.

She paused, one corner of her mouth quirking up in a half-smile as she considered the question. "No certain insights yet," she said, her tone contemplative as she gestured toward the tent's entrance we were securing. "I need to meditate on our findings, but I can feel the power. Considering the quick advancement I've experienced, I'm certain it's something formidable."

The thought lingered between us, the implications of such potential power painting both exciting and daunting possibilities for the future. There was a brief silence, the forest around us coming alive with the sounds of evening: a distant owl's call, the scuttle of nocturnal creatures through the brush.

Just as I opened my mouth to speak again, our intimate bubble burst with the sound of Leigh's voice calling from nearby. "Dinner's ready, you two! Come and get it!"

At the same time, Diane's form materialized from the dusky woods, her report ready. "The area's clear — no signs of any beasts or threats. We're good for now," she assured us, brushing off a few clinging leaves from her sleeves.

We finished up with the tent and headed toward the campfire, where the alluring smell of our evening meal wafted through the cool air. Leigh had outdone herself, the simple cuisine appearing as a feast thanks to the hunger our strenuous day had fostered.

The campsite was alive with light and warmth, the fire crackling as Celeste laid out bowls and utensils on a large flat rock for us to use. Her knack for creating pockets of home in the wilderness never failed to impress me.

Yeska and I joined the others beside the fire, the orange glow reflecting off our faces as we took our seats on fallen logs and smoothed stones. It was a makeshift setting, but we had all we needed, from pots and pans to provisions. A collective effort had turned a spot in the forest into another branch of our homestead.

The smells of boiling broth and roasting root vegetables mingled together. It reminded us that comfort was not solely found within walls, but in the company we kept and the way we adapted to the earth we shared.

As we prepared to eat, our conversation steered toward recollections of the day — the icy challenge within the barrow, the battles won, and the threats overcome.

Diane shared a particularly harrowing moment, replicating the crash of ice and the fear she had felt, her theatrical portrayal eliciting a round of laughter that cut through the darkness like a beacon. I enjoyed it with generous laughter, for it was rare that Diane took the stage.

And indeed, she seemed to blush at the laughter and then sidled up against me as if for safety, while Leigh recounted details of the battle with the ghouls at the beginning, once again praising my ingenuity at coming up with the bottleneck strategy.

"This is what it's about, isn't it?" Leigh said after

the brief silence that followed her tale, a thoughtful expression softening her usual merriment. "Facing what the world throws at us and still managing to sit here, around a fire, as a family."

Celeste nodded, her gaze wandering over our faces, her lips curling in an unspoken agreement that encompassed all the emotions that had passed through us during our journey.

Yeska caught me looking at her, and a shared smile formed between us — a recognition of the remarkable changes we'd faced together, how they bound us to the same thread of destiny.

"Alright," I said. "Let's eat. I think we earned it today..."

The evening sky began to embrace the hues of night as we settled down around the simmering campfire. Our stomachs were eager for the warmth of the meal Leigh had prepared. The scent of the stew, filled with the spoils of our foraging and the supplies we had brought, embraced the campsite. We huddled closer, sharing the comforting space with the spreading chill of the forest night.

Diane reached for the ladle first, serving generous portions into our bowls. "Nothing like a good stew to end the day," she said, her voice carrying a tired satisfaction. I watched her spoon the broth, observing the precise movements that spoke of her inherent meticulous nature.

Yeska sat across from me, the light of the fire reflecting off her eyes, giving them an eerie glow that seemed to embody the mysteries of the Dungeon we had faced together. She caught me looking her way and offered a faint smile before breaking the silence. "I think it's fascinating, really, the way we all manage to work together when it counts," she mused.

Leigh nodded in agreement, spooning a mouthful of stew, her earlier boisterous laughter now subdued into a contented quiet. "Yeah, it's like we've found our rhythm as a team," she added, a hum of approval in her throat as the flavors of the food hit home.

Celeste, who had been busy unpacking the rest of our supplies, joined us with her own bowl. Her usually animated gestures were now replaced with the calm motions of someone winding down from the day's exertions. "What we've encountered today, the things we've seen... it's a lot to take in," she said, a thoughtful expression softening her delicate features.

Conversation flowed naturally as we shared our meal, with everyone reflecting on the events that had unfolded in the depths of the barrow. We recounted close calls and clever tactics, each story underscoring the strength we found in unity and quick thinking.

Diane looked over at Yeska curiously, echoing the question I had asked earlier by the tent. "Have you come to any conclusions about David's Bloodline?" she asked with a tone gentle but inquisitive.

Yeska mirrored the smile she had given me not too long ago, her head tilting slightly. "No certain insights yet," she repeated with a reflective look in her eyes. "It will take some time to meditate on what we've experienced. But I'm certain it's something special."

As the fire crackled and popped, Celeste began to hum softly, her gaze drifting to the flames. Inspired by the moment and the day's adventure, she began to sing an improvised tune, her voice as clear as the Copperwinde air.

Diane chuckled, a sound of delight and encouragement. Picking up on Celeste's melody, she lent her own voice to the song, adding words to commemorate our journey through the Dungeon:

"In the depths where shadows cling,
Together brave, we've faced the king.
Specters fell before our might,
With teamwork strong, we won the night."

Celeste's voice mingled with Diane's, a duet crafted in the spur of the moment yet holding the profound weight of our shared experiences. Their song rose to the treetops, carried on the breeze as an ode to our courage and camaraderie.

"The barrow's secrets ours to claim,
United force, we end the game.

A prize now won, a quest complete,
With hearts resolved, we shan't retreat."

The soothing strains of the improvised song danced around the fire, drawing smiles from Leigh and Yeska. It was a shared moment of peaceful reflection on the trials we had faced and the victory we had achieved.

As the final notes of the song dissolved into the whispers of the Copperwinde night, compliments flowed freely from one to the other.

"That was beautiful," Yeska said, her voice full of earnest admiration. "You both have a way with words... and tunes," she added with a wistful note that spoke to her appreciation for the arts.

Leigh's applause was soft, her hands coming together in quiet praise. "What a way to remember the day," she remarked, her grin returning, as infectious as ever. "Should've known you'd turn our escapade into a melody, Celeste."

Celeste blushed lightly, a modest dip of her head acknowledging both the praise and the shared sentiment behind the song. "It just felt right," she said, her voice carrying the warmth of the fire before us.

With the hours stretching late and our bodies craving the rest that would prepare us for the journey back, I looked up from my empty stew bowl. "I'll take the first watch," I suggested again, but before I could stand, Diane placed a gentle hand on my arm.

"I'll sit with you for a while," she offered, her eyes not leaving mine. "The fire's warmth is too inviting, and I want to talk." The unspoken layers of her simple desire hinted at a conversation laced with something deeper than the night's vigil.

Agreeing to her request, the two of us settled by the dwindling fire, our legs stretched out toward the remaining embers. The others bid us goodnight, retreating to their tents with yawns and the satisfying exhaustion that promised a deep slumber.

Yeska gave me a knowing smile as she departed, the shadows of the night cloaking her retreat. I returned the gesture, contemplating the bond that had been forged between us all, tight and unbreakable.

The forest around us sighed as it settled into repose, the sounds of nocturnal creatures the only whispers that dared encroach upon the silence that had fallen. The fire's heat was subtle, a lingering touch against the coolness that seeped in through the treetops.

Chapter 39

As the others tucked themselves away in their tents, the silence of the night enveloped us, leaving Diane and I seated on a blanket by the fire's dying embers. I looked at her, the crackle from the campfire casting a warm glow on her delicate features. She scooted closer, seeking warmth in the cold night air of Copperwinde Forest and found it in my arms.

With the subtle ease of familiarity, Diane nestled against me, and I wrapped an arm around her. The weight of the day's events seemed to melt away as we settled into the comfort of each other's embrace. The surrounding forest remained still, as if holding its breath in reverence to our private moment.

The campfire's glow danced across our faces, and in its light, Diane's sapphire eyes glistened with tranquility. Tentatively, I placed my hand on her belly, feeling the faintest stir of life within.

"How's the little one?" I asked softly, a whisper of wonder tugging at the edges of my words.

Diane's hand rested atop mine, her touch light and reassuring. "As restless as the wind out here," she replied with a tender chuckle. "But he'll be here in a few months... Or she?"

"A few... *months...*" I muttered and blinked. "You mean seven months?"

Now it was her turn to blink, confused. "No, my love... Four."

It took me a moment to process that. "You're that

far along? Five months?"

"No... Just two."

Was I going insane? I did the math again, and Diane must've read my confusion. "How... How long do you think a pregnancy lasts?" she asked.

"Well, nine months," I replied, immediately realizing that there might be something else at play here.

"They last six with us," Diane said, realizing the same thing. Then she laughed and covered her mouth. "Oh no! I should've told you. I didn't know that human women..."

I laughed and held up my hand. "No, no!" I said. "How could you have known? Six is normal for your kind, and nine is normal for mine. I didn't even consider it might be different, but it makes sense, I suppose."

She grinned and placed her pretty head on my shoulder. "It does not scare you?"

"Of course not," I said. "I'm only happy that it'll happen sooner rather than later... Although there are some preparations I'll need to move up..."

The realization that our time to prepare was

shorter than anticipated made my mind shoot into overtime. Four months. The house had to be made ready sooner, and with that knowledge, the future felt closer, almost tangible. It was a thought that brought both joy and a twinge of anxiety.

"We'll be fine, my love," Diane said. "Even if we make no preparations at all."

I smiled and held her close. She was right, after all. But still, there were things I wanted to do. Luckily, the duergar summon could help.

As the forest around us settled into the rhythms of the night, I turned the conversation. "Diane," I began, the flicker of the fire reflected in my eyes, "what are your thoughts on Yeska?" The question lingered in the quiet space between us.

She glanced up at me, her features softening. After a moment's thought, she admitted, "At first, I wasn't sure I liked her. But these past days... we've bonded." Positivity colored her words, the truth in them a relief to my ears.

"I'm glad to hear that," I said, comforted by her admission. "It's important that we're all on the same page." I paused, allowing a moment for the sincerity of my statement to sink in.

Diane's voice held a hint of curiosity as she posed a question of her own. "David, are you attracted to her?" Her gaze locked with mine, searching, inquisitive.

I took a moment to reflect, choosing honesty over obfuscation. "Yes," I admitted, feeling no point in concealing the undeniable. "But you know me, Diane. My will is strong, and I would never let anything get in the way of us."

Diane listened, her quiet acceptance and understanding a testament to the trust we shared. "You mean I have nothing to fear from Yeska then?" she asked.

"Nothing," I assured her with gentle firmness, reinforcing the commitment we had made to each other. "Your feelings are important to me. If you aren't comfortable with her, that's all I need to know. While I'm open to seeing Yeska as a friend and ally — maybe even more — I wouldn't do that if you weren't on board."

A smile graced Diane's face, and she leaned in to press her lips to mine. The kiss was deep, and I felt her hum against my mouth.

"You are sweet, my love," she hummed. "I have not yet made up my mind, but she has surprised me in a positive way more than once. We will see what the coming days hold."

She then placed a soft hand on my chest, her sapphire eyes boring deep into mine. "But I've wanted you for myself these past few days," she whispered with a hint of desire in her voice. "I know I share you, but I treasure these moments together as well."

Her hands found their way to my hair, pulling me closer as our kiss grew more passionate. The sound of her purr was mesmerizing, almost intoxicating, and I felt a surge of warmth rush over me.

She deepened the kiss, and I responded in kind, feeling the connection between us strengthen with each second. There was an urgency we both shared, a fervor that only nights like this could ignite.

A tenderness permeated our embrace, born from the profound bond we had forged over time. It was in moments like these that I found myself most grateful for Diane and the love we shared.

Suddenly, Diane pulled back slightly, gazing into my eyes with a mix of fondness and anticipation. A playful glint sparkled in her eyes as she whispered, "I have something special in store for you."

I arched an eyebrow, intrigued by her words. "Oh?" I asked, feeling my curiosity pique.

Diane leaned in once more, her lips brushing against mine as she murmured, "Just wait and see."

Chapter 40

Diane gracefully repositioned herself onto my lap, her sapphire eyes glowing with anticipation under the silvery hue of the moonlight.

Her black hair spilled over her shoulders, catching the glow of stray embers that popped from the fire. As her fox tail curled around us, a distinctive yet pleasant hint of lavender filled my senses, causing an involuntary shiver of excitement to ripple through my body.

With a demure smile, she let her slender hand drift downwards, deftly removing the barriers posed by my clothing, and found their way to my hardened manhood. Her touch was feather-light yet held a potency that was intoxicating. As she softly kneaded me, I found myself biting playfully onto her lower lip, an unspoken dare between lovers.

"Oh, David," she whispered. "I want to feel you inside me tonight. Just me and you." Her words came out in breathy syllables that left no room for misinterpretations. Her movements became more deliberate, her body squirming seductively in my lap.

Diane's innocence had given way to a newfound boldness, and I couldn't help but enjoy the liberation she now experienced.

The anticipation in her eyes stoked the flames of my own desire, and together we moved in silent understanding. Lifting her gently off my lap, I laid her on the soft, dew-laden blanket. Her clothes removed piece by piece, each one revealing another tantalizing facet of her flawlessly sculpted form.

Diane's body was a hypnotizing spectacle, fit and toned, her curves generously lined in all the right places. Moonlight painted her skin with a gentle glow, highlighting each curve and crevice as her bosom heaved, excitement and arousal firing her up. She was divine, a goddess of the foxkin draped in human desires and vulnerability.

My hands roamed her exposed body, tracing her form and the gentle swell of her baby bump with an intimate familiarity. My fingers ran over her soft, pert breasts, circling her areolas before gently kneading the supple mounds. Her nipples were hard pebbles under my touch, a potent indication of her arousal.

Her hand reached up with the hem of my shirt clenched tightly in her lithe fingers. In a surprising display of strength and urgency, the fabric ripped apart as it was pulled over my head. Her actions, bold and raw, elicited a hint of laughter from my lips.

"Eager, are you?" I playfully teased, and watched as a roguish smirk grew across her face.

With a coy smile, she pushed me over, taking firm control. Straddling me, she made quick work of removing my trousers, freeing my hardness swiftly.

"I *am* eager," she admitted. "I'm always eager for you, my love."

She cradled my manhood in her soft hands before slowly easing her mouth onto it. I groaned with delight at the searing contact, the warmth of her mouth enveloping me in an intimate cocoon of pleasure. She took her time, pleasuring me with her mouth, every wave of sensation more potent than the last.

Her tongue twirled and caressed, sending tremors of bliss tingling down my spine. She was nothing short of a magnificent artist, painting my body with her amorous brushstrokes. I reveled in the sensation, each wave pushing me further onto the precipice of pure ecstasy.

Slowly, Diane withdrew, a trail of saliva still connecting us. Looking up, she maintained the tantalizing eye contact. She pressed my swollen manhood between her firm breasts, using them as warm pillows to stimulate me further.

"Oh, Diane," I groaned. "That… That feels so good!"

Her gaze was teasing, almost challenging, as she rubbed her breasts rhythmically against my hardened length. For a moment, I noticed her eyes dart somewhere behind me as if she had seen something, and a coy smile appeared on her plump lips. But I was too preoccupied with my own impending release to ponder over it for long.

As Diane moved faster and faster, I could feel the orgasm building within me. Her breasts, slick with spit, heated with the friction against me. Pulsating in rhythmic waves, lips forming pleas, she urged me, watching closely as I approached my climax.

"Cum on me, David," she begged. "Let me feel your seed on my skin."

There was nothing I could do — even if I wanted to. My pleasure erupted over her breasts, overwhelming in its intensity. I released myself, coating her breasts with my cum. It was an electrifying sight, my seed gleaming on her heaving chest against the silvery moonlight.

But my euphoria did not ebb away. Instead, it transformed into a raw, primal lust for the woman writhing on top of me.

On the edge of this precipice, we remained suspended for a moment, ready to plunge into a realm of pleasure again.

No sooner had my seed cooled on Diane's breasts when she reached for me once again. Resting her soft hands against me, she guided my still hard cock towards her, allowing me to slip inside her center.

To describe the sensation as heavenly would be an understatement. It felt like being held in delicious warmth, a sensation that was both comforting and arousing.

"David," she moaned. "Oh, it feels so good!"

Diane began to move, her hips gyrating in

motions that served to enhance our connection. With each rise and fall, I became more entrenched within her. The smile on her face was one of joy, a candid expression that echoed the affection we shared.

Everything about Diane while she rode me was enchanting — from her soft hair that brushed against me, to the way her eyes glowed under the moonlit sky. Her body, slick with a sheen of perspiration, bobbed in rhythm to her movements.

I watched, mesmerized, as my seed still shining on her bosom, glistened with her movements. She was mine, claimed in every way, and I enjoyed her as deeply as she did me.

As she rode me, one of her hands dipped down to tease her little nub — to give herself pleasure. I released a deep groan at the sight of her arching her back, touching herself as she rode me in the moonlight, as if we were gods of the old world, free and loving in nature's heart.

And as she pleasured herself, I felt her tighten around me. Her body reacting to her own touch. I savored the delicious torment it brought me. It felt as though we had become an extension of each other's pleasure, a shared conduit for our desires.

My hands gripped her hips and set the rhythm, bouncing her on my lap at the pace I desired, and she mewled with happy lust as her deft fingers moved faster and faster. Soon, she would cum, and I would give her my second load, but I wanted to postpone the moment, to make our dirty dance in the moonlight last but a while longer.

Her eyes interrupted their focus on me and flitted away, drawing my attention towards something that interested her, and again she grinned before focusing on me and intensifying her efforts.

"David," she hummed. "Oh… It feels so good… David!"

"That's it," I grunted, slamming her down in my lap again. "I'm gonna fill you up!"

"Yes!" she mewled. "Oh, yes! David!"

Her body trembled, signaling her release was imminent, instilling in me a deeper lust still, knowing that I had facilitated her ecstasy. She clung to me with one hand, her nails pressing little circles on my chest as her climax washed over her.

"I'm… I'm cumming, David!"

I slammed her down again, then winced as her nails dug into my skin. Then, she gasped and trembled. The intense tightening around me created a delectable friction that sent me spiraling into my own climax.

I raised her again, slammed her down, and gave a deep grunt of delight as I spurted my seed into Diane, quivering and trembling as she came on my cock. It was a sea of pleasure that coursed through my veins, and I succumbed to it, releasing all of my essence inside her in an explosion that matched her glory.

Then, her movements slowed, and she panted for breath. And as the waves of pleasure subsided, there was a moment of utter tranquility. Cushioned against the soft soil and enveloped in each other's scent, I realized there was no place I'd rather be.

This, to me, was utter perfection.

Diane fell into fits of light giggles, her body quivering against mine as she toppled over, her face next to mine — lips seeking mine.

"That was delicious," she murmured when she withdrew from our kiss.

"Indeed, it was," I agreed, my voice husky from exertion. I turned to her, "I hope we haven't woken anyone up." I ventured, keeping my curiosity subtle.

Diane rolled off me, landing lightly on the now crumpled blanket beside me. Her eyes held a hint of mischief, her body a tempting canvas illuminated by the dying embers of the fire. "We *may* have," she finally admitted, her grin bright against the dark.

As she said this, my eyes were drawn to a streak of my seed trickling down her thigh. The sight, far from being distasteful, held a primal allure.

She chuckled, prompting me to look up. "Who did we wake?" I asked, my voice echoing in the silent forest. I considered the others in our party, their tents tucked away in the shadowy veils of the Copperwinde night.

Diane's sapphire eyes twinkled with mischief. "I am not *entirely* sure. It looked like someone with a cat's tail," she confided with a wink, her voice carrying a teasing note.

Yeska, of course…

The thought of Yeska witnessing our intimate moment sent a thrill through me. It was unexpected, but not unwelcome. Diane seemed undisturbed by it, and that was good. After all, if she didn't find Yeska watching us make love disturbing, she might like the catkin woman better than I hoped.

I found myself smiling at the revelation. The dynamics of our group were changing and in ways that held my interest.

"Interesting," I just mused.

Diane winked again before she yawned, her gorgeous body stretching out on the blanket, unfazed by the open sky above or the dew-laden soil beneath. In that moment, I appreciated just how genuinely beautiful she truly was. All thoughts of our unseen audience faded into the background.

"Why don't you get some sleep?" I told her. "I'll finish my watch. We have a long day ahead of us tomorrow."

She smiled and nodded. "Sleep sounds really good right now…" Her eyes were already shut.

I laughed, rolled her over, and slammed her hard on her butt. She yelped, then reached around to cradle where I'd smacked her before chuckling.

"Go on!" I said. "Into the tent with you before I have my way with you a second time!" I gave her another teasing slap on her other cheek. "If you stay out here to distract me, anything could sneak up on us."

She laughed and hopped to her feet before gathering up her clothes. She then shot me a loving look, blew me a kiss, and scampered off toward the tent, leaving me to my reflections and the quiet night.

Lying in the quiet stillness of the Copperwinde Forest for one more moment before I would gather my things, I let out a sigh of relief, arms folded behind my head.

This little adventure had thickened the plot with Yeska. But rather than anxiety, I felt a bubbling anticipation for what lay ahead. A tantalizing puzzle, a captivating mystery of love and attraction, that was just beginning to unfold.

I had a feeling that Yeska might still play a larger part…

Chapter 41

The first light hadn't yet given way to a clear blue sky when I stirred from my makeshift bed, the remnants of last night still humming in the back of my mind. Diane was already up, shadows playing over her as she packed her stuff with quiet care, already preparing for the journey home.

We all set about breaking camp with a rhythm born of necessity, the larroling watching us with mild interest as we loaded our bags onto its back. For a moment, I watched the creature, its shaggy body offsetting the more delicate shapes of the tents and packs, and I was thankful that we had it along for the ride.

"We should make good time today," I remarked to the group, "Gladdenfield will welcome us back in about three days." There was comfort in knowing our direction, and a growing warmth in the thought of returning to the town that had become a haven.

Our journey began anew as we left the clearing, Copperwinde Forest wrapping around us like a familiar cloak. Diane walked close beside me, her hand occasionally brushing against mine, a silent echo of the previous night's intimacy.

Our path meandered through the magical realm, the Tannorian blue bees buzzing idly around us and the distant roar of a larroling calling out to its kin. It was in those moments, surrounded by otherworldly flora and fauna, that I felt a profound connection to this place.

The atmosphere among us was one of shared contentment, as if the forest lent us its peace. Steps untroubled, we made our way. The ground beneath us was soft with ancient moss and the scent of thyme thick in the air.

Evening drew near all too soon, and the light of day faded as we settled in a new clearing. Once more, tents were erected, each motion speaking volumes of our familiarity with the task.

The forest around us settled as we worked, the bustling of day creatures giving way to the soft pad of nocturnal life. Our campfire crackled to life, a beacon amid the emerald expanse of Copperwinde.

Dinner preparations were a communal affair; Leigh unpacked our leftover provisions while Yeska started the fire, her movements more assured than the days before. The dance of flames against the growing night was almost hypnotic.

Our meal consisted of smoked fish and root vegetables, a simple offering that tasted of home and wilderness melded into one. We sat around the fire, savoring each bite as if it were both our last and our first.

As we ate, the conversation ebbed and flowed, a gentle stream of laughter and recollection, now made lighter because the job at the Dungeon was finished. There was an easy companionship among us, a congeniality born of shared experiences.

This night, I listened more than I spoke, content to absorb the warm interaction and reflect on victories past. Diane sat to my right, her glow in the firelight matching the sparks that rose into the evening sky. She reached out, her fingers tracing a line on the back of my hand — a tactile reminder of our connection.

The night deepened, and one by one the girls made their way to their respective tents. I volunteered for the first watch, a quiet alone time I sought. Leigh's whispered, "Goodnight, baby," followed by Diane's softer "See you in the morning," left echoes of tenderness in the air.

With the camp settled and the fire reduced to glowing embers, I found myself alone with the steady pulse of the forest. The rhythmic chirring of insects, the occasional rustle of a creature moving through the underbrush, the soft hoot of an owl — the nighttime wonder of the living forest that I had grown to love.

The tranquil chorus of Copperwinde's night kept me company, a steady reminder that life teemed all around, unseen but vibrant in the veil of darkness.

I added another log to the fire, watching the sparks jump and dance before being swallowed by the night. The wood caught quickly, sending fresh warmth radiating out into the small camp.

With the others asleep, I enjoyed the solitary peace, letting the sounds of the forest seep deep into my consciousness — a balm to the day's weariness and the echo of adventures past.

I poured myself a cup of water, taking in the simple purity of the forest air mixing with the cool liquid. Even here, so far from what we called civilization, I found a home in the cadence of nature's breath.

Settling back, I let my vigilance relax ever so slightly, embracing the night's embrace. My thoughts drifted to Diane, to the warmth of her smile, the softness of her voice, and the life we were soon to welcome together.

Then, in the silent, eternal watch of night, a sound caught my ear — a delicate disruption. My eyes turned towards the tents.

There it was— the subtle noise of a tent's zipper, a faint but unmistakable reminder that, even as some slept, others stirred.

I rose, curious to see who was still awake.

Chapter 42

I turned to find Yeska stepping out of her tent and into the cool night. She zeroed in on my solitary form by the now smoldering fire. Her approach was unhurried, the sync of her steps with the forest's nocturnal rhythm a familiar dance.

"Can't sleep?" I asked with a low voice to match

the night's tender notes, my question hanging between us like the mist of breaths in the air.

Her nod came with a small shrug and a smile, her silhouette outlined by the receding glow of the embers. "My mind is too active." She took a seat beside me on the log, her presence a welcome addition to the quiet watch.

Together, we settled into the tranquil vigil, the scene of the forest night manifesting a play of shadow and starlight. It was a display that tempted one's thoughts to wander the infinite paths between the heavens.

Our conversation, a mere trickle at first, soon flowed, meandering through topics as varied as the stars above. At first, we spoke of the barrow's secrets that we had learned and the battles fought under the earth with the sigh of relief that the forest seemed to share with us. Later, we turned to the wonder all around us.

"It's beautiful out here, isn't it?" Yeska finally mused, tracing a finger along the log, her words as much an observation as they were an embrace of the moment.

"It is," I agreed, allowing my gaze to lift skyward. The stars, scattered across the night canvas, reminded us of our place amidst the vast gentle wild.

I pointed to a cluster of stars that winked back with an ancient gleam. "See that? That's Pegasus," I told her. "The flying horse of Greek mythology."

Yeska followed my gesture, her eyes seeking the celestial artwork I had outlined. "I've seen it from many forests," she said. "It's almost overwhelming to think of the rich history of Earth before the Upheaval. So much has happened here, like on our world." She chuckled. "I wonder if anyone could ever learn the histories of both places."

I smiled and nodded, wondering that same thing myself.

The following shared silence was comfortable, the kind that only arose between individuals with a mutual understanding of nature's untamed beauty.

Eventually, I broke the calm by inquiring further. "So, what's keeping you up, Yeska?" My curiosity was genuine, seeking the root of her restlessness.

"My mind… It's just *grinding* away." Her voice

carried a contemplative softness. "Being with you and your wives… It has awakened something."

I looked at her sideways, my curiosity definitely roused. "And what is that?" I asked.

"Well, I've always lived on the move, offering my Bloodmage services. Bloodmages are rare enough, and our services are always in demand..." She hesitated. "But now, I've seen your homestead, your life here, your..." She trailed off, seeming to grapple with a newfound aspiration.

I nodded, absorbing her confessions, internally gauging her words and their implications. "You're thinking you might want a life like ours?" I ventured, probing the change that stirred within her.

"I might," she admitted, a note of certainty creeping into her timbre. "I'm looking forward to the coming months at the homestead. A steady life, if that makes sense."

My smile, upon hearing her affirmation, was one of anticipation. Seeing her connect with the girls had sparked a hope in me for a harmonious future.

"It makes perfect sense, and I am looking

forward to it, too," I said, my own thoughts turning to the potential within Yeska, the possible kinship beyond just allyship. "It'll be good to see how things unfold."

She reached out, her action instinctual, and her arms wrapped around me in a heartfelt hug. The gesture was filled with the appreciation of the bond we were fostering.

Holding Yeska, I felt a myriad of emotions envelop us, much like the night did with its serenity. There was something blossoming, a delicate bloom nurtured by shared experiences and the promise of tranquil days ahead.

I returned the embrace, my hands gently rubbing her back, the warmth of her nearness speaking volumes more than any exchange of words could.

As we sat in comfortable silence, my mind wandered to the bonds formed and forming within my homestead with my other women. Yeska was right: our lives were rich, full, and vibrant. The homestead itself was an intricate weave of personalities and spirits that I hoped would welcome Yeska as one of our own.

The forest bore witness to the quiet moments between us, the hoot of the owl and the whisper of the wind through the leaves a soft underscore to our companionship.

Yeska pulled back but remained close, her eyes reflecting the last light from the dying fire. Her features were softened by the dim light and the comfort found in shared affection.

"Whatever your future holds," she whispered, "I'm glad to be part of it, even if only for a while." Her voice carried the weight of sincerity and an unspoken yearning for permanence.

I replied with a quiet optimism, "The future looks bright, Yeska. I know the others will feel the same." My words wrapped around us, a vow made beneath the stoic presence of ancient trees and stars. "Let's enjoy the time that's coming, and we will see what we will see after that."

We held each other, feeling the tranquility of Copperwinde Forest around us and the stars above. I felt my desire and appreciation for the cat girl rise, understanding that feelings were blossoming between us and hoping that the other women would accept Yeska.

Chapter 43

Dawn ushered in the promise of our last day in Copperwinde Forest before we would hit the more familiar grounds of Springfield Forest. Birdsong wove through the crisp air, and the world outside awakened to the touch of dawn. Inside our shared tent, I lay for a moment longer, the grogginess of sleep still clinging to my limbs.

The rustle of movement stirred me from my slumber as Celeste, bright and chipper from her last watch, peeked into our tent. "Time to rise, everyone," she called out softly, her voice a gentle harbinger of the day ahead. Leigh, Diane, and I exchanged sleepy glances before we began to untangle ourselves from our blankets.

Outside, the chill of the morning greeted us, but the activity warmed our bones. Yeska was already up, tending to the dying embers of our campfire, coaxing them back to life for a quick breakfast. We gathered around the revived flames as Diane prepared a pot of oatmeal with dried fruits we had stored away, the simple smells inviting us to a hearty start.

Conversation was light, the soft laughs and easy banter washing away the hold of night. We savored our breakfast, spooning the warm oatmeal into our mouths with contented sighs — a satisfying prelude to breaking camp.

With nourishment settling comfortably within us, we packed our belongings and took down the tents. The larroling watched patiently, its presence a steadfast reminder of our journey's end drawing near. We loaded our gear onto the creature, its frame well-suited for the burden, as we prepared to re-enter Springfield Forest.

Soon enough, we hit Red River and the bridge that crossed it — the border between Copperwinde Forest and Springfield Forest — and we once again set foot on familiar trails. As we walked along the paths Diane knew better, the forest enveloped us in a comforting embrace.

The trees of Springfield Forest, a symphony of green hues, felt like old friends welcoming us back. Our conversations flowed naturally, returning to cherished topics and recollections of our recent adventure that already felt like distant memories.

We spoke of the barrow, the challenges within, and the triumph of retrieving the staff. Joyous laughter rippled through our group as I recounted the moments of tension turned into victory, with Diane adding her recollections of scouting the unknown. Leigh's hearty chuckles punctuated our tales, her spirit never flagging.

The hours hiking passed with the ease of a well-loved story. We traversed the leafy paths, breathed in the scents of wildflowers, and watched as the sun cast dappled patterns on the forest floor. Our steps were buoyed by the anticipation of home drawing closer with each mile covered.

As the second evening of our hike back approached, the shadows of the trees grew longer, pulling the cloak of dusk tight around the world. Diane's keen eye picked out a suitable spot for our night's rest — a small clearing nestled within the woods, protected and serene.

We set up camp with a practiced efficiency that spoke volumes of our shared experiences. Tents rose, and the campfire was lit, its flickering light a beacon against the advancing night. The forest around us eased into quiet, the creatures settling down as we did the same.

After a dinner of the remaining travel rations, Yeska and I found ourselves seated away from the others, enjoying a moment of peace. It was then I seized the opportunity to inquire further about her work on my Bloodline, knowing that her observation of us in a Dungeon had been one of the prerequisites of her finishing her work.

"What else do you need, Yeska, for your observations?" I asked, eager to know the extent of my lineage's powers.

She turned to me, the reflection of the fire in her curious eyes. "I think now that observing you for the remaining time — a little under four months — at the homestead should suffice," she said earnestly. "To study your interactions, your life there — all of it will help me determine the true nature of your Bloodline."

I nodded, satisfied with her response. It was a fair timeline, and the thought of her integrating further into our daily life was a welcome one. With all she'd done alongside us, she was becoming less of an outsider and more a part of our story.

The evening drew on, and conversation turned back to laughter and shared memories. The warm glow of the fire illuminated the faces I had come to care for so deeply. Diane's gentle smiles, Leigh's animated tales, and Celeste's soft hums filled the air with Yeska's inclusion in our circle completing the picture.

As the camp settled into the night, the last embers of our fire casting a dying hue on the encampment, I found myself reflecting on the journey we had undertaken. From the homestead to the depths of a barrow, and back through magical woods, we had weathered it all together, and our ties were stronger for it.

We had made good time, and tomorrow would see us arrive in Gladdenfield Outpost. The thought of returning brought a sense of excitement. Turning in the quest, purchasing some supplies, and returning to the homestead — the steps were laid out before us, simple and clear.

Still, I looked forward to sharing the success of our mission with Lernoval. The satisfaction of a task accomplished was a joy in itself, and to deliver on a promise was a duty I held in high regard. And contrary to many Dungeon runs for wealth or items or ingredients, this quest allowed Lernoval a measure of peace in reclaiming an artifact that belonged to his family.

I understood the need well. Sometimes, simple

objects linked us to the lives of those who came before us, who even paved the way for us. *We are who we are today because of them — for better or worse.* And while those objects were still what they always were, their meaning changed to us, and we held onto them as keepsakes of people loved and lost. I was happy to assist Lernoval with that, as I would have wanted others to help me, had I been incapable of doing it myself.

However, the thought of obtaining new supplies brought more practical considerations to mind. The homestead needed more than our presence to thrive. It needed our care and providence, and I looked forward to stocking our stores. I also wanted to get started on my Ranching skill, and I figured chickens would be a nice start!

The night deepened around us, shrouding the forest in a veil of quiet mystery. The sounds of the wild were hushed whispers that mingled with my contemplations of the morrow and the days to come.

Diane, Leigh, and Celeste slipped into their tents after saying goodnight — I would take first watch again. I watched their silhouettes through the canvas as they made ready for sleep, a smile touching my lips as their forms settled down in their sleeping bags.

Yeska rose from her seat by the fire, stretching languidly as she made her way to her own tent. Her graceful exit was a reminder of the ease with which she had slipped into the cadence of our days — a new piece in the puzzle that was our life.

I took a moment to stir the ashes of our fire, ensuring it would remain safely contained throughout the night. The responsibility for our camp's safety lay on my shoulders, but it was a task borne of love — a guardianship I took seriously.

After we ate breakfast the following morning, we packed up and departed early. We all noticed a drop in temperature — sudden as it can be when nature shifts seasons. There were more red and golden hues among the trees, it seemed, than on our way in. Autumn is a beautiful time of year, and we all enjoyed the sights in silence as we completed the last leg of our journey.

Gladdenfield awaited us with its familiar bustle and rustic charm. As we entered the town, its wooden palisades stood sturdy and welcoming, like the embrace of an old friend.

Diane led the larroling to the livery stable at the edge of town, where the stablemaster greeted us with a warm nod. We left our trusty beast in his care, knowing it would be well-tended during our stay.

The streets of Gladdenfield were lively, filled with the sound of merchants calling out their wares and children darting amongst the bustling crowds. The scent of freshly baked bread and the tang of smoked meats wafted from the stalls that lined the main thoroughfare, beckoning passersby.

We made our way along the familiar paths, nodding to faces I recognized while Leigh's playful banter with some of the townsfolk she knew well from her days as the shopkeeper added a pleasant note to our return.

The Wild Outrider loomed ahead, its weathered sign creaking gently as we approached. Its doors swung open to reveal the lively interior, a scene of laughter and spirited conversation that drew us in. As usual, early patrons were enjoying a meal or a drink, and there was a company of dwarves that were starting drinking early today.

Darny was behind the bar, his presence a sturdy fixture in the room as he poured a drink for a patron. Upon seeing us, a broad smile broke across his face, lighting up his eyes beneath the curve of his gray mustache.

Diane and Yeska scanned the common room and selected a table near the window, its light spilling onto the worn wood. Leigh followed, chiming about being parched after our trek, while Celeste settled beside them with a soft sigh.

"Find yourselves a seat, I'll catch up with you shortly," I said as I headed toward the bar where Darny stood wiping down the counter.

As I approached, Darny leaned on the bar with a knowing look. "Well, I'll be — the Dragon-Slayer returns, and I see the crew's all in one piece. Looks like another quest under your belt, huh?"

"Something like that, Darny," I replied with a chuckle, the weariness of travel slipping from my shoulders. "You know how it is with these Dungeon runs. They're never quite as straightforward as you hope."

Darny laughed, his voice booming across the room. "That's what keeps life interesting on the frontier, don't it? So, tell me, how'd it go?"

"Better than we could have planned," I said, resting my elbows on the bar. "We retrieved an elven staff from the barrow — Lernoval's heirloom. But it wasn't without its share of hurdles — spectral mages and such."

Darny's eyes widened, an appreciative whistle escaping him. "Oof. Sounds like quite the adventure. You and your group never cease to amaze me, David. Always comin' through, no matter what comes your way."

"Thanks, Darny," I said, tipping an imaginary hat. "We just try to do what's right, keep the town safe, and honor our commitments."

Our conversation drifted to the goings-on of Gladdenfield, Darny filling me in on the little changes that had taken place during our venture. "Some new traders passing through, a wagon wheel broke on Main. Buncha dwarves lookin' for work. You know, the usual frontier stuff," he said with a grin.

After a few moments of hearing the gossip, I glanced up toward the stairs leading to the upper floors of the inn. "So, you wouldn't have happened to see Lernoval around, would you? I have a staff to return to its rightful owner."

"Ah, old Lernoval's upstairs, probably buried in one of his books," Darny replied, tilting his head toward the staircase. "He ain't much for the common room. Anyway, was asking about you just yesterday, wondering when you'd be back."

I straightened up, nodding my gratitude. "I appreciate it, Darny. Time to turn in the quest."

"Third door on the left, my friend," Darny said.

With a final pat on the bar and a smile at Darny, I turned toward the stairs, each step carrying the weight of a quest nearing its end. At the top of the stairs, I paused in front of the third door on the left.

Chapter 44

With a measured knock, I rapped on the heavy wooden door, the sound echoing back to me. The creak of the hinges broke the pause, and Lernoval's figure filled the doorway with an expectant presence that seemed to brighten the dimly lit hall.

The elder elf's eyes widened at the sight of me,

and his lips curled into what I could only describe as a smile of mingled relief and joy. "David, you've returned! Please, come in — I've been waiting for this news," he said.

Stepping into Lernoval's room, I offered the elder a smile. Books and scrolls lay meticulously arranged on the small table near the window as his life's work was displayed in a quiet order. I was not going to keep the poor elf in suspense, so I came to the heart of the matter right away.

"I have something for you," I began, unclasping my pack and reaching inside. The staff, carefully wrapped in protective cloth, emerged from its confines, as significant and unassuming as it had been within the barrow's depths.

I handed the staff to Lernoval, and his hands trembled with reverence as he unwrapped it — the familiarity of its intricate craftsmanship evident in the way his fingertips lingered over the runes that spiraled its length.

As the last fold of cloth fell away, the true form of the staff was revealed in the modest light of the room. Lernoval's breath hitched, his rheumy eyes glistening, as if the staff had brought forth a tide of memories and emotions that he struggled to contain.

"My ancestors' work... I had almost lost hope of ever seeing it again," he said, his voice thick with a sentiment that resonated within the confines of the room, an almost audible cadence to the weight of his gratitude. "Thank you," he breathed, his voice almost inaudible.

A small pouch, heavy and filled to the brim, exchanged hands as Lernoval offered it to me. "Take this, with my deepest thanks," he said, his grip on my hand firm within the folds of fabric and coin.

As the pouch's weight settled in my grasp, I gave a respectful nod. "If you're ever in need of aid, you have but to ask," I said, offering a promise to the mage who had entrusted me with more than just a quest.

Lernoval met my offer with a soft chuckle, the years momentarily fading from his face. "I may take you up on that, especially since I'm planning on building a small place of my own around here

— a home for my studies."

The idea of Lernoval establishing a residence in the area sparked a genuine interest within me. We had many homesteaders, but not so many mages. It was good to have one around. "If you need assistance, my summons are skilled in building. And we know the land — you won't find better guides than us."

He regarded me for a moment, clearly assessing the sincerity behind my offer. "I appreciate that, I truly do. Your help would be... most welcome."

We shook hands and smiled at one another.

"But you appear tired from your journey and your adventure," Lernoval observed, sitting back in his chair with a comfort that time had granted him. "You must be eager to return home."

I smiled at his perceptiveness, glancing around the room that had become his temporary watchtower over Gladdenfield. "Yes, the road home is always the sweetest part of any quest."

"Well, I will send a message if I have need of your help. And the same goes for you, my friend. I am a Frost Mage. Should you ever need someone with such skills, I will gladly lend you my assistance."

"I appreciate that, Lernoval," I said. "And I will keep your kind offer in mind."

With cordial farewells exchanged, I took my leave, exiting the room with a sense of completion – a mission brought full circle with the grace of successful outcomes and the promise of future collaboration.

The stairs creaked underfoot as I descended back into the common bustle of the Wild Outrider. The inn's voice was louder here, a chorus of morning greetings and the sound of Darny attending to his patrons echoed welcomingly.

The hearty sounds of life within the Wild Outrider filled me as I headed towards our table. The women were immersed in lively conversation, and I smiled at seeing them so happily engaged with each other, Yeska included. Diane was the first to look up as I approached, her sapphire eyes bright with curiosity, ready to hear the news of my meeting with Lernoval.

With a smile, I sat down beside her.

As I rejoined the table with my companions, the light streamed through the tavern windows, casting soft light on the worn wooden surfaces of the Wild Outrider. With a smile, I pulled out the heavy pouch that Lernoval had given me, placing it on the table with an audible clink.

The sound drew the attention of Diane, Leigh, Celeste, and Yeska. "Not a bad haul for our troubles," I said, watching their faces brighten at the sight.

Leigh leaned forward, her eyes weighing the pouch with a merchant's practiced gaze. "That's more than enough for the supplies we need, and then some!" she said, the prospect of successful bartering lifting her spirits even higher.

Celeste, ever mindful of the group's needs, chimed in with a gentle nod. "It's good timing, too. We're running low on a few things at the homestead," she remarked.

Yeska looked impressed. "This is generous indeed. Lernoval is a man of his word," she observed, a note of satisfaction in her voice.

Diane's smile was one of contentment as she scooped up the pouch, weighing it in her palm. "We'll need to stock up on essentials — cheese, eggs, bread, and more," she said, already picturing the supplies in her mind. "All the stuff we don't make ourselves… yet."

I voiced the idea of adding chickens to our homestead with excitement. "I also want to buy hens and a rooster," I announced. "It's time we have a few animals around."

Diane's nod came quick, and she cast a glance toward the others. "Fresh eggs? Count me in," she said, her support immediate and firm.

"Oh, I can picture them already, scratching around in the yard!" Leigh said with an enthusiastic grin. "Let's do it. And you can level your Ranchin' skill with 'em."

"Exactly," I agreed.

Celeste's lips curled into a soft smile. "Chickens will make a lovely addition," she agreed, her voice carrying the warmth she held for all good creatures, great and small.

Encouraged by their enthusiasm, I rose from my seat. I looked over at Darny, offering a wave of farewell. "We're off to the marketplace. Thanks for everything, Darny," I said.

"You're always welcome here," Darny replied, his tone warm as always. "Good luck with your shopping!"

We made our way through the tavern's busy interior, the chatter of patrons a pleasant backdrop to our departure. As we stepped out into Gladdenfield's lively streets, the marketplace already bustled with activity.

Vendors called out from their stalls, displaying an array of colorful produce and goods that turned our heads with interest. Diane and Yeska headed straight to a farmer's stand, pointing out fresh cheeses and selecting the best for purchase.

Leigh and Celeste wandered over to the baker's cart, entranced by the smell of fresh loaves and pastries. They filled a basket with a variety of breads, their banter light and happy.

My eyes were drawn to the eggs, their pale shells promising the simple pleasures of home-cooked meals. I collected a few dozen, imagining the breakfasts we'd enjoy once back at the homestead.

The final stop was at a small pen where chickens clucked and pecked at the ground. The seller, a friendly sort with a wide-brimmed hat, helped us choose three hens and a rooster who seemed lively and healthy.

Yeska held the wooden cage as we secured our feathered friends inside. "They're charming," she said, a grin spreading across her face as the chickens settled into their temporary quarters.

With our purchases made, we retraced our steps toward the livery stable. The larroling greeted us with a low grunt, ready to continue our journey back to the homestead.

We loaded up the creature with our supplies, the chickens in their cage balanced securely among the other items. It was a sight that brought a chuckle to us all, the reality of our growing family both human and animal alike. Plus, the larroling looked kind of comical all covered in bags and cages with chickens that gave nervous clucks at the sight and smell of an animal like the larroling.

The marketplace began to quiet as the afternoon drew on, and our footsteps mingled with the softening sounds of commerce coming to its daily pause. It was time for us to head out; if we left now, we would make it to the homestead before dark.

"Come on, girls," I said. "Let's go home!"

My suggestion was greeted with enthusiasm, and we soon headed toward the gates. Once there, we paused, taking in a deep breath of the fresh air. The familiar path that would lead us home lay ahead, calling us back to the homestead we had all invested so much in.

And as we moved away from Gladdenfield, the anticipation of returning to our lives at the homestead warmed us all.

Chapter 45

The rise and fall of our boots along the road was a familiar rhythm, reminding me of the countless journeys we've taken together back to the homestead. The transactions at Gladdenfield were still fresh in our packs, and the jingle of coins kept time with our pace. Diane walked beside me, her profile outlined against the burgeoning day, while Leigh's banter with Celeste brought a light air to our departure from the outpost.

Weaving through Springfield Forest, our path was marked by the lively chirrups of birds and the scurry of small forest creatures. The sun spread warmth still across our backs, as if urging us onward.

Our conversation meandered as we hiked, touching on memories of past adventures and speculations about future plans. The sense of community between us was palpable in this stretch of wilderness; it was more than just forest — it was the connective tissue between our outpost lives and the homestead sanctuary awaiting our return.

As the midday sun reached its zenith, we found a quiet spot off the road where moss blanketed the ground softly. Here we decided to take a respite, the green canvas inviting us to spread out the dried meats and bread we'd brought from Gladdenfield. The simpler the meal, the more profound its taste seemed in the forest setting.

The urgency of hunger abated with each bite, the

quiet chomping and subtle sounds of our quick lunch were a comforting chorus. We didn't dwell long on the repast; our bodies were eager to resume the journey, fueled by the shared sustenance and the company we kept.

As we packed up and continued on our way, the mood remained light, the little details of our surroundings — a dew-spotted spiderweb, a bird's sudden flight — became markers of our progress, elements of a forest canvas we were all a part of, in that moment.

We pressed forward until the familiar shape of the old cottonwood tree came into view, a natural landmark signaling the turn onto the smaller road that led to my homestead. We followed it with rising hearts, eager to be home again.

The homestead gradually came into sight; the wooden fence and farmland plots a confirmation of our roots. As we approached, Mr. Drizzles and the other storm elementals materialized from their patrols of the property to greet us, their presence a welcome committee.

Our steps quickened at the sight of home, the

familiarity a needless reprieve, and as we came closer, I felt the pull of joy firmly rooted in this piece of earth. Our connection to the homestead, the appreciation for its constancy, swelled within me. We unloaded the larroling together once we reached the porch, and the larroling gave a pleased grunt at being rid of the burdens before venturing off to roam the expanses it knew so well.

The chickens clucked curiously as I set them free in the pasture with a nod. "Go on, peck around," I told them, confident that the larroling and elementals would keep an eye on them. My mind couldn't help but drift to the plans I had for them. A sturdy fence and coop were imminent additions to this growing homestead.

But for now, the chickens pecked at the soil, their newness to this place seemed not to faze them. I watched them a moment longer, a gentle contentment within me at having my first animals at the homestead.

I looked to the house as I placed my hand on the wood of the pasture fence, my gaze lingering on the home that had seen so many sunrises and sunsets, its windows now reflecting the afternoon light. My girls were already bustling about with that happiness that being home brought. Diane was off to inspect the wider terrain, while Leigh, Celeste, and Yeska had gone inside.

And I wanted to do a round of my own. My feet carried me around the homestead, a quick inspection to ensure all was as it should be. The ground responded to my familiar steps, and each corner of the property held memories — of laughter, of work, of moments both quiet and filled with life.

The Magebread flowers, Thauma Root, and Wispsilk leaves stood tall in their plot, their magical properties a cascading nod to the care we'd given them. The produce plot was a colorful quilt, vegetables promising meals and stories yet to come.

The water of the Silverthread river ran clear and soothing. A fish jumped, creating ripples that mimicked the ever-expanding influence of our presence in this forest.

A sigh of satisfaction escaped me as I completed

the familiar route, the setting sun casting long shadows across the yard. My heart held pride for what we created here, for the ties that bound us not just to this land but to each other.

I looked back toward the forest, the wild beauty of Tannoris and Earth blended here, and a peaceful symphony of evening sounds rose. Springfield Forest was lush, so full of promise and mystery. And it was home.

As the sun sank, the homestead settled into the comfort of an ordinary evening, and I finished my round and headed over to the house. The wooden steps creaked beneath my feet as I climbed the porch, a sound that felt like the greeting of an old friend.

I was home again.

Chapter 46

Sitting at the kitchen table after dinner with Diane, Leigh, Celeste, and Yeska, I never felt more content to be back within the sturdy walls of my homestead. The whispers of the world outside were subdued by the warmth of the room and the familiar scent of wood-smoke from the stove.

Diane, to my right, was discussing the little details of our journey back, and I could hear that she was as happy as I was to be back again.

Leigh, her feet tapping gently against the floorboards, leaned in with a slight twinkle in her eye. "So, Yeska," she began, her curiosity unmistakable, "you've been with us for a bit now. Notice anything... interesting about David's Bloodline yet?"

I had to smile. She had the same curiosity about the whole Bloodline thing as I did. And who could blame her? If our rapid advancement was indeed due to my Bloodline's powers, then it was of interest to us all.

Yeska, who had settled across from me with a cup of tea cradled in her hands, seemed to blush just the slightest bit at Leigh's question. She took a moment, perhaps gathering her thoughts, then nodded slowly.

"Observing David has been... enlightening," she said. "But understanding his Bloodline will take more time. As I told David, I shall remain with you for about four more months."

"You'll likely see a lot of things in that time," Leigh purred, the little light in her eyes betraying that she wasn't talking about just farming and ranching.

Diane and Celeste chimed in with playful glances at each other and then at me. It was clear that they were enjoying the playful interrogation Leigh had stirred up.

"What kind of *observations* do you need to make?" Diane asked, her tone laced with amusement.

"Well, I need to see how David reacts in different situations, how his presence affects those around him," Yeska explained, now looking directly at me. There was a tremor of seriousness beneath her words that told me she was genuinely dedicated to the task.

Leigh perked up at that, leaning forward, elbows on the table. "Does that include seeing David naked?"

The question was out before anyone could react, and sudden giggles erupted around the table.

Celeste covered her mouth with one hand, her

cheeks rosy with laughter, while Diane snickered, shaking her head at Leigh's boldness. I could feel myself grinning wide, appreciating the direction this conversation was heading.

Yeska's initial shyness seemed to dip away, bolstered by the laughter and because she was very open about such things. "Actually," she said boldly, clearing her throat, "seeing David naked would, um, provide *vital insights.*"

A momentary hush followed her assertion, then a round of chuckles filled the kitchen. I watched as Leigh slapped the table with delight, while Celeste's eyes widened with bashful surprise. Diane hesitated for a split second, then a mischievous twinkle appeared in her eye as she acquiesced with a playful nod.

"I guess," Diane said playfully, "since I expect Yeska has already seen us in our intimate moments from a distance, a second time shouldn't matter." Her gaze shifted to Yeska, teasing.

Yeska blushed only a little at Diane mentioning she had spied on us, but that blush told me enough to know it was the truth. Still, she held Diane's gaze and gave a mysterious smile. I could already tell Yeska knew little shame.

I leaned back in my chair, arms folded behind my head, utterly amused with the turn of events. "Well, no one's watching me until after I've had a bath," I declared, earning more giggles from the girls. "I'm dusty from being on the trail."

"And we could use a bath ourselves," Leigh added, still chuckling as she stood up from the table. Celeste followed suit, nodding in agreement with a shy smile still etched across her face.

Yeska, now more comfortable with the playful banter, gave a small nod. "I suppose a bath is in order," she said gracefully.

"I'll be up in a minute," I said. "You girls go on ahead."

"We'll prepare the bath for you," Celeste said with a promise in her eyes.

"Yes, and we'll join you once you're in," Leigh added, and Diane gave a playful giggle. "And then Yeska can do her… observations."

The cat girl bit her lip, her eyes hazy with a desire that spoke of an eagerness to explore this proposal. I felt the same way and shot her a smile.

As the women dispersed with plans to freshen up — Diane and Celeste toward the stairs leading to the bathroom and Leigh to her room — I glanced around the kitchen and just enjoyed being back. For a while, I sat in silent appreciation of my home as the girls upstairs ran a bath, laughed, and joked.

The room carried traces of dinner; dishes stacked to the side, crumbs from the bread we had brought back from Gladdenfield. It was a comforting mess — the sign of life being lived fully. Soon, the domesticants would clean it all up, but there was a simple kind of joy in seeing the signs of a house well-lived in.

I stood, feeling moved by these reminders of the life we had built within these walls. My hand idled over the back of the chair where Yeska had sat, the warmth of our exchanges almost palpable. I was happy the girls were teasing her a little — good-natured stuff that showed promise for the future.

As I turned to follow the others' path toward getting cleaned, my mind was a whirl of anticipation. Yeska's newfound boldness, mixed with the open mirth from Diane and Celeste, and Leigh's brazen teasing, set the stage for something more thrilling than simple cleanliness.

With a quiet chuckle to myself, I made my way to the large stove, checking to make sure the fires were out before leaving the room. The stoic cast iron held the heat well, securing it within its metal clasp even as the day unfolded beyond it.

My hands found the coolness of the banister I had made myself as I ascended the stairs, each step an echo as I already heard the girls giggling upstairs. I felt the adventure of the day melting away, replaced by the anticipation of a different sort of quest, a more personal one.

The second-floor corridor opened before me, the doors of the bedrooms standing like silent ushers. I approached the bathroom door, my hand hovering over the handle. The sound of running water, not heated but fresh from our well, promised the cleansing luxury of a bath.

With a turn of the knob, I opened the door to the bathroom, eager to see what spectacle was waiting for me here…

Chapter 47

Water lapped gently against the porcelain edges of the tub, a tranquil rhythm that eased my thoughts. Seated in the bath, I watched as Diane, Leigh, Celeste, and Yeska made their graceful entrance into the steam-filled room. The air, heavy with warmth and scented soap, grew richer with the promise of their presence.

Diane was the first to start the delicate dance of undress, her movements deliberate and tender. She slid off her simple dress, her form emerging like a creature of pure grace.

The light caught on the curves of her body, defining the contours that I knew and cherished so well. In this light, I could now see the slight swell of her tummy, betraying the presence of the life growing within, and that things did indeed move faster with the foxkin.

Leigh followed, her giggles a curtain of sound that muffled the rustle of her discarding her clothes. Her freckled skin peeked out, an array of tiny constellations that adorned her form with an allure that was both innocent and intoxicating. And the way her long blonde hair cascaded down her fit back to almost touch her firm and round bottom quickened my heart.

Celeste, with a quiet elegance, unfastened her garments, revealing the amber waves of her hair that fell and framed the perfection of her elven curves. The serene beauty in her unfolding form stilled the room, a silent awe at the artistry of her being.

Across the room, Yeska's gaze sparkled with a vibrancy that was new and arresting. She watched me and my trio of women with a hunger that was clear in her wide, green eyes. She wore a tight skirt and top that showed the outline of her voluptuous body and full curved, amplifying the hunger rising within me with all these naked beauties on display for me.

Leigh, her blue eyes gleaming with mischief, turned her gaze toward me, a playful tilt to her lips. "David, why don't you stand and give Yeska a proper view?" Her words, spoken with a teasing lilt, sent a ripple of excitement through the room.

No bashfulness withheld me, and if the woman wanted to see me naked, she could. With a grin that matched Leigh's playful challenge, I rose from the bath, water cascading down the planes of my body. The cool autumn air coming in from the window brushed against my wet skin, heightening the sensation as I stood before them.

Yeska's gaze locked onto mine for a moment

before drifting downward, a rosy flush coloring her cheeks as her eyes traced every line of my form. She bit her lip and released a sigh that betrayed arousal. I watched, a curious thrill blooming within me, as her hands began an anxious journey over her bare thighs.

Diane, Leigh, and Celeste, with a fluid grace that seemed to challenge the very water they stepped into, made their entrance into the tub. Their bodies eased into the depths beside me, their skin shimmering beneath the surface as they found their places close — very close.

The proximity of their supple forms against mine was electrifying. A current of desire surged through me as I felt the slick glide of their bodies, the gentle brush of skin on skin.

Diane's warmth melded with my left side, a soft contrast to the cooler waters that lapped lazily around us. Her hands, hesitant at first, began to wash over her own form, and inevitably, mine — creating a connection both cleansing and provocative.

I groaned with pleasure, enjoying those hands on

my skin. They were familiar by now, her touch a frequent thing, but I would never, ever grow tired of it.

Leigh settled to my right, her smile warm and edged with lustful promise as she playfully splashed water at us. Her body, a symphony of curves, found its rhythm against my form, her movements sending waves through the bath.

Celeste, her front pressing gently into my back, moved behind me with an artist's sensibility. Her hands swept through the water as she tended to me with a careful touch that spoke of a quiet passion, kneading my back and making my muscles give up the tensions of the last few days of travel and questing.

The sensation was overwhelming — the warmth of the water, the heat of their skin, the soft sounds of the bath punctuated by their caring ministrations. Every touch heightened my arousal, a building pressure that coiled within me, ready and waiting.

"Getting a good view?" Leigh asked Yeska, that teasing edge to her voice, and Celeste and Leigh gave soft giggles at the question.

"Very good," Yeska confirmed, her eyes still on me. Her hands, still exploring the smoothness of her own skin, ventured higher, a stark outline against her defined silhouette.

My gaze settled on her with hunger as her fingers paused, then continued their trail, her breath catching as her attention wavered between self-pleasure and the intimate display before her. My lust for her rose, but I would not hurry things. Harmony and love in this elven marriage were my priorities.

Diane's fingers grazed over me with a gentleness that was almost a caress, her touch lingering on places that urged me to lose myself in the sensation. The water, once just an element of cleanliness, now felt like a conductor for the electricity between us.

Leigh's form against mine was an unspoken invitation, a playful dare that seemed to ask for more to show Yeska — to show our potential new companion the depths of our love and pleasure.

Celeste's serene strokes, the careful way she

tended to my back, as if she were crafting a masterpiece on my back, only added depth to my desire. The intimate knowledge between us surged like the water that surrounded us.

Leigh leaned in, pressing a soft kiss to my shoulder, a whisper of a touch that somehow spoke volumes, urging me closer to the edge of restraint. Her full breast brushed me, the nipple poking against my skin, begging to be touched.

My arousal was evident, a physical truth that could not be concealed by the water, and the girls cooed and crooned as their gazes regularly dipped to my ready cock. The pulsing need thrummed through me, a rhythm that sought release, that sought to claim the beauty they generously offered before me.

Leigh's voice, a sultry tone entwined with the steam, broke the quiet that had settled over us. "We're all clean now..." she said with a smile that suggested a myriad of possibilities.

I caught the flicker of agreement in Diane's and Celeste's expressions, a silent understanding that transcended words — a shared readiness for the 'real fun' that lay beyond the curtain of falling water.

As the water stilled, and we rinsed the soap from our bodies, I sensed the moment moving on — a prelude nearing its crescendo. The room was thick with steam and unspoken expectation. My manhood was throbbing, and I was eager to claim my women, turned on by the idea of Yeska watching me.

As the last droplets cascaded down from the bathing women, the air within the bathroom hugged our damp skin in a delicate dance of warmth and coolness.

Diane, her raven hair framing her face in rivulets, looked up at me with eyes that sparkled, reflecting the fire of my own. She encircled her hands around the firmness of my arousal, her touch igniting sparks that flickered through my entire being.

"Hmm," she purred as she touched my firm

weapon. "David... It's so hard."

Leigh's soft giggle vibrated with a throaty undertone, her gaze flitting between Diane, Celeste, and me. "Looks like someone's very eager," she teased, sliding her fingers along the length of me, taking her turn with a stroke that pulled a throaty groan from my lungs, even as Diane's fingers caressed my full balls.

I gave a crooked smile as I buried my hands into Leigh's blonde locks, making her look up at me with those baby-blue eyes I loved so much. She gave a pleased hum at the gentle tug I gave her.

Celeste, with her elven grace, came around and knelt before me in the water, adding her touch to the symphony of strokes and caresses. Her fingers clasped gently around the base, guiding and coaxing with a rhythm that felt like the ebb and flow of the Silverthread River itself.

"So firm," she purred, going almost cross-eyed as she sat on her knees, worshipping my cock.

The warmth of their hands, the rhythmic tending, left me swaying in the waters of burgeoning lust. I stole a glance toward Yeska, her expression rapt with the scene unfolding before her, her chest heaving with what seemed like an anticipatory breath.

Yeska's fingers, now stray and bold, tiptoed along the firm slopes of her bosom as she pulled down the collar of her top, unveiling her firm breasts to the room. The sight of her soft and inviting skin, the peaks of her full breasts cradled in her palms, sent an additional surge through my yearning flesh.

The giggles from Diane, Leigh, and Celeste surged into fervent murmurs while they shared their task. The air grew thick with an intoxicating blend of steam and desire, enveloping the room in an ambrosial haze that tickled the senses and called forth deeper cravings.

The women, their delicate hands working in tandem, tended to me, their voices joining in soft giggles and moans as they lavished attention upon my rock-hard cock. Leigh, ever the wordsmith among us when it came to the bedroom, whispered things too lewd that were laced every dirty promise meant to stoke the fire already roused.

"David," she hummed, her big eyes on me as she stroked me. "I think Yeska needs to see you fuck us, baby. I want her to look at you when you cum — I need her to see how you release yourself on us, in us..."

My breaths turned shallow, the tightness in my abdomen winding into a persistent coil of want. Leigh's words, intertwined with the harmonious attention from Diane and Celeste, fired up a crude yearning that draped heavily over my thoughts.

Yeska's gaze upon us was a golden thread in the tapestry. Her eyes smoldered with the reflections of the scene, her own touch upon her bosom growing more poignant with every moment. She rolled her swollen nipples between her thumb and forefingers. Her plump lips were moist as she moaned at the pleasure of her own touch.

I reached out, instinct guiding my hand to the back of Diane's head, drawing her in closer, diving into the depths of the arousal that clouded the room. The steamy air vibrated with each stroke, each tug, and the soft sound of Diane's giggle against my aroused self.

She obeyed my bidding and lowered herself to kneel beside her harem sister, Celeste. I gave her a look of approval, wanting to feel her lips on my cock before I turned my gaze back to Yeska.

Through the haze of yearning, I watched as Yeska's hand ventured lower, past the curve of her hips, lifting the skirt that draped her thighs. A fleeting glimpse of the allure underneath peeked out, heightening the already heady atmosphere.

And then, Diane's lips parted, encircling me with an eagerness that sent the room spinning. The soft touch of her lips on my cock was beyond anything I could take, and I inhaled sharply, hissing as I submerged myself in the pleasure she gave with her mouth.

"That looks so pretty," Leigh crooned as her hand stroked what part of me Diane had not taken into her mouth.

And to my infinite delight, Celeste leaned in as well, joining Diane's efforts. Their mouths left a trail of warmth as they kissed and licked my firm member, pulsing with their touch, and I had to fight to keep from shooting my load over their pretty faces.

Yeska, entranced, lowered her skirt, drawing away the last scrap of fabric that concealed her warmth. A blaze of desire lit up within me as she revealed her pretty pussy, soft and pink with a cute landing strip of black hair. Her eyes remained fixed on mine as her touch became an exploration, a study in self-delight that mirrored the pleasure we were sharing.

"Doesn't that look cute?" Leigh hummed when she saw Yeska touch herself. "Guess it's part of the magical research..."

I chuckled, and Yeska released a playful smile at the blonde's comment, but she was not ashamed, and she did not stop.

The room's temperature seemed to climb with these actions and words. With the mounting need, a palpable presence grew, as Yeska's parted her lips with desire, her hand delving into her own longing.

I watched Yeska pleasure herself even as Celeste and Diane were on their knees, worshipping my cock, while Leigh whispered her dirty words into my ear. I had my hands buried in their luscious locks, directing them, and I felt a king among men.

Yeska's fingers shifted, delving and moving in a silent symphony that played upon her own form. Intensity flickered across her features, transforming the scholarly observer into a being of pure sensuality.

"I think she's gonna cum," Leigh whispered as she pushed her delicious breasts against me. "That little minx is hornier than the four of us together." Her blue eyes turned to me. "Still, we need to show her how you fuck us, baby. She needs to see."

I groaned my agreement as my awareness narrowed to the heady sensation, the tender encasement, to Leigh's throatier whispers that spoke of all we could do while Yeska bore witness in the name of her research. My gaze dipped down as Diane took my cock as deep into her mouth as she could, gently urged on by her elven harem sister.

I hissed with delight as she gagged on my weapon, her big sapphire eyes fixed on me, seeking approval, which I gave with a delighted moan.

Then, she released, a strand of spit connecting her lips to my glistening cock, before Celeste took over and wrapped her soft lips around me, making me moan with pleasure as she, too, deep-throated me.

Leigh caught my gaze as Diane and Celeste continued their work, her smirk blossoming into a bold declaration. "Seems like a good time for a personal demonstration, right?" Her tone lingered in the air, playful and laden with promise.

The suggestion, woven with the sight of Yeska's unabashed touch upon herself, draped over me like a lure. The urge to claim them, to heed the call of our lust in front of our newest audience member, flashed through me, urgent and compelling.

Diane and Celeste's movements grew more fervent, their knowing hands reading my body like a treasured script. My readiness thrummed, a hum of anticipation that sang through my hardness.

Leigh met my gaze, the heated intensity in her eyes offering silent permission, a mutual understanding that she, too, was eager to escalate our delicate waltz.

Yeska's gaze remained locked upon us, her self-pleasure nearing a fever pitch. Her fingers, a blur of motion, echoed the rhythm that Diane, Leigh, and Celeste played upon my body, each of us dancing on the edge of a precipice we longed to leap from.

The flickering candles cast shifting shadows across us as the women's pleasuring intensity grew, turning the bathroom into a haven for primal beats and breathless whimpers.

I stood braced between worlds, the heat of their hands and mouths on me, the glint in Yeska's eyes stoking the fire within. I was ready to claim my women in front of Yeska and show her the depth of our passions.

As the two women rose from their kneeling positions, Leigh cast a coy glance my way, her voice husky with desire. "David, baby," she purred, "how do you want us now?"

The thick air of the bathroom felt charged with

our collective arousal, my own desire reaching its peak as I met her gaze.

I slid down into the bath, the water embracing my heated skin as I beckoned Celeste closer, her soft and curvy body just what I wanted right now.

"Celeste, come here," I said softly. "I want you to ride me."

A hint of scarlet flushed her fair cheeks, but with little hesitation, she complied, settling onto my lap with a shiver that wasn't from the cold. I held her, my fingers digging into her lush butt cheeks as she positioned herself, her velvet hands on my cock as she placed the tip against her entrance.

"Like that," I groaned. "Put it in."

She bit her plump lip as the other women cooed their admiration, and then she guided me in. Her pussy enveloped me — tight at first, but soft like velvet as she lowered herself and took me deeper.

Leigh and Diane took their places on either side of the bathtub, their approving purrs a welcome soundtrack to Celeste's tentative movements. The slow rise and fall of her hips began at a measured pace, her breath hitching slightly with every dip.

The joy that blossomed within me at the sensation of Celeste's warmth enveloping me was indescribable. I watched, entranced, as her ample bosom bounced in unison with her increasing speed, creating ripples across the water's surface and making the bath water slosh against the edges of the tub.

Leigh's voice was a teasing whisper in the background, her dirty talk adding a tantalizing layer to the unfolding scene. "That's it, Celeste," she encouraged. "Ride him. Show him how much you adore him."

Yeska observed from the edge of the bath with her eyes wide, burning with a hunger that spoke of her own burgeoning needs. The sight of us together, the air thick with steam and longing, was surely providing her with ample material for her Bloodline studies. Her fingers dipped into her wetness on occasion before going back to circling her swollen clit. As Celeste bounced on my lap, my mind raged with the promise of soon fucking Yeska.

My roaming hands traced the curves of Celeste's

body, gliding over her skin with a possessive tenderness that only heightened the intimacy. Her slick flesh under my fingertips felt like the most natural thing in the world as she moved.

"Oh, David," she moaned. "It… It's so good!"

Celeste's pace quickened, her breathing growing erratic as she sought her release. The water around us echoed her urgency, the sounds of splashing and panting a chorus of desire that filled the room.

Leigh's bawdy encouragement fanned the flames within Celeste, who was now lost to the rhythm she'd set. "Look at that," she purred, her tone laced with pride and heat. "You're such a good girl for David!"

Yeska — almost involuntarily — released a moan as she fingered her tight little pussy. The way her breath caught and the flush of her skin told me she was as affected as any of us by the encounter. My gaze raked her, and it only seemed to turn her on more.

Then, Celeste's body tensed around me, a crescendo building within her as I continued to move my hands in time with our dance, my fingers digging into the ample flesh of her full ass. Every thrust was met with her own, the water barely able to contain the passion that surged between us.

"Cum for me," I groaned in her ear. "I want to feel it."

"Ahnn!" she moaned, releasing herself as she bounced on my cock. "David! Gods! I'm cumming!"

The moment of Celeste's climax was a spectacle of beauty and intensity, her body shuddering as waves of pleasure overtook her. Her moans, echoing against the walls, were the sweetest music, declaring her ecstasy to the entire room. Her pussy clamped on me, eager for my seed, but I postponed my pleasure, wanting to fuck my other girls too.

As she trembled in my arms, spent from her high, I gently eased her off me and turned to Leigh with a grin. "Your turn," I beckoned, my arousal still very much evident in the sight of my glistening cock.

"Thought you'd never ask, baby," Leigh teased as, with a cheeky glint in her eye, she slipped into my lap. Her soft and curvy body was a delight for me, and my hands were always hungry to explore my sultry blonde. She positioned herself above my eager manhood. Her movements were unabashed, her gaze locked on mine as she lowered herself onto me.

The sensation of Leigh's tender pussy around my cock was like coming home. The perfect fit, and I reached up to knead her full breasts, pinch her hard nipples as she moaned with delight and began to ride me with a confidence that sent ripples through the water.

"Oh, baby," she moaned. "Your cock feels so good inside me!" She moved faster, slapping down wetly in my lap.

Leigh's rhythm was relentless, her body moving atop mine like a nymph at the dawn of time. Each downward motion drove me deeper into her, her pleasure mounting with every thrust. My balls were full and ready to spurt my seed into her welcoming pussy, but I fought it off tooth and nail, knowing I wanted to fuck Diane too.

And as my hands clamped down on Leigh, my eyes drifted to Yeska. Her clothes disheveled and pushed aside, the cat girl was fingering herself vigorously, moaning as her half-lidded eyes watched my cock slip in and out of Leigh — no doubt wishing it was her riding me.

And with Yeska still watching intently, Leigh reached her climax, her release a symphony of gasps and cries that only spurred me on further. I could feel my own peak drawing nearer still as I grabbed her by her lush hips and slammed her down hard on my cock, splashing bath water around.

For once, Leigh had no words. She collapsed against my chest, breathless from her orgasm, and I gently eased her off, seeing how Celeste and Diane admired us, their cheeks rosy.

"Now, it's your turn, my love," I said to Diane, and she bit her lower lip as she rose from the water and turned before me, presenting the delicious body I would now claim.

As she did so, her eyes lingered on Yeska for a moment, and I sensed that Diane approved of it — that she wanted Yeska to see how I would fuck her and bring her to a climax, and I hoped it signified the growing bond between the two.

I rose to my feet, water cascading off my form. "Bend over," I said to Diane.

Diane gave a squeal of excitement and desire as I bent her over the lip of the tub. We both had a full view of Yeska, who was pleasuring herself with abandon.

With our new position, we were close to one another — close enough to touch — and I reveled in the sight of her. She was not abashed, meeting my eyes with boldness as she kept touching herself.

The voyeuristic thrill fueled my movements as I gave Diane's round ass a smack that made her yelp and giggle. Then, pushing my throbbing tip against her pink little pussy, I entered Diane from behind.

She was tight but dripping wet, and I knew the idea of Yeska watching us turned her on even more than I had expected.

"Hmm," Leigh moaned, her voice still hoarse from her own orgasm, "look at that pretty sight."

"So... beautiful..." Yeska hummed, still pleasuring herself.

Diane's moans filled the room as I plunged into her, her voice gaining volume with every thrust. I grabbed her fox tail and pulled on it, winning a mewl of lust from Diane. Her pretty ass bounced as I savagely claimed her, and I could already feel her tightening around my cock.

"I'm… I'm gonna cum," she hissed, breathless.

Leigh and Celeste gave naughty giggles, and Yeska bit her lip, watching me fuck Diane from behind with savage power. Her green eyes never left ours, her fingers a blur as she chased her own pleasure. Her admiration was clear, the approval in her moans matching the tempo of our union.

Then, her eyes rolled up in their sockets, and her tongue lolled out as her delicious thighs began quaking. At the same time, Diane moaned and tightened on me, her body trembling as her climax synchronized with that of Yesksa.

It was a cacophony of pleasure, their moans mingling in exclamation as they both found sweet release. As they peaked, Diane's plea broke through.

"David," she moaned, "give… g-give it to

Yeska!"

"Yes!" Leigh crooned. "Give her your cum! Let her taste it."

"Give her your seed, my love!" Celeste agreed.

And as they spoke, Yeska slipped forward to her knees, her face now next to the back of Diane's head.

"Y-yes," Yeska mumbled, still carried by the height of pleasure. "Give it to me!"

My women's moans of consent were all I needed. With a guttural groan, I withdrew from Diane and aimed my cock at Yeska's pretty face. Then, I released my pent-up passion even as Yeska opened her mouth and closed her eyes to receive it.

My first rope was thick and shot far, splattering across Yeska's pretty face and one of her cat ears as I hissed with delight at the release. She gasped as I covered her face, but I was not done yet, leaning on Diane's panting body as I shot rope after rope of warm cum, releasing my passion across Yeska's face and breasts, some of it spilling into her eager mouth.

"Look at that!" Leigh exclaimed.

"Beautiful!" Celeste agreed. Diane just gave a mewl of approval as she scooped up some of the cum that had spilled on her butt and brought it to her lips.

"So good," Yeska moaned, her hazy green eyes fixed on me.,

Satisfied, I sank back into the tub, surrounded by a chorus of giggles from Diane, Leigh, Celeste, and Yeska. Soon enough, my girls draped themselves around me, with Yeska seated on the edge of the tub, bathing her feet and wearing only her disheveled skirt.

"This was lovely," I said to them as I pulled them close with a voice still husky.

"It was," Diane agreed, shooting Yeska a warm smile before she added — a little teasingly. "I hope it helped your *research*."

Yeska grinned, her chest still heaving lightly, and the other girls joined in with giggles. "It did," Yeska said. "Although perhaps we might have to do it again sometime to heighten the effect."

We all laughed at that, and I couldn't help but hope that this meant she was being accepted by the other women, which would allow me to act on my desire to have her around more.

Chapter 48

Evening settled softly upon the homestead like a well-worn quilt, tucking the landscape into gentle shadows. The last rays of sunlight brushed against the sturdy oak log walls of the house, casting a golden glow that seemed to hold the last of the day's warmth tight against the encroaching cool of the night and autumn.

I stepped off the porch, my boots crunching on the gravel pathway that led around the house. The rifle felt familiar as it hung over my shoulder, its weight a companionable presence as I began my final patrol of the day.

The farmland stretched out before me, silent sentinels of Magebread flowers and Wispsilk leaves standing guard over the day's end. They swayed slightly in the tender breeze, their magical nature a subtle hum in the fabric of the homestead.

I walked past the vegetable plot, where the produce had thrived under our care. The magically imbued tomatoes, onions, beans, carrots, and lettuce seemed to hold onto the day's light, their vibrant colors a soft contrast to the dimming skies.

The wooden fence that enclosed our farming plots cast long, slender shadows as I moved through them, a security made of simple things. The chickens clucked happily in their enclosure, roofless for now, but I would soon solve that.

As the sound of the Silverthread River reached my ears, its waters murmuring stories only a river could tell, I felt a wave of contentment. The river, constant in its journey, ran like the vein of life through the heart of the land we called home.

I paused by the water's edge, watching as fish broke the surface in silver arcs, catching the evening's final light. Finally, I turned my gaze back to the log house, its two stories now just shapes against the twilight.

My patrol led me along the well-trodden paths that snaked around the house — the places where we lived, loved, and labored. The last of the day's heat soaked into my skin, a promise to hold close against the night's certain chill.

As I stood there, the thought of Yeska once again occupied my mind, her quest to unravel the mystery of my Bloodline. Her presence was equal parts enchanting and enigmatic, and I was more and more falling for her. I hoped that she would stay — that the others would accept her. With our little play together, however, things were looking good.

And another thought weighed on my mind -- a happy one. In four months' time, our homestead would be pierced by a new life's cry. The prospect of fatherhood was a vista as broad and beautiful as the land that stretched out before me. I had many pleasant memories from childhood, and I had many ideas about being a father.

It would happen this winter…

Plans for winter jostled with hopes for the spring. There would be a wedding party to organize, a celebration of bonds already forged under elven law but deserving of a day filled with mirth and company — a day when family and friends would join us, witnessing the joy we had cultivated on this frontier.

And as I watched the stars, a certain formation of them reminded me of something else that might come to pass in the future — something threatening. For in the back of my mind loomed the shadow of the dragon Father. His vengeance, a potential threat to the peace we had crafted, was a disquieting thought amidst the gentle hum of the evening.

Still, a sigh escaped my lips as I pushed concerns of dragons and Bloodlines aside. The night was not a canvas for worries but a time for rest, and for now, the homestead was safety embodied.

The cool kiss of the evening air brought clarity, a reminder that our lives here were a dance with nature — a give and take that was both subtle and profoundly changing. I let my eyes linger on the dusky horizon, where the last trace of light was surrendering to the shadows.

I took a final look at the farm, at the fences and the growth within. Tomorrow would bring its toil, but tonight, the homestead would rest.

With a final sweep of my gaze, I ensured all was as it should be. Then, finishing up my patrol, I turned in for the night. Whatever the future might hold, tonight I'd spend in my bed, warmed by my women.

Finished and eager for early access to my next book? Check out my Patreon: patreon.com/jackbryce

THANK YOU FOR READING!

If you enjoyed this book, please check out my other work on Amazon.

Be sure to **leave me a review on Amazon** to let me know if you liked this book! Like most independent authors, I use the feedback from your review to improve my work and to decide what to focus on next, so your review can make a difference.

If you want early access to my work, consider joining my Patreon (https://patreon.com/jackbryce)!

If you want to stay up-to-date on my releases, you can join my newsletter by entering the following link into any web browser: https://fierce-thinker-305.ck.page/45f709af30. You can also join my Discord, where the madness never ends… Join by entering the following invite manually in your browser or Discord app: https://discord.gg/uqXaTMQQhr.

Jack Bryce's Books

Below you'll find a list of my work, all available through Amazon.

Frontier Summoner (ongoing series)

Frontier Summoner 1

Frontier Summoner 2

Frontier Summoner 3

Frontier Summoner 4

Frontier Summoner 5

Frontier Summoner 6

Country Mage (completed series)

Country Mage 1

Country Mage 2

Country Mage 3

Country Mage 4

Country Mage 5

Country Mage 6

Country Mage 7

Country Mage 8

Country Mage 9

Country Mage 10

<u>Warped Earth (completed series)</u>

Apocalypse Cultivator 1

Apocalypse Cultivator 2

Apocalypse Cultivator 3

Apocalypse Cultivator 4

Apocalypse Cultivator 5

<u>Aerda Online (completed series)</u>

Phylomancer

Demon Tamer

Clanfather

<u>Highway Hero (ongoing series)</u>

Highway Hero 1

Highway Hero 2

A SPECIAL THANKS TO...

My patron in the Godlike tier: Lynderyn!
My patrons in the High Mage tier: Christian Smith, Eddie Fields, Michael Sroufe, Christopher Eichman, Theophilus, Jason, William Hayes, and James Hunt!

All of my other patrons at patreon.com/jackbryce!

Stoham Baginbott, Louis Wu, Joseph S., and Scott D. for beta reading. You guys are absolute kings.

If you're interested in beta reading for me, hit me up on discord (JauntyHavoc#8836) or send an e-mail to lordjackbryce@gmail.com. The list is currently full, but spots might open up in the future.